BREEDER
PROTOCOL

DAVID ALLAN HAMILTON

DeeBee

For information contact:
David@davidallanhamilton.net
http://www.davidallanhamilton.net
ISBN: 9781896794853

First Edition: May 2025

10 9 8 7 6 5 4 3 2 1

BREEDER
PROTOCOL

For Susan

It is a rule with few exceptions
that what a man fishes for
he is most likely to catch.

Charles M. Spurgeon

HISTORICAL NOTE

WELCOME TO THE TORFINN GALAXY—WILD, VAST, AND largely unexplored.

Scattered across hundreds of planets, the remnants of Terran colonists and alien settlers live under the watchful eye of the struggling Torfinn Galaxy Governing Council, headquartered on the planet Asteria. But interplanetary peace and cooperation is an illusion.

Bound by the Ethical Protocol on Non-Interference, the Council forbids planets from meddling in each other's affairs—a law that's supposed to protect, but too often shields corruption, cruelty, and silent suffering.

Piper Madison, a brilliant young Asterian research scientist, finds her sheltered life turned upside down when she uncovers cruel injustices on Robos 7 quite by accident. Despite being raised by the Chancellor of the Governing Council, Piper despises politics, preferring exploration, discovery, and opportunity for all. Where others see inevitable bureaucracy, she finds bone-crushing betrayal.

Where others stay silent, she takes a stand.

Driven by a fierce sense of justice, Piper dares to cross the lines no one else will—to challenge tyranny, expose lies, and where necessary, ignite revolutions across the stars.

These are her stories.

ONE

PIPER MADISON HAD TO REMIND HERSELF THAT KITTO was nothing more than a simulacrum—a face she designed to give the main computer at the Olavus Research Lab on Hauntor a human touch. He wasn't the real man himself, even though she treated him as if he were still alive.

A crazy exercise that only a crazy person might do, she thought.

But Piper Madison wasn't in her right mind.

"The weather seems to be holding," the digital image said. *"I take it you'll proceed with the scheduled survey?"*

She dropped into a chair at the central work station, brushed a long strand of blond hair from her face, and pulled up the weather maps. "Yeah. There's a two-hour window before the next storm hits," she said, studying the pressure gradients and winds. "Half hour there, an hour to investigate, and a half hour back. I'll leave for the caverns now. She closed the maps, headed to the other side of the laboratory, and began pulling on her boots and thick longcoat. She slung the scanning equipment across her chest and secured a battered pair of goggles on her face. "Keep me updated on any sudden weather changes."

"Perhaps we can play a round of fizzpaw when you return?" Kitto's graphics shifted to display her mentor settling down with a book in front of a struggling fire.

"Count on it."

She swung open the heavy door. A gust of cold wind swirled into the workspace, and she pulled her longcoat tight against the near-freezing temperature. Piper clanked down the grated ramp to the dusty surface where the station's mule sat charging in the maintenance shed. After disconnecting the energy cables and onboard data links, Piper fired up the vehicle, kicked it into gear, and crawled over the desolate plains toward a distant outcrop of caverns.

Mostly, her time at the isolated research facility provided the tonic she needed in the aftermath of her encounter with the sadistic Zadicus Verman back home on Asteria. She'd overcome her physical injuries in short order, but the bone-deep emotional scars remained. Adding to her troubles, Captain Jay Carstairs had once again vanished like a coward after battling alongside her. The Tealian counsellor she saw suggested easing into work at the Asterian Technical Institute as a way to encourage healing. Instead, she volunteered to take up residence on Hauntor with her supervisor's reluctant permission... the only soul at this remote station on the edge of the Torfinn Galaxy.

I'm not simply running away from him, she lied to herself, shivering against the biting wind.

After clattering across the grey, rock-strewn plain for half an hour, Piper arrived at the ridge of caves jutting up from the cracked ground like a crooked mouth with their split-tooth openings. Scientists and engineers in the ATI tasked her with studying this planet's curious magnetic traits, which suggested that Hauntor acted as a natural relay station for long-range, low frequency EM interplanetary comms. If she could determine the mechanism behind these spurious transmissions, they may exploit the planet for future deep space soundings.

Up to this point, her general survey of the caverns revealed nothing unusual, so the bulk of her research focused more on specific mineral properties rather than on any large-scale structural phenomena. That suited her fine. Either way, she loved the work, and loved being alone even more.

The Nav device on the mule blinked, targeting the opening in front of her for the day's observations. She confirmed the location coordinates with Kitto, shut down the cart and leaned into the swirling wind that slashed past the entrance.

"Begin recording," she said. The monitor on her chest sprang to life. Her body cam engaged as well.

Piper stepped into the dark cave, removed her goggles, and squinted into the gloomy space. She flipped on the torch strapped around her forehead and followed the light as it danced along the black jagged walls and ceiling of the subterranean hollow.

"At first glance, this cavern is the same as the others. Nothing specific jumping out at me, at least, nothing visual." The machine detected no radiation or toxic air. Only rocks full of hematite and magnetite. Some tourmalines.

The darkness sloped downward at a steep angle, and Piper unlatched her longcoat to gain better mobility as she descended the tunnel structure. Wind gusts that, moments before, threatened to flatten her were now barely audible, and a remarkable silence descended over her. She steadied herself against the rock wall when, from nowhere, a faint whisper-like voice filled her head, then rapidly disappeared. Thick shadows blanketed her. The hairs on the back of her neck bristled.

She froze, holding her breath, and listened.

"Kitto, is that you? Do you copy?"

A burst of static returned her call, but she failed to decipher any words. Not surprising given the density of these metallic rocks and her depth in this cave. Even so, though she was the only intelligent lifeform on the planet, she failed to overcome a sudden and intense feeling of being watched.

Not from without.

From within.

After 20 meters of constant descent, the ground flattened, exposing an odd, subterranean clearing. Piper halted and flashed the torch around a chamber-like opening. In the other caves she investigated, she'd seen nothing comparable. Considering Hauntor's arid environment, she wondered what created such a space.

Almost artificial.

Several meters away, something sparkled on the ground as her light swept over it. She confirmed that her scanner continued recording, then followed the beam toward the brilliant patches.

As she approached the scintillating rocks, Piper gulped. Her eyes widened. Blue-grey stones the size of plums littered the area, glistening as if covered in water. To Piper's amazement, dozens of these pebbles formed concentric circles in the centre of the seemingly random fragments scattered over the dusty floor.

Someone placed them here this way.

She glanced around the chamber with nervous apprehension. Her heart pounded in her ears.

"Are you seeing this, Kitto?"

No response.

"Kitto?"

She knew this world, much like many dark planets, was

mostly unexplored. But that didn't mean others hadn't been here before the early Asterian settlers arrived. Adrenaline coursed through her body and her fight-or-flight instinct screamed at her to get out.

Yet, she found the odd, luminescent stones arranged in perfect circles compelling, and she couldn't turn off her scientific curiosity. The smooth pebbles suggested they'd come from a water-rich environment, and ranged in size from a few centimeters in diameter to that of her palm.

They all appeared to be of similar composition. Random rocks surrounded the circular design, reminding her of how children often built things out of wooden blocks. She scanned them for any potential radiation, but they remained inert, so she knelt, removed her gloves, then declared, "Here goes."

Piper reached out and brushed her fingers across one specimen, then picked it up. She blew a layer of dust from the rock. It felt light to the touch. Thin. She rubbed the remaining coating away and brought it close to her face. Flecks of green and yellow danced in the blue-grey, and Piper wondered if this rock belonged to the feldspar group, or perhaps it was a rare feldspathoid. A geochemical analysis back at the lab would confirm either way.

She studied the stone pattern for several more minutes, taking images and readings, then stood and muttered, "The geologists will enjoy poking around these, but I've gotta keep moving if I hope to beat that storm."

After she marked the dimensions of this odd chamber and the unnatural patterns, a pebble in an outer circle appeared to glow. Not sparkling in the torchlight like before, but presenting as a living, pulsating piece of rock.

A trick of the mind? Strained vision?

She ignored it and continued surveying the surrounding space.

Several more stones glowed.

This time, she stepped across the random pebbles and scrutinized the circular pattern, scanning and recording it with her sensor. No odd findings appeared on her equipment, other than a set of perfect circles that had no business being in an underground cave. Piper licked her lips, bent down, and picked up one of the radiant gems.

Without warning, the entire collection of concentric rings burst into a brilliant bluish light. She collapsed, covering her face as the pulses filled the chamber. The scanner sparked and crackled, its circuits overloading.

Piper scrabbled toward the tunnel on her hands and knees. The stones thumped, casting warm light as bright as any Asterian morning back home.

"What the hell have I done!"

Mild tremors shook the surrounding ground. Whiffs of dust belched from the ceiling. The pebbles continued shining.

That's when she heard *them*.

The faint whispers again.

Not from the cavern itself, no. These ghost-like voices invaded every interstitial cavity from within her mind. She pulled herself up, groping the thick wall for support, and stared at the terrifying light show unfolding before her. Having regained her footing, she quickly lurched forward through the tunnel, stumbling toward the cavern's entrance and the howling winds beyond. The blue glow followed her, dancing off the rock walls, mocking her every step.

Meanwhile, ghostly whispers persisted.

More desperate than before.

They filled her with a singular, raw, and ancient emotion that no word she knew could describe.

A jagged presence ripped into her soul, flooding her with the darkest fear she had ever felt in her life.

"Help us, Piper... Please..."

She fell to her knees, clutching her head.

TWO

"ARIEL?"

A fleeting image of Piper's half-sister on Robos 7—millions of kilometers away—teased her mind. The ground shuddered again. She gathered her senses and stumbled out of the cave, shielding her face from the relentless gusts and dust whorls. She searched the rocky landscape for her goggles and specimen bag, but both had vanished.

Piper leaned against the rock wall by the entrance and caught her breath. How could she see her half-sister imploring her to help? Ariel's image, no longer visible in her thoughts, frightened her. The young woman's face, pleading and distressed, was far too vivid to be a hallucination.

And where was her husband, Dolian?

Those ghostly utterances continued echoing through her consciousness. They were unlike any of the other voices she normally encountered.

Like her mother's chiding.

Or Neris's soothing words after they'd made love under the Asterian moons, before he rejected his life and career in Capital City—and her—to become some ember-root farmer in the Valley, of all things.

Or Jay Carstairs, Captain of the *Dauntless*. Grade A Asshole.

No, these whispers fumbled in a turbid, synesthetic kaleidoscope of colours that reminded her of musical notes. Dissonant. Hurried. Like residual flashes of the sparkling rock symbols in that damned cave.

She shook it off, attempting to stay present and focused. *The wind.*

Piper ducked into the rocky opening, surprised to find the mysterious pebble still in her hand. She pocketed the stone and glanced around for her missing gear.

She staggered to the mule, buckling her longcoat as she stumbled through the heavy sand drifts. Dust scratched her eyes and collected in her nostrils. The aural circus in her head diminished, but the sense of foreboding and doom remained, biting into her conscious thoughts. Her fingers trembled as she sank into the cart's cockpit and searched in a storage container for another set of eye protectors. She located one usable pair—a cracked lens, but sufficiently functional—and pulled them on. The howling gale intensified, slashing over the brittle, rocky plains and whistling through the ridge of caverns. She turned her back to it, forcing tears to clear the grit from her vision.

"Piper, do you copy?"

A clash of words.

The whispers receded into a haunted memory.

"Piper, are you there?"

She cleared her head and hit her comms device. "Yes, Kitto, I read you. Heading back to Olavus now." She gathered her strength. "By the way, did you pick up any odd readings from these coordinates?"

The radio crackled. *"Negative. Everything seems normal."*

"Okay. I've got a rock specimen for you to analyze. Apparent electromagnetic properties." She kept the voices to herself, but added, "I thought about Ariel when I was in the cave. Did she contact the lab while I was incommunicado?"

"Heavens, no. The distance between Hauntor and Robos 7 is too vast for normal communications to be successful. Unless she happened to be close to us, perhaps in a spaceship. Did you expect her to call?"

Piper smirked. "Not really. Just curious. Returning now."

"Acknowledged," Kitto said. *"Oh, the approaching storm is strengthening, and the wind has shifted. You'd better get going."*

She took a deep breath and blinked more grit away. "Sure, if I can squeeze 20 clicks out of this mule, I'll be fine. See you soon."

After pulling a filter scarf from the storage container and wrapping it around her nose and mouth, Piper fired up the rover and kicked the accelerator. She pulled away from the toothy ridge, glanced over her shoulder and wiped a finger over her goggles. Through the waves of dust swirls and murk, she swore a thin blue light shone from the cave opening.

THE CART RATTLED AND COUGHED AS IT APPROACHED the research lab with more speed than its design called for. The ferocious wind gusts morphed into a gale, darkening the muted sky and leaving her visually disoriented. Piper monitored her course and position on the Nav panel. She couldn't see more than a few meters ahead and relied on the onboard navigation system to guide her safely to the station. Finally, at the onset of panic, the massive rotating beacon lamp towering over the facility beckoned to her like a lighthouse.

Piper eased into the maintenance shed, dismounted, plugged the rover into its power source and re-engaged the computer links. The well of fear that threatened to drown her in the cave had almost disappeared, but adrenaline continued pumping and paranoia lived in her thoughts. She climbed the metal ramp, boots clanking up the open grate, and entered the station.

The first thing she noticed after muscling the thick doors shut was how quiet the facility seemed compared to the fury outside. She exhaled long and slow, as if she'd been holding her breath all this time, releasing the pent up stress.

"Welcome back," Kitto said. Dimmed lab lights increased in brightness as the smart building detected her presence. The avatar appeared on several screens throughout the main work area in the foyer. Piper dropped onto the change bench, lifted the worn scanner over her head, and removed her longcoat and boots. Dust fell everywhere. She stepped over to a cleaning station and swished the grit from her mouth before splashing her face with water.

"I'm glad you returned before the brunt of the storm hit. It promises to be significant."

The wind moaned like an injured animal. "Sure, I'm thrilled to be here, too." The sound of her voice shocked her: distant, bereft of the confidence she'd known most of her life, bordering on sarcastic. She cleared her throat, grabbed the scanner and marched to the workbench where the primary analytical computers hummed.

"Kitto, I'd like you to begin an analysis of my survey data right away. Some of its circuits overloaded."

She linked the scanning unit to the main computer and placed the stone specimen in a clear plastic bag.

"I take it you found an item of interest, hm?" The man

cocked his head at her from a handful of screens.

"Not sure. I had a... a possible hallucination, or maybe some local interference from the iron-rich rocks messed up my head." She stared off into space. "But I'm not right."

Kitto opened the link to the scanner, then began uploading. Data files scrolled over the primary screen in front of her.

She ran her fingers through her dirt-laden hair, looking forward to a hot shower and fresh clothes. "I found a collection of stones with luminescent properties. Brought this one back and I'll do some geochem on it tomorrow. The other rocks themselves aren't unusual, but these were..." She squeezed her eyes tight, striving to hear any whispers again, but with no luck. "These were..."

"What were they, Piper?"

"Well, several of these fragments formed a series of concentric circles. Not sure of the origin. An artefact from previous visitors, perhaps? I'm curious if anyone's observed this pattern before. I got images of them on the scanner. Cross-link with the Torfinn Libraries, will you?"

"Fascinating... the idea that earlier explorers traveled here is exciting."

She grimaced. "Sure, but that's not the—" Piper swallowed hard, recalling the desperate spectral cries and the strange blue auras. "That's not..."

Concern filled Kitto's expression. *"What happened out there, Piper? What else did you see?"*

She licked her lips and recounted the events as best she could for the record, up until the kaleidoscopic whispers flooded her mind. At that point, she couldn't find the right words to explain the immense depth of fear and foreboding. "The closest thing I can suggest is a collective cry of thousands of people all facing..." She searched her mind. "...their own deaths." She glanced at the avatar. "Does that make any sense at all? Could these stones somehow tap into other civilizations?"

Kitto stroked his chin before saying, *"Well, that is curious. Let's see what my analysis of your observations reveals, hm?"* He then added, *"Do you still detect these whispers?"*

"No," she said. "Not anymore. And that heavy feeling of dread has pretty much disappeared."

"Which suggests some local phenomenon at that particular cavern."

"It would seem."

Kitto scratched his head. *"But we only have one data point to work with. The preliminary analysis will take hours, Piper, and with that storm, there's little more we can do right now. Perhaps you should rest. Enter your observations in the log, or grab some down time."*

Piper leaned forward at the workbench. "Forget it. I have something else to do first."

"What's that?"

She stood. "I want you to analyse my brain activity."

"Your brain? That's an odd request."

"Some strange occurrence happened in that cavern, Kitto, and I have to make sure we consider all possibilities. Getting a mental baseline might show something."

"I understand," the digital man said. *"Your insatiable curiosity was always your strongest trait."*

Piper cleared the examination table and pulled down the imager from its overhead perch. Since she arrived on Hauntor, she had suffered no health issues except for her recurring nightmares, and therefore had no use for the modest medical supplies and diagnostic tools available in the lab. By any normal standards, the equipment and medicines would be adequate. She'd performed a full body baseline scan her first day on the job, following Olavus protocols, and had no reason to do any more.

Until now.

She adjusted the scanning plate for two functions. First, a reading of her entire body to compare with her baseline record. Second, a more intense and thorough diagnostic reading of her brain. She punched the power supply and programmed in the protocols. After hopping on the table, she lay on her back and waited for the plate to begin its methodical sequence.

"The analyzer is operational, Piper, and I'll start a full spectrum sweep of your body and brain waves in a moment. Can you tell me what we're looking for?"

She tapped her fingers on her flat stomach, regulating her breathing. "I don't know yet. Whatever anomalies you come across. But listen, Kitto." She turned toward the old man's avatar on a nearby screen. "Something's not right in my mind. My thoughts are muddled, and I gotta figure out what those... those *things* out there did to me."

She also burned to contact Ariel, but not until she understood what had penetrated her consciousness first.

Piper stared past the analyzer to the ceiling, tracing the spider web of conduits and cables, valves and ventilator shafts, visualising where they intersected with the station's operational computers and air exchangers, releasing her tight shoulder muscles under the soothing, warm light beams of the scanning plate.

As she lay there relaxing, something—or someone—in the recesses of her mind, whispered.

You're not crazy, Piper.
You're not.

THREE

"I MAY BE TOTALLY CRAZY, KITTO, BUT I SAW WHAT I SAW out there," Piper said in a calm voice waving her arm at the large viewing window. Thin morning light struggled to shine through residual dust whorls from the storm. "And even after a good night's sleep, I'm pretty sure I heard what I heard in here," she added, tapping her temple.

"I believe you, Piper. The data you recorded in the cavern has been most intriguing. A strange, unprecedented phenomenon obviously transpired. But as for your body, I found no significant physiological changes since you arrived here three months ago."

She bit into a protein bar and wiped her mouth. "And nothing in my brain waves, either?"

"Correct."

She scrunched her face and swallowed. "So it's a mystery then, because I sure as hell am not nuts."

Piper brushed some crumbs from her hands and washed the meal down with a mug of coffee. She turned from the window and approached the central computer bank. "Kitto, were you able to cross-reference those stone circles with the Torfinn Libraries?"

"Yes, and I confirm we have no recordings like these in our archives."

"Anything close?"

"No," the man said. *"Let's avoid premature conclusions. Remember, the dark planets in the galaxy far outnumber those in the organized cluster. Any speculation about their origin would be... well, imprudent."*

She sat in front of the primary screen and pulled up the recordings she'd taken in the cavern. The glowing circles caused her to wince at the mental memory. But their odd patterns and spectral nature weren't the reason; it was the damn whispers.

Kitto, as if reading her thoughts, inquired, *"More strange voices this morning?"*

Piper shrugged. "No. Not a whimper. And they weren't really voices. More like sensations."

"Intuition, perhaps?" he asked. *"These odd stones may have triggered a kind of second sight in you."* A moment passed before he continued. *"Your biometrics suggest an elevated degree of prescience. If that's the case, the stones could possibly unlock numerous psychic breakthroughs."*

"I've experienced nothing like that before," she said. "I don't go for that ESP stuff, but let's not discount it right away."

Kitto stated, *"More research into this business is required."*

Piper agreed. She had already closed the records and opened the files to a long-range communications propagation theory she'd been studying, suggesting that this planet—and perhaps others like it—could indeed act as repeaters or signal mirrors. In times such as this, she missed her old lab at the Asterian Technical Institute, with its abundant resources and chats with colleagues. Regardless, she needed to continue her investigation here, mapping the mineral resource distribution on Hauntor and modeling its effect on subspace electromagnetic signals.

And put the cave stone through a proper study.

"Kitto, I'd like you to do the geochem analysis on that specimen and figure out its composition and structure. Also, check for luminosity. I'm heading down to Optics to keep working on the EM modeling project."

She positioned the stone on a diagnostic plate adjacent to the geochemical sensor and thumbed the equipment on. Kitto's computers hummed.

The smooth stone piqued her curiosity. Although the analyzer would list its chemical properties and confirm its luminosity, along with the overall atomic structure of the sample, its origin held the most intrigue for her.

Highly unlikely that it formed in the cave by itself.

Perhaps earlier, unknown explorers brought the stones here, arranging them in that pattern. But the ATI had no evidence of earlier settlements or visitors near Hauntor.

And why were the stones placed in concentric circles? This mystified her the most. Some intelligence was behind it. But who?

Or what?

Piper strode down the corridor leading to the Optics Lab. Her thoughts turned to running one of the daily experiments that predicted EM subspace transmissions—the kind used for deep space communications—against changes in mineral distributions.

She swung the Optics door open and stepped into the tiny, stuffy room. After turning on a small task light, she set up the test parameters for her EM model and keyed them into the computer. At the side of the work station, she had already coded and separated a collection of luminescent mineral specimens on a thick table and placed them into a geochem analyzer.

The native sodalite among the samples sparkled like amber diamonds under the infrared spectrum.

Beautiful.

The intricate machines operated flawlessly, a perfect marriage of art and science. This was the work she longed for.

Not farming with Neris in some backwater river bed.

Not entering Mother's political world and that... that... She shivered at the thought of her father, the deceased Governor of Robos 7, ruling that planet with an iron fist.

And sure as hell not gallivanting across the galaxy in a beat-up bucket with Jay Carstairs.

It relieved her to believe there was hope that, perhaps soon, her life and work would return to normal. She'd finish up this project in a couple more months, and resume her old job at the ATI.

She cocked her head and listened to her surroundings.

Her heartbeat.

The thrum of the station life support systems.

The whirr of the computers running through their data crunching and analyses.

And, yes, something else.

Something *other.*

"Piper, help us..."

She bolted upright on the chair. This was no hallucination.

"Kitto, what's the status of the mule?"

"The rummage cart is fully charged and ready to go, but there is a slight issue..."

"Alright, listen. I'm going back to that ridge of caves. I've started another suite of data runs here, and they'll take a few hours to complete." She double-checked the inputs. "I'm hearing them again, Kitto."

She stood and exited the lab. Harsh corridor light

blinded her.

"Are you talking about the mysterious whispers?" The avatar appeared on a pair of screens in the hallway.

"Yes. I'm stopping off to change at my cabin. Can you load the scanner with atomic filters? I'll investigate that end of the light spectrum if I get those stones to shine again."

She headed to the sleeping quarters, running her fingers along the concrete wall. Her footsteps echoed through the stark concrete hallway.

"Understood, but there's something else—"

"Kitto, whatever it is, can't it wait?"

Piper entered her modest room and threw on her dusty outdoor work clothes.

"I don't think so."

"Fine," she huffed, pulling a neck protector over her head. "I'll be down in a sec."

She grabbed a set of gloves and left for the main foyer. Entering the room, she said, "I planned a longer stay at the—"

The monitors flashed an urgent warning. The cave stone she'd placed on the diagnostic plate emitted a hazy, but unmistakeable, blue light.

"Apparently, this specimen you harvested is unique, Piper," the avatar remarked. *"Its structure and chemical composition are unlike anything discovered to date."*

As she drew closer to the strange stone, the ominous spectral whispers grew louder in her skull. They were real. And unsettling. Getting to the bottom of this phenomenon just became her top priority.

Piper read the geochem analysis summary that Kitto prepared. She expected to see atomic lattices, chemical composition, magnetic and electrical properties, luminosity, hardness and mineral ratios. Some of those appeared, but the structure remained hidden, replaced by a simple finding: *Insufficient data.*

She ran the test again with Kitto, waited several minutes, and observed the same result.

"Dammit, I'm heading to the ridge to gather more information on those stones and circles. The scanner works?"

"I loaded the molecular filters in a working unit and confirmed their operability."

She picked up the device from its interface on the workbench and disconnected it from the computer. "We need more data for a proper analysis. I won't be away too long, and in the meantime, run a diagnostic on the equipment. I want to real out any technical problems."

"Very good. I'll also monitor the experiment's progress in the Optics Lab while you're gone."

Piper marched to the doorway, pulled on her boots and longcoat. Then, after slinging the scanner across her chest, she drew a thermal flux gun from the nearby armory.

She slipped on her gloves and goggles. "Oh, and check the perimeter defenses just in case, okay?"

"That seems unnecessary, Piper. None of the reports identify any other lifeforms in this vicinity."

"Perhaps, but I've got a strange feeling about all this business."

Piper heaved open the weighty doors and clanked down the ramp to fetch the mule. She detached the cables, climbed into the cart and churned away from the research lab, snaking through the rocky debris toward the ridge.

Kitto's voice interrupted her thoughts. *"The skies are clear, Piper. No active storms in the area for at least another 24 hours."*

"Understood," she said. "Listen, I'm going to be incommunicado until I reach the caves. Will check in then, okay?"

"Any reason I should know about?"

Piper grimaced. "Nah, I just want some quiet time to

figure things out."

"*Acknowledged.*"

The heart is born solitary, she remembered Neris telling her once, *and after years of struggle to reach into the shadows for existential validation, it didn't recognize itself anymore.*

When the fledgling sunlight peeked through the high, hazy cloud cover like it did this morning, Piper observed that Hauntor held a natural, mysterious beauty, reminding her of the frozen polar regions on Coomus and, for that matter, on Asteria itself.

Except Hauntor's climate was milder. The early surveyors mapped some sub-freezing areas to the west of Olavus, but nothing too harsh at all. The incessant wind made it feel so much colder.

As the mule rumbled across the land, she marvelled at the muted tones of a lavender, eggshell horizon.

This didn't stop the spectral cacophony in her head from intensifying, and she couldn't stop thinking about her half-sister.

But what made this possible?

The lack of biophysical data from her medical scan bothered her. Given yesterday's events, the tool should have detected *some* heightened mental activity at least. How could she have aural hallucinations without increased brain function? Perhaps, like Kitto mused, the stone unleashed some latent perceptive abilities. Second sight? Possibly.

Or something else is going on.

The rover hit a rough patch of debris, and she slowed to manoeuvre around the rocks and crevices. From out of the blue, she remembered Neris and how he torpedoed his science career to take up farming. That began on a crisp fall morning after they'd spent the night in each other's arms. He kissed her cheek, rubbed the stubble on his chin and announced he'd made a life-changing decision. He described to her the chunk of land he purchased in the Valley, and his ambition to grow ember-root crops.

At first, she dismissed his decision as ridiculous, confident he'd change his mind and return to the ATI. But he never did. After several weeks, she feared he abandoned her.

At the transportation platform on a dreary wet afternoon, before he disappeared for good, Neris said to her, "I'd ask you to come with me, Piper. You know I love you."

She stood before him, studying his face as confusion and pain ping-ponged through her body. Drops of rain trickled down her cheek.

"But your future doesn't lie in the soft earth and gentle rains of the Valley, does it?"

Her lips trembled. "I don't understand what you're talking about. We should be together, Neris. Our lives are here in Capital City. Our future is here, together."

The bastard shrugged.

"The truth is I can't stay here, and you'd be beyond miserable farming ember-root. No," he said, "what your future holds may be a mystery, but we both know it's not with me."

He turned and leapt on the shuttle he'd hired to carry him to his new land. Piper remained paralyzed on the platform, sobering rain beating down on her shoulders.

The solitary heart...

The memory of Neris peacefully watching her as the runabout lifted off caused her to relive all that pain. He was the man who got away, of that she was certain. Not because of anything she'd *done*, but because of who she *was*. Or at least, who *Neris thought* she was. A scientist. The daughter of the Torfinn Governing Council's Chancellor. Unwilling to compromise.

And here we are, she thought.

The dark ridge emerged in the distance.

When Jay Carstairs arrived in her life, he dropped in, quite by accident, as an out–of–work pilot. She never counted on falling in love again, but he changed her mind. They teamed up well together against the myrmidons during the Robos 7 crisis, and he helped her overcome the initial shock of learning that Morden Graves was her father. He sealed some Council agreement by hopping into bed with the Chancellor, and nine months later, Piper was born.

But that damn Carstairs…

The captain told her, after she'd fallen hard and given herself to him, that a long time ago he also made love to her own mother in order to save his career. It cost him his wife and his job, and invited the demons in to play.

Still, he showed up for her again when Zadicus Verman from Borta attempted to break her. He ended that creep's life and ensured that her corrupt mother would face justice. He even remained by her side in the hospital while she recovered.

And then the asshole disappeared, too.

Her shoulder muscles tightened. It seemed the closer she got to the caves, the more powerful the spectral whispers grew.

If only I could understand their meaning.

After weeks of searching for the captain, sending him numerous messages only to have them returned unread, she finally let him go and volunteered for the isolated posting on Hauntor. *Some future*, she thought. *Banging on rocks in the middle of nowhere. Messed up and terribly lonely.*

As long as she buried herself in work, her emotional issues remained unhealed. She hadn't even allowed the wounds to develop scars. They remained fresh, toxic, lurking right beneath the thin veneer of her normal life at the lab.

Eventually, she'd have to confront them. She

understood that to heal the pain, she'd have to face the pain. All of it. But not yet. The solitary, forsaken heart would crumble in the face of it.

That weakness filled her with disgust.

THE MULE RATTLED AND CLANKED TOWARD THE YAWNING entrance of the peculiar cavern. The mottled ridge of caves seemed far less intimidating in the spare daylight and absence of yesterday's storms, and Piper looked forward to working on the mystery of the stones by gathering more fundamental data. She began recording and surveyed the cave opening for residual luminescence. The scanner showed nothing unusual. No evidence of the eerie blue light.

"I'm at the ridge now, Kitto. Gonna unload the seismic gear and set up in a few minutes."

"Acknowledged. I'll continue monitoring your position along with environmental parameters."

She prepared a sample bag and a toolkit. The battery on the portable seismograph held a full charge, and she tested the unit's functions to ensure they operated properly. She planned to monitor the cave's structural integrity, specifically detecting any ground vibrations if the stones chose to get busy again.

Piper drew a small container from the pocket in her longcoat and opened it. Two thin round electrodes, the size of buttons, sat there in plastic holders. She removed her goggles, yanked the sensors out, unfolded the backing paper, and stuck one on each temple. The other ends served as input connectors for the scanner. Normally, these pickups analyzed acoustic waves in tiny objects or rocks, but she was determined to capture her brain activity with them if the phenomenon reoccurred.

With the sensors secured in place, she strapped on the headlamp and carried the equipment toward the cave entrance, then headed into the darkness.

Spectral whispers echoing in the background of her mind now burst forward and flooded it. She leaned against the rock wall and focused on the mental sounds, attempting to distinguish one from the rest to make sense of the racket. But her effort yielded nothing helpful. The jumbled noises persisted in languages she didn't understand. After unclasping her longcoat, Piper hefted the seismometer and descended toward the dark chamber.

Not crazy, she reminded herself.

Not one bit.

As she stepped over debris, she paid close attention to the visible striations on the walls and the sodalite deposits that glittered under her infrared scanner. By the time she arrived at the subterranean hollow, the whispers filled her mind, echoing back and forth as if they bounced through her skull, leaving her with fear and dread.

The circle patterns had not moved, and the gems remained dormant—the same way she'd seen them yesterday, so it didn't appear that any other living creature lived down here. She prepared the seismometer and activated it, then planted a handful of geophones throughout the chamber.

Piper then grabbed the scanner and raised it to her face. In the headlamp's light, she observed several readings on the chemistry of the surrounding rocks and circles themselves. With the molecular filters, she delineated the rock structure and composition with more accuracy and precision—nothing compared to the resolution in the Optics Lab, but useful in the field. The scanning device dutifully recorded these observations.

She switched screens to her temple sensors and the familiar wave patterns of brain signals appeared. Piper was no medical expert, but she knew enough to recognize that, like Kitto's findings, the brain function seemed normal.

Waves oscillated in the 40 to 100 Hz range. Standard magnetic and electrical components. No overt cause behind these strange sounds presented itself in her brainwaves.

Thoughts themselves comprised EM energy too, and since she could hear the whispers internally, she expected to find an assortment of anomalies in her regular thinking patterns.

Such was not the case.

Where are these ghostly voices coming from? Why are they so intense in this cave?

Piper recalibrated the scanner to check that it functioned normally. Again, despite hearing cries in her head, her brain waves appeared normal. Her only conclusion was that the noises were simply undetectable with her rudimentary equipment. They had to exist on a different dimensional plane altogether. A spectral one, perhaps. Her heart began pounding.

The scanner's alarm shrieked, and she flipped screens away from her brain pattern to the molecular readings screen. Among the nondescript observations of intrusive igneous minerals, several anomalies appeared. She expected some impurities in the findings, so these measurements were not unexpected. However, the precise nature of these data eluded the device's ability to delineate and identify them.

She held the device closer to the stone circles, and the readings scattered. The tool could not resolve the chemical composition of the stones. They were unlike anything she understood about the geochemistry of rocks and minerals.

Regardless, the scanner recorded a high concentration of magnetite and secondary ferro-magnetic rocks in the chamber. The findings made sense to Piper, given the complete black out of communications being filtered by the magnetic properties.

"Well," she said out loud, "maybe Kitto can tackle these spectral whispers when I return to the lab."

Her voice died in the stale, confined space of the hollow.

But before returning to Olavus, Piper wanted to activate the concentric circles again. She knelt in front of the outer rim closest to her and studied the pattern more closely this time. Kitto reported no record of these circles in the archives, so relating them to anything she observed already would be futile.

She scanned the gems by applying the molecular filter, but observed no solid readings. When she touched them yesterday, she activated a torrent of blue light and a ferocious roar of spectral sounds and emotions, leaving her wallowing in loss and pain... not something she desired to experience again. But her curiosity wouldn't allow her to leave well enough alone.

Piper inhaled, held her breath, and reached for the stones.

FOUR

CAPTAIN JAY CARSTAIRS LINGERED IN THE SHADOWS OF A local flophouse in the town of North Kalmut on the remote planet Occion. He peered across a mud-filled street at Tilley's Outpost, one of the filthiest, most violent, and nastiest watering holes in the galaxy.

His kind of tavern.

Humid night air cloaked the place. He glanced up and down the dark road before whispering in his comms device.

"Quirp, keep the engines warm."

The QRP-705 ship computer sing-songed, *"As you wish, Captain. The Dauntless is flight ready the moment you need her."* Then Quirp added, *"Are you sure you want to risk this meeting? Perhaps there are other alternatives to—"*

"We've been over this. But don't worry, I'll be careful." He instinctively felt for the thermal flux gun strapped around his waist.

"Thank you. I do not wish to be marooned at these

coordinates for the rest of my operational life."

"Just keep the ship on standby, Quirp." Carstairs licked his lips and puffed out his chest. "It's time."

The unmistakable laughter and shouts of drunkards poured from Tilley's long before he climbed the wooden steps to the main door. When he entered, pushing his way through a gaggle of curious traders, the sweet aroma of jangle-weed hit him hard. A few pilots and runners from various species watched him enter, then turned back to their drinks or gambling. An out of tune house band played in the far corner, and several provocative Rilmorian women lounged at the bar, waving and posing. Their thin strips of clothing left little to the imagination.

But Jay Carstairs was not here for that sort of pleasure. His sole objective was to find the old Asterian trader Dhollot and get some work... return to a normal life... and run as far away from his own past as he could.

The wily merchant sat by himself, back against the wall, nursing a drink and cracking jangle-weed on the tabletop. He acknowledged the fellow and squeezed toward him.

"Thought you might have chickened out, Captain," the older man rumbled. "So, you've been hanging out on Izillon, eh? That's a long way from Asteria."

Carstairs pulled up a stool, waving at the thick perfumed smoke. "You're right, Dhollot, but I needed to get away for a bit, and Izillon is a beautiful little planet. If you don't mind the creepy simian beasts, that is. Gives me a chance to think about things, you understand."

The cagey trader observed him with mild curiosity. "People everywhere have been doing a lot of thinking these days, it seems."

"Well," he continued, "these are... interesting times in the Torfinn Cluster." He surveyed the room. "I recognize many of these runners from the old days. I gather life's been tough for all of us."

Dhollot sipped his drink. "Quite so. Ever since that dirty business with Chancellor Madison being deposed, and the Asterian Battle Fleet patrolling trade lanes, it's been challenging getting any contract, legit or otherwise." He cracked one of the jangle-weed roots with a knuckle. The pod released its smoky intoxicant into the air.

The stocky man invited Carstairs to partake. "Some other time, perhaps. I can't stay long."

Dhollot snorted. "Smart." After waving the sweet smoke in his face, he inhaled long and deep. "Well," he said, his words on the cusp of slurring, "this is your meeting. How can I help you?"

The captain leaned forward on the table and lowered his voice. "I'm looking for a contract. Maybe you know someone. Do me a favour?"

The man sniffed with disdain. "We all understand the reality of our situation, Captain. There are no contracts. Following Borta's fall and the Robosian government's upheaval, the Torfinn Council's surveillance is pervasive. Even here."

"What are you saying?"

"Until and unless the galaxy stabilizes, we're all out of work. The regular black market trade routes aren't safe. Too many patrols, you see. Those of us who've been in the game a long time can afford to wait it out within reason, but these other clowns won't last much longer." He sniggered. "Look around. It's in their eyes... the feral expression of desperation."

Carstairs studied the men who, despite their apparent economic duress, numbed their senses with drink and expensive drugs. A pair of toughs leaning against the bar sneered at him and whispered to each other.

He faced the grizzled old trader. "Surely there must be some work. Maybe not under-the-radar jobs, but still..."

Dhollot leaned back and studied him. "There is

nothing. Why do you think we're hanging out here in this dump?" He glanced about nervously, licked his lips, and hinted in a coy way. "Well, almost nothing."

"You... you have something?"

The playful merchant shook his head. "You're not the right person for it. Never mind."

Carstairs reached across the table and grabbed him by his jacket. "Tell me. I'm going crazy on Izillon. I need the work."

Dhollot brushed his hands away and straightened. His pupils gleamed like glass with violent intensity. "Such a brash fellow," he said. "I'm surprised you're still alive, to be honest. Come," he added, changing his demeanour, "join me in the jangle-weed incense. You'll feel better, you know. And none of this," he waved his hand with a flourish, "will matter anymore."

The beautiful, full aroma of the weed tempted him without a doubt. His battle with drink remained ongoing, and it took all of his willpower and guilt to resist Dhollot's invitation.

He'd been a worthless drunk in his younger days. Ruined many lives. Made plenty of poor decisions. Piper's youthful face flashed in his mind, and he recalled the promise he made to himself when he ditched her at the hospital: to give an honest shot at being an Izillonian fish supplier to the outer planets.

But that wasn't really him.

He needed something more than just excitement.

He needed something... darker.

Carstairs was surprised to find his hands gripping the edge of the table with harsh ferocity. "Tell me," he demanded. "What sort of job?"

Dhollot's eyes narrowed. "If you're up for it, Captain, I know of an open contract released by the Black Bond cartel yesterday. More money than you've ever seen in your miserable life. But no pilot here will go near it. That should tell you something."

If nothing else, Dhollot's assessment made sense. Since the desperate traders and flyboys wasting themselves in Tilley's Outpost wouldn't take on the cartel's business, it had to be suicidal.

"Interested?"

Carstairs clenched his teeth. The danger didn't bother him; he'd been in and out of snares most of his life. And cartel money could be attractive. But Piper kept invading his thoughts, as if she watched his every move.

As if she *knew*.

He pushed her away and raised his head to stare into Dhollot's weathered face. "Tell me more."

Before he learned about the contract details, the pair of toughs who watched him earlier appeared beside their table. Dhollot's hand slid to his thigh. "Something we can help you with, boys?"

The taller one with a missing front tooth spoke first. "We got no quarrel with you, Dhollot. But this here asshole," he said, pointing a crooked thumb at Carstairs, "is trouble. We'd like to, er, invite him outside for a wee chat."

"Yeah, yeah," the other tough echoed. "Invite him outside, yeah, uh-huh."

The captain stood. He glared at the tall stranger. "Tell you what, friend. Let me treat you both to a few drinks before we go our separate ways." His fingers pulled back his jacket to reveal his weapon.

"Here's a better idea," the leader slurred. "You come with us instead."

Carstairs scowled. "Or what, exactly?"

The man moved with impossible speed. Before the captain took his next breath, the toothless one held a blade to his throat. "Outside. Now."

Adrenaline surged through Carstairs' body, and when

that happened, someone usually got hurt. He turned to Dhollot. "We'll carry on our conversation in a minute."

The merchant raised his glass to him and slammed back the dregs of his drink.

"And put that knife away, would you? You're causing a scene."

Carstairs headed for the door, aware of the room going quiet and many of the patrons staring at him. After exiting Tilley's, the captain faced the thugs in the street. "Listen, boys. I don't want any trouble. What's up?"

The tall one spat on the ground and muttered, "You're a slug, flyboy. And we knows what you did to ruin the trade for everybody. Put a lot of runners outta commission with your interference."

The captain shrugged. "What are you prattling on about? I'm in the same boat as you. Can't find an honest run to save my life."

"That's not how we sees it, old man."

"Well then, you'd better explain because right now, I find your tone irritating. And I don't like it." He flexed his fingers.

The squat sidekick produced a weapon in his palm and cackled. Tallboy pushed him away. "Here's the skinny. You and that Madison girl destroyed our livelihoods in the Fairfield Sector when you overthrew the Governor on Robos 7. Then, you messed up our trade with Borta 'cause she wouldn't play nice with the man, and you took it upon yourself to be some freakin' hero."

"You got that all wrong, friend. And I'm done with these accusations."

"Yeah? Whatcha gonna do, ya old puke?"

Carstairs considered reaching for his weapon, but these two already had the drop on him. To get rid of them and pick up the conversation with Dhollot, he needed a better tactic.

And fast.

"Hey, lose the name-calling, *friend.* You want credits? Travel somewhere? Let's talk. Otherwise, we're done."

The taller thug lashed out at him with the blade, narrowly missing his ear and grazing his jacket. The smaller grunt cackled with glee.

That unfortunate move was all he needed. The man lunged again; Carstairs countered, sweeping his leg, sending the man sprawling, face-down in the mud. He spun and grabbed the sidekick's wrist and snapped it, causing him to drop his weapon and stagger away in pain.

"Quirp!" he shouted into his comms. "Fire the engines."

The leader rose, reaching for a sidearm.

But Carstairs anticipated the move. His flux gun was already in his hand. "I wouldn't do that if I were you, *friend.*"

The man hesitated, glanced at the gathering crowd, then reached for his weapon, anyway.

Carstairs fired a bolt into his chest, searing the man's ribs and spilling his steaming guts into the mud.

The wild assortment of onlookers cheered them on, clinking their mugs.

"Quirp?"

"We are standing by, Captain."

Carstairs peered around, searching for Dhollot among the faces, but couldn't see him anywhere. He backed away from the Outpost, holding his weapon steady at the onlookers in front of him. When he reached a nearby machine shop, he turned and raced toward the ship. Shouts rose behind him and several shots flared overhead.

"Open the portal, Quirp!"

Carstairs fired high and wide over his shoulder, hoping to slow down whoever else wanted a piece of him. His boots clanked up the ramp to the entry port, and he dove inside the *Dauntless* as a laser flare ricocheted off the ship's shields.

"Fire thrusters and get us the hell out of here!"

"As you wish."

The light cruiser exploded straight up into the night.

Jay Carstairs picked himself off the deck, stumbled onto the bridge, and sank into the command chair.

"That was a close call tonight, Quirp." He exhaled and smiled. "Pretty awesome."

FIVE

A SURGE OF ENERGY SCREAMED UP PIPER'S SPINE AS HER fingers quivered over the stones in the outer ring. Harsh blue light flooded the chamber. She recoiled, aching to seek distance from the stones, but her own wonder—like a separate, objective being—kept pushing her on.

Voices, if she could call them that, intensified, shrieking with a pain so deep and foreign that it crushed her soul. She fought to read the scanner. The molecular filtering showed nothing. In the eerie glow of the chamber, she flipped the screens to check her brain wave patterns.

Sweet mother of...

The readings were unlike anything she'd ever observed before. They comprised the Normal EM waves around 100 Hz, but now also spiked into a much higher frequency range. She double-checked the screen. No doubt about it: whatever she triggered in the stones—or more to the point, whatever they triggered in her—was being recorded through her agitated and highly active brain.

The whispers became wails.

Piper winced at the sudden rush of pain that careened through her skull. Again, she deciphered no words, no recognizable language of anything remotely familiar. Instead, the whispers left impressions: panic, intense brutality, instant death.

The cutting of flesh and bone.

What are you telling me?

No response came.

Piper moved her fingers across the other stones, sending more light splaying over the chamber walls. The seismograph alarm coincided with renewed ground vibrations. Dust clouds puffed from the ceiling.

"Who are you?" she shouted, her voice throaty and distant.

The mental screams intensified, such that Piper began losing consciousness from the explosions of pain ripping into her mind.

Pull away… pull away…

She couldn't tell if the cry was her own thought or a spectral impression, but the sense of immediate danger smothered her. She wrenched her fingers from the gems and a shock of energy threw her backwards.

Through her fluttering eyelids, the haunting light swirled around. She lay on her back against the craggy rock wall, catching her breath. The howls in her head refused to diminish, and she squeezed her temples in her palms and cried out, then sank down on the cold stoney ground. Black spots filled her vision, and just before she lost consciousness, Ariel's image appeared, and there was no mistaking her words.

Help us.

WHEN PIPER REGAINED CONSCIOUSNESS, SHE HAD NO idea how long she'd been out. A few minutes? An hour? All she remembered was the intensity of emotions from the strange voices coursing through her.

And Ariel's terrified face.

Her head continued pounding, but the fury had diminished. Blue-grey light floated around the room and up the ramp toward the cave entrance, like traveling cosmic auroras.

The seismograph alert shrieked anew. The ground rumbled and the chamber walls cracked. Dust and rocks tumbled from above. Piper hauled herself up. *Time to get out.*

The incline leading to the entrance shuddered and several large boulders burst from the surrounding rock. Eerie light continued to bathe her in a swath of blue. She staggered and fell to one knee, fighting for breath as the dust whipped around, choking her throat and filling her nostrils.

She peered up.

There!

Light marking the cave entrance appeared, and she scrabbled toward it. Without warning, a horrific thunderclap crashed behind her and rubble exploded over the ramp. The blue light flickered and disappeared. Piper glanced back to see nothing but a crumbled rock wall from the explosion.

The cave continued heaving.

Run, Piper.

She staggered toward the entrance, avoiding more rocks bursting from the top of the cave and exploding from the surrounding walls. Before she reached the opening, a fist-sized rock flew at her from the darkness and clipped her knee, spinning her around and dropping her against the rocky ground.

Half-blind and crippled, Piper crawled toward the light. A menacing crack in the entrance's archway threatened to bring the entire cave down.

A few more meters...

Debris shattered around her. Then, as the archway began disintegrating, she gathered as much remaining strength as she could, and propelled herself through the entrance and rolled free, just as the opening crumbled in a heap, sealing off the cave in a flurry of dust and boulders.

Piper rolled away from the cave toward the rover. Sharp rocks scraped at her face and hands as she scrambled to put as much distance between her and the destruction as possible. Dust prevented her from seeing clearly, and she strained to breathe through the grit in her mouth and lungs. Piper coughed and tried to spit, but she produced no saliva. She lay on her back beside the mule, digging at the grit collecting in her eyes.

Mercifully, the ground stopped shaking.

The scanner across her chest had disappeared. Her goggles dangled around her neck. Piper struggled into a sitting position and, in a panic, glanced around. No sign of her equipment. She tried standing, but her damaged knee refused to hold any weight. The lack of blood on the wound indicated that, fortunately, no artery had been hit, but she suspected the patella was fractured, or worse, shattered. No way to tell until she returned to the lab.

Piper dragged herself closer to the rover and leaned against its wheel hub. With the urgency of the cave-in over, she noticed the voices in her mind had dissipated into mere hints of whispers—present, but not debilitating.

And in that moment of confused chaos, with her injury and knowing she'd have to return to the cave to recover the scanner—the only evidence she had of the spikes in her brain waves—she thought of *him*. The man appeared just beyond the edge of feeling, nudging memories into the forefront, teasing her heart with cruel pulses.

Where is he?

Why did he bail without saying a word?

And why won't his damn memory leave me alone?

Piper shook her head. As the adrenaline diminished, the stab in her knee cried for attention and her back and chest felt heavy, throbbing with pain from the narrow escape.

She pulled herself up and rummaged in the storage area for the first aid kit. She found it buried at the back of the container, pulled out a painkiller and swallowed it. Then she took an inflatable tension belt and wrapped it around her knee. Once she hit the compression, it provided support to her leg so she could at least put some weight on it.

The critical task now was to find the scanner. She pulled on the goggles and punched her comms badge. "Kitto, I ran into a bit of a problem here." Her vision blurred as the painkiller took effect. "Will explain when I return."

"Acknowledged."

She peered at the cave opening and the wall of rock and debris that sealed it shut. Gaining access would take forever without the proper equipment, and she was in no condition to do the heavy lifting on her own. For the first time since she'd arrived on Hauntor, she wished she wasn't alone.

SIX

SCYTHER ENTERED THE DARK, FAMILIAR REGENERATION Room 22 and marched to the station where his chief medical advisor waited for him. He'd struggled with his organic arm for over two months now, and it refused to function within acceptable operating parameters.

They could delay the procedure no longer.

Dr. Sheilor inspected the fetid arm with her ocular scanner, grunted, and instructed the Protoran leader to sit. She placed his rotting limb on the table before her and rolled back the thick, vulcanized rubber protection. Flesh peeled off the arm and fell away like thin bits of paper. He sensed her observing him.

"This is well overdue, Scyther."

"I am aware," he shrugged.

"The organics are unlike our mechanical parts, my Liege. You know this."

Scyther scanned the doctor's physical parameters and said, "I am more fully integrated into the machine world than you, Dr. Sheilor. I can withstand greater periods of time with flesh of dubious origins."

"Regardless," the doctor muttered, grabbing an arm restraint, "let's get you fixed up."

Scyther shut down several of his non-essential systems for the procedure, including his optics. What flashed in front of him was no longer the constant data stream awaiting his synthesis. Instead, his neural lattice detected only what the medical practitioner performed.

"Someone is here to see you, my Lord," she said matter-of-factly.

Scyther boosted energy to his primary network, engaged optical scanners, and viewed his senior tactical officer, Martok, entering the regeneration room and maintaining a respectful distance.

"Approach, Martok. We have not yet begun the procedure."

"By your grace, Lord Scyther. I bring news from Robos 7."

Scyther's systems retrieved the internal data pack for Robos 7 and processed what had been happening there since the former Chancellor's daughter disrupted their way of life. "What is it?"

"The internal conflict continues, my Liege. No substantive change. Various factions continue fighting for control of the mineral trade and government powers."

"Then why interrupt me, Martok, if there are no significant changes? I am busy." Scyther pointed at the medical advisor to continue the procedure of replacing his decaying organic arm with a freshly harvested appendage.

Sheilor prepared to remove his rancid limb.

"Liege," Martok continued, "what's new is a report that the Robosians are operating reproduction farms to supply their workforce. Apparently, the ruling class, the Heads, have been breeding workers for decades."

Scyther grimaced as Sheilor finished removing his old arm and began attaching the nerve endings of a fresh appendage to his input port. "Do you have evidence these farms truly exist?"

"Yes, Liege. We intercepted satellite transmissions showing the precise location of the facilities. They remain intact. Fully functional. Fully organic."

"Production?"

"Thousands of younglings every year."

The Protoran leader's mind separated. One section focused on the integration of the new flesh arm; the other considered the ramifications of this surprising information. "Martok, access to these farms would have a significant impact on our people. And you're certain they weren't damaged in the rebel uprisings? How strange."

"Yes, sir." He glanced at his tablet. "Satellite imagery taken in the last hour shows the facilities received no damage. The fighting, it seems, is confined to Edenfall and a few sparsely populated industrial outposts."

Throughout his long Fairfield Sector existence, Scyther had never encountered organic humanoid farming. But with the galactic Ethical Protocol on Non-Interference in place, some member planets refused to divulge their internal private affairs. He flinched as Sheilor tugged on his shoulder mechanics. "Who's in charge over there? One of the old Governor's idiot ministers, or has the Torfinn Chancellor interceded?"

"Neither, my Lord. Our spies tell us that Feryn Graves, the former Governor's son, along with a small group of progressives are leading the planet during the crisis. However, many factions continue fighting for power and influence, so perhaps his hold is tenuous."

"Naturally."

Sheilor stepped back and adjusted the automated surgery pod. She glanced at Scyther and he redistributed his internal energy field to permit integration of the new arm.

"Martok," he said, his speech slowing. "Along with the Robosians and the Bortans, we are the only other developed planet in the Fairfield Sector aligned with the Torfinn Governing Council. We have respected the Ethical Protocol since its initial implementation, and we must not allow recent events on Robos 7 to change our position."

"Yes, my Liege." The officer could not hide the disappointment in his artificial voice.

"But we must all preserve our individual and collective ways of life, no matter the consequences."

"My Lord, are you... are you suggesting we ignore the Protocol and interfere with Robos 7's affairs in order to—"

"Not at all, Martok. The policy remains in effect. But we mustn't grow complacent. These breeding facilities are cause enough for our people—across the entire transhuman spectrum—to have hope for our future. Imagine... a long-term supply of organics for the taking."

"Yes, Liege."

Scyther winced at the searing pain of the organic nerves being attached. "As such, I'd like you to pull a diplomatic team together and arrange a conference with Feryn Graves on Robos 7."

"What purpose for the meeting shall I give them, my Liege? They will demand to know. These diplomats are skittish, and more so when they're given orders on short notice."

The large Protoran considered the options presenting themselves in his artificial mind.

Martok remained silent.

"Tell them I want to discuss the status of the Robosian reproduction farms. Let's see if we can negotiate a deal for their manufactured organics. Perhaps the Head leadership is no longer tethered to the idea of autonomy for the labourers, now that chaos rules that planet. In exchange, they may desire additional military resources to help secure young Feryn Graves in his position as leader. Quell the uprising for him, so to speak."

"By your grace, my Liege." Martok saluted, pivoted and exited the room.

After a few moments passed, Scyther glanced at Sheilor. "I trust my plan to negotiate access to their organics is appropriate?"

"You don't need to hear from me about such political tripe, my Lord."

"Perhaps not. But I value your input."

She ignored him and focused on her work.

"If there's something on your mind, then speak, Sheilor. You are my oldest, dearest friend."

Sheilor continued monitoring her equipment as the fresh organic pathways replaced the old in the Protoran leader's arm. "Regarding Robos 7 and the Ethical Protocol, I have remained silent." She turned to him.

"Go on."

"Protorans will do whatever you tell them. That's a tremendous responsibility weighing on your shoulders. Our population continues to decay and cease functioning because of the lack of fresh organic material available to us, and the rate of loss increases daily. Our indigenous creatures are completely diminished, and the people worry that our entire civilization may soon become extinct, or reduced to microchips in a computer. The organics shortage must be addressed, of course, and I know you're doing everything you can about that."

She moved closer and held his good hand.

"But I suggest you consider any action against Robos 7 with extreme caution. The worker Hands are proven, formidable fighters, and they even had outside help from the Chancellor's daughter to overthrow the previous government. Mind your step, old friend." She backed away and glanced at her machines.

Scyther began shutting down his non-essential functions. Immediately, the pain from the nerve endings ceased.

Sheilor was correct. He understood all too well the need for importing fresh organics to supplement their mechanical bodies. But he was determined to make a deal with the young Graves to access their reproduction farms, and then his own people would never worry about decay again. Should Graves refuse, however, then he would be forced to find a different solution.

Tephera Madison, that cagey old Chancellor, would understand my people's needs.

"Thank you for your concern, Doctor, but do not worry. I know exactly what I must do to save our world."

ALTHOUGH THE PAINKILLERS HAD TAKEN FULL EFFECT, and Piper now hobbled more efficiently around the mule, she knew they only provided false relief. As soon as the pills wore off, her knee would bark at her again and shut down, so she avoided putting any unnecessary weight on it.

The rover contained no massive drilling equipment that might break through the rock debris covering the cave entrance, and Piper concluded the scanner must have fallen inside somewhere. She considered transporting the old excavation machinery that the engineers used to build Olavus, but that would require more time, several trips, many more hands, and she needed to understand what the spectral voices meant. Now.

What would Carstairs do?

The question kept circling through her wooly thoughts. Piper staggered to the entrance, looking for an air pocket. She shone her beam into the crevices, tore a few light rocks away, but the opening was closed up tight. Trying to move these boulders out of the way by hand would be futile. After several minutes spent poking around the barrier, she rested on a large flat stone that had tumbled from the cave.

Was the scanner all that important? Could she retrieve it some other day? While always an option, the odd whispers in her mind lingered, ever-present and intertwined with the stones in the lower chamber. More importantly, the device had captured spikes in her brain wave activity. Clues to what happened, if not the answers, had to be there.

No, abandoning the scanner was not an option.

Piper limped several meters from the entrance, drew her thermal flux gun, set it on maximum force, and aimed at one of the larger stones at the centre of the pile. She squeezed the trigger.

The beam splashed against the boulders. Several small rocks splintered away under the power of the weapon. Tiny shards bounced off her goggles.

Piper stopped firing and approached the entrance to inspect the impact. Other than some pebbles being displaced, the heavier rocks remained intact. She shook her head and holstered the flux gun. *Works great in combat; less so in mining operations*, she thought.

What she really needed was a large, industrial drill bit… some kind of foraging implement. The rover had no such tool; however, other pieces of equipment hung from the vehicle, held by thick straps and metal holders. A couple of shovels and cable assemblies covered one side, and clamped to the rover's rear was a light duty scraper used to sweep debris and dust drifts off the ramp at Olavus. Its low profile and jagged leading edge might help clear some rocks from the entrance.

She released the tool from its hold, and it dropped hard to the ground. Piper dragged the scraper to the front of the mule and secured it.

The extra weight over the engine caused the rover to

dip forward. Piper activated the mule, proceeded to the rock face and excavated the point of loosest debris. The blade swiftly removed it, exposing further rocks and boulders. She poked at the pile with the blade, to no avail.

Breaking through would require a lot more power.

Piper backed the rover up, tilted the blade at an angle, and sped toward the rock face. She rammed into the pile, and a few stones loosened and fell away. She took another run, targeting the loose rocks. The rover smashed into the wall, and the sudden impact caused her body to launch into the steering wheel, winding her momentarily.

She eased away and pulled herself out of the mule to assess the result. A thin opening appeared. After climbing up the rock pile for a better view, she judged the opening to be too narrow, yet felt she could squeeze through if she ditched her coat and weapon.

She shone her torch around the hole. The inside of the cave—at least at the entrance—seemed relatively clear. Rocks and other debris blanketed the ground, but it was passable. She aimed the light through the crack, relieved to see enough space for standing and a clear path leading down to the lower chamber.

Piper slipped out of the longcoat, removed the weapon from its holster, and strapped the torch around her head. She pulled some of the looser material away and placed her arms through the tiny opening. *This'll be a tight fit.* Then, she kicked with her good leg and thrust herself into the hole. Rocks pinched her shoulders and hips, and she scraped her body anew as she wriggled through. Finally, her hands reached the other side, and she hauled herself into the dark cave.

Her knee screamed at her as the painkillers slowly lost their effectiveness. She didn't have much time left before becoming completely debilitated.

Piper removed her goggles and inspected the area.

Scattered rocks littered the ground. The ceiling showed fresh cuts where debris had broken off. Despite searching everywhere for the scanner, nothing appeared.

She staggered down toward the chamber. Further ahead, the headlamp showed more rocks; a cave-in blocked her entry. She prayed the scanner hadn't been torn off there.

Rocks covered most of the slate floor, and Piper moved with caution, trying to secure her footing as best she could. Approaching the boulders, she frantically searched for the missing equipment, finding nothing. The rock wall prevented her from descending any further. Sweat poured from her face, partly from the exertion and mostly from her pain.

No way to get the rover down here, even if she could smash a hole in the cave opening. She leaned against the uneven wall, her breathing strained, and carefully shone the light over the ground.

The rock walls trembled, spilling a plume of dust from the ceiling on her head. Piper gulped. The stability of the cavern itself was questionable. She resigned to losing the scanner and, using the tunnel sides for support, crept back toward the entrance.

On her way through the boulders, she stretched around the debris, lost her balance, and fell. Fresh pain shot up her injured leg. Piper winced, struggling to hoist herself up.

A glint in the lamplight across the rubble caught her attention. She crawled over the debris, scraping her legs and hands. A shimmering light flashed in the gloom.

The scanner, or what remained of it, sparkled like a jewel. The falling rocks had crushed it, leaving the device mostly covered in dirt, its strap shredded.

Piper grabbed the mangled machine and brought it to her face. A fresh cloud of dust fell from above. Punching the power button produced nothing. *Perhaps Kitto can still pull some information from it back at the lab.*

The tunnel continued groaning. She staggered to the entrance, tossed the scanner through the access hole, and heard it skitter down the far side. Then she pulled her way through. Loose rocks in the passage hinted at the structure's imminent demise.

She kicked, ignoring the pain of the sharp rocks gouging into her hips and thighs. Her hands broke through and she tumbled out just as the hole behind her collapsed and the cave walls imploded.

Piper rolled across the hard terrain as dust and dirt bloomed into the surrounding air. When the ground stopped rumbling, she opened her eyes. The cave had turned to rubble. She grabbed the crushed scanner and tossed it in the rover, then retrieved her longcoat and grimaced as she pulled it over her battered arms and shoulders.

The first aid kit contained no additional painkillers. Piper shrieked as she hoisted her injured leg into the mule and climbed behind the wheel. A long ride back to the lab lay ahead, and she prayed her injuries wouldn't cause her to black out on the way.

She floored the mule and headed out, and realized this was *exactly* what the Captain of the *Dauntless* would have done. And in that same moment, she also understood how alone and scared she truly was.

PIPER TOSSED THE BROKEN SCANNER OVER THE LAB bench, where it clattered in front of Kitto's sensors. She retrieved more pain medication pills from the dispensary, slammed a couple down her throat, and slumped on a stool.

"I'm reading dangerous bio-markers in your overall health," Kitto said. *"You require medical attention."*

"I'm okay," she muttered. "Can you retrieve anything from the scanner?" Sleep and fatigue overwhelmed her as she fought to remain awake.

The sensors whirred and hovered over the device, and the computer chugged. *"There is nothing to salvage from this unit, Piper. The memory circuits, including backups, are too damaged."* Kitto's avatar flashed on the screen. *"Sorry."*

Piper arched her back and stretched. "That's alright. I'll head out tomorrow for another look."

"I do not think that's in your best interest," the computer said. *"Your knee requires immediate attention or you may never have its full use again. There are several deep contusions and lacerations across your body as well. You need to see a doctor, and fortunately, there's a mobile hospital at the Second Point outpost en route to Asteria."*

Kitto's demeanour softened.

"Time to go home, Piper. The medics can assess and treat your knee, and you can use the ATI labs to analyze the unknown stone much better than I can here."

Piper suddenly felt the depth of all those aches and pains. The avatar was correct, but returning home now soured her.

"Besides," Kitto continued, *"your observations of the whisper stone and a cache full of others are of significant strategic importance to the Torfinn Governing Council. Show them the sample, as they may wish to protect this area. You'll also be able to contact your half-sister and assess that apparent connection."*

She reached into her pocket and felt the stone with her fingers. If it fell into the wrong hands and produced the same visions in others, immeasurable chaos could ensue. But in the right hands, perhaps some good could be achieved.

She dropped her head, feeling the full weight of defeat. "Okay, Kitto. Bring the shuttle online and begin pre-flight preparations. Alert the ATI that I'm coming home once I see the medics on Second Point."

SEVEN

THE DAUNTLESS SHUDDERED AS SHE TOOK DIRECT FIRE from the security ships patrolling Occion's orbit. The impact threw Carstairs from the command chair, slamming him into the bulkhead near the vacant tactical station.

"Dammit, Quirp! Get those shields up!"

"As you wish, Captain."

He picked himself up and glanced at the overhead screen. A pair of gunships appeared off starboard, in hot pursuit. A gaggle of others followed at a distance.

"Incoming message, Captain."

"Put it up."

The viewer blinked and a sharply dressed woman sitting erect in an oversized command chair materialized, replacing the purple planetary horizon. She clenched her jaw with purpose and gripped the chair's armrests. Her slick, dark hair stretched back from her face, and her cold eyes glared directly at him.

"Captain Carstairs, I am Commander Gutizenda of the

Occion Orbital Security Force. You are hereby ordered to return to the planet immediately. Is that understood?"

Carstairs leaned on the command console, inspecting his fingernails. "Sorry, I can't do that, Commander. I'm already late for another appointment."

Her lips thinned. *"That response is unacceptable. Land your ship now, or suffer the consequences."*

He muted the transmission. "Quirp, can we outrun those patrols?"

"Affirmative. This class of gunship lacks long range flight capabilities and velocity. The patrols are primarily used for suborbital engagements only."

"All right. Well, I suppose this getaway will only add to the legend of the *Dauntless*, hm? Plot a random course for Suna. Stand by to punch it."

"As you wish, Captain."

He unmuted the comms channel and frowned at the stern-faced officer.

Gutizenda bristled. *"Carstairs, I won't ask you again. Return to Occion now!"*

"Sorry, Commander, no can do. It'll have to wait until the next time I'm back your way."

He hit the main thrusters, and the *Dauntless* blasted out of orbit, leaving the patrols far behind.

THE LIGHT CRUISER RACED THROUGH THE CORRIDOR OF dark planets, transmitting false transponder signals as a matter of course to dissuade any other ships—friendly or hostile—from finding their location. Jay Carstairs entered the bridge after taking a quick nap and assumed the helm. He sniffed the air and pulled a face.

"What's that smell, Quirp?"

The ship's computer said, "It appears to be emanating from the cargo area, Captain, since it comprises the unmistakable scent of the fish you harvested on Izillon and prepared for delivery."

He grimaced and sighed. "How much longer before we reach Suna?"

"Three hours, forty-two minutes at current velocity. I have contacted the Bolutian settlement there and they are preparing to meet at the designated rendezvous location."

"Great," he said. "I can't wait to get this order off my ship." He leaned over the navigation console, shaking his head. "Look what's happened to us, Quirp. The *Dauntless* smells like an old fish scow. What have I done to her?"

Quirp, in his often annoying sing-song voice, replied, "You have been a fish merchant since leaving Asteria a couple months ago, Captain. Earning... what did you call it? An *honest* living. Is that not so?"

Carstairs caressed the back of the seat at the communications station Piper once occupied. "Yes," he replied. Turning to the bridge viewer, he muttered, "Quirp, you should have stopped me."

"If you recall, Captain, I had suggested at the time that you forsake a fishing excursion to Izillon and instead help Ms. Madison with her physical recovery and transition back to a normal life. You chose to go fishing."

Carstairs scratched the stubble on his chin, recalling the spontaneous decision he'd made to leave her at the hospital.

"Yes, well, here we are. I came close to getting a job through Dhollot, Quirp. If it wasn't for those clowns blaming me for the ills of the universe, we could've been en route to another exciting adventure."

The ship mind said, "May I remind you, Captain, that you almost lost your life at Tilley's Outpost. If that happened, I imagine the mob would have turned me into a dishwasher. Perhaps meeting with Mr. Dhollot, like fishing, was not one of your better ideas."

Carstairs shrugged. It had been a stylish exit from the watering hole, followed by a brief chase through orbit before they all returned to whatever they'd been doing before. He hadn't gone looking for trouble, but sometimes, he'd learned that trouble had a way of finding him regardless. *Like a magnet.* Still, the adrenaline rush and near death experience reminded him of who he was, and what he enjoyed doing most.

Stirring things up.

Taking chances.

Not slinging fish, no matter how respectable and honest the profession, or how much he enjoyed it as a sport.

"Well," he conceded, "once we deliver this order, let's take a break for a while, hm? Find something less… smelly to do until the trade routes open up again."

"I serve at your pleasure, Captain."

A comms alert sounded on the navigation board. Carstairs ignored it until Quirp said, "Captain, we have received an encoded incoming transmission from the Occion system."

"Sender?"

"Unknown. Shall I decode it?"

Carstairs lingered at the main console, wondering if the security force had more to say. *Or it could be…*

"Go ahead, Quirp."

The secure message flashed before them… a pre-recording with a covering shot of Dhollot the trader standing in front of an interplanetary cruiser in some space dock.

"Play it."

The static image flickered and Dhollot now appeared from his own bridge. *"Listen, Carstairs. I watched what you did at Tilley's, and I've given some thought to our discussion. Turns out, I may have been wrong about you."* The man shifted in his command chair, leaning toward the camera. Despite his bloodshot eyes, he was all business. *"In fact, I think you might be exactly the right pilot for the job, so listen up. The cartel requires a diversion… someone or something that will cause the Asterian Battle Fleet to abandon its trade route patrols. Efforts to date have proven unsatisfactory. You already understand what that means for us."*

The old trader licked his lips and coughed. *"They'd pay you a handsome sum, Carstairs. More than you could ever imagine. You can count on that. But more importantly, you'll restore your credibility with the other traders and pilots. Become one of the team again, so to speak. No more grubs trying to take you out at drinking holes."*

He leaned back with a smug, self-satisfied grin. *"So I tell you what. I'm going to be in Capital City on Asteria in a few days. If you're interested, meet me at the Hillsborg Hollows for a more fulsome conversation. You're familiar with those geologic structures east of the city? Coordinates and rendezvous time attached to this message. I'll find you there if you have the courage to show up."*

The message broke off abruptly.

"Shall I play it again, Captain?"

Carstairs rubbed his chin. His mind raced like a comet. *A diversion involving the Fleet?* The *Fleet? What did that mean? Everyone knew these cartel freaks were insane and dangerous to work with. No wonder Dhollot couldn't find any takers. Still though…*

"Captain?"

"Hm? No, Quirp, not necessary."

He peered up at the screen. Deep space replaced Dhollot's message. Long range scanning detected the remote planet Suna, sparkling like an emerald in the distance.

"May I ask what your plan is?"

Carstairs brushed his hands together. "We're going to deliver our fish order to the Bolutian colony."

"As you wish. I will also set a post-delivery course for Izillon."

The Captain relaxed, staring at the screen, half-watching the blanket of stars streak by. What harm would there be in talking to Dhollot and gathering more details about this contract? None. Yet, could he justify taking on this shadowy business to himself? To Piper?

"No, Quirp. Not Izillon. I've got something else in mind."

SECOND POINT WAS A MODEST COMMUNITY OF SEVERAL thousand scientists, engineers, and miners and their families, built on an asteroid orbiting Madus. Its importance to the Torfinn Governing Council resided not only in its strategic location between Asteria and the dark planets, but also in its rich mineral resources. The community also happened to be the closest service centre to Hauntor with a fully-functional medical clinic and surgery.

The doctors wasted no time hustling Piper into an operating theatre moments after she landed. They repaired her knee temporarily—sufficient to get her home to Asteria where specialists would have to finish the job, and already, after a few days of recovery, her pain had all but dissipated. She continued her journey in a better frame of mind and looked forward to analyzing the whisper stone at the ATI's labs.

She arrived at a remote airfield outside Capital City, choosing to keep a low profile given the instability of the Council, and hopped on a mag train destined for the downtown core.

The Institute's marble and brick low-rise facade glistered in a naturally pristine section of the city. Piper kept her head down, avoiding eye contact with passersby on her way through the shop-lined streets and micro-parks. As she marched up the steps to the ATI's main entrance—testing her repaired knee—she glanced up at the floor where she'd spent the last few years researching and teaching deep space communications, a profession she adored until her crash landing on Robos 7 when returning from that conference on Dunanas.

Regardless, she soaked up the memories as she stepped through the doors and breathed in the familiar musty smell of the building. She pulled back the hood covering most of her face and adjusted her back pack. She was among friends here. Instead of returning to her flat immediately, she could distract herself from recent galactic events by enjoying the comfortable, safe setting here.

Her scanning ID still worked, despite her not having any contact with her supervisor in the research unit. When the windowed doors hissed open and she waltzed into the lab area, Piper didn't recognize half the faces.

But they clearly recognized her.

Many scientists stopped their work and conversations and stared. An awkward silence descended over the room. Blood rose to her cheeks and a peculiar sensation blanketed her. A sudden urge to turn and run pounded in her brain, until Melbon, her old Thudoran colleague, called her name.

Piper turned and the humanoid researcher with the light-green skin raced toward her. They embraced.

But Piper's confusion with the others persisted. Melbon said in a low voice, "Follow me."

They walked together down a corridor to a private meeting area. Piper entered the familiar room first. Melbon closed the door behind her.

"Piper," she said tenderly, "it's so wonderful to see you again. Thank you for bringing the Chance—well, your mother into custody. My sister…" A dark shadow crossed her face. "She and I had many discussions about stopping the abuses of the Ethical Protocol. But we were powerless, of course."

"Why didn't you talk to me before all this happened, Mel?" Piper already knew the answer: they couldn't or wouldn't trust her as the daughter of a sociopath.

"I know better now, Piper. But listen." She lowered her voice to a whisper. "You are not safe here."

"What do you mean? This is where I work. You are my friends... well, except for all the new recruits out there."

"That's just it," the Thudoran said. "Following the Chancellor's arrest, numerous loyalists either left or faced termination. Other scientists, myself included, had to swear an oath not to contact your mother's people. It's madness."

The pain in Melbon's face burned. Piper noticed the fresh wrinkles and worry lines since they'd last seen each other.

"I can't believe politics infiltrated our work. What is that all about?" Piper took a seat at the round table in the corner.

"Who knows?" Melbon said with a hint of sadness in her voice. "People don't like change, or perhaps they don't like the stress that change brings. Either way, when everything happened and your mother was arrested, I guess many of the workers here feared the unknown more than they feared supporting her regime."

"Well," Piper said, regaining some of her ease, "I'm back now, so I can help. In fact, I'm kind of looking forward to picking up my projects again. And I've got a new one. On Hauntor, I found this cave and—"

"You can't do that, Piper." Melbon grimaced. "Talk to Supervisor Bornham, and see if a suitable position exists for you."

"Oh, you can't be serious, Mel. This is my work."

"This *was* your work, Piper, but everything's changed now. No one trusts anyone these days. The researchers who stayed, like me, don't trust the new ones, so we all keep to ourselves, discuss nothing but the projects. We don't socialize, we don't laugh anymore."

So much had changed over the past few months, and where was Piper? Licking her wounds alone on the mysterious Hauntor, oblivious to all these social ills spreading through Capital City like a virus.

"Maybe I should rethink my purpose, Melbon. I'd rather not go to my flat just yet, but if what you say is true, I sure don't belong here at the ATI either."

"Speak with Bornham," she said. "But just know that everything is different since we worked together. The science remains, but it's…" she pursed her lips. "It's strange now."

Piper stood and straightened her clothing. She slung her pack over her shoulder and said, "I'll see Bornham straight away."

Melbon's face darkened again.

Piper placed her hand on the Thudoran's shoulder. "What is it, my friend? What's bothering you?"

Suddenly, the whisper stone in Piper's pocket began humming in the back of her mind, triggering a fresh wave of foresight.

"Is it true my sister… helped you escape from the indoctrination machine? We get so little information from the grown-ups."

Piper reflected on that afternoon in the lab deep in the basement of the Governing Council building. She'd been strapped to the mind-cleansing device, under guard, when Melbon's sister, Heso, not only released her ties but also created a timely diversion, allowing Piper to escape. But in the ensuing firefight, an Asterian security officer gunned her down.

"Yes. Without her, I'd probably be working alongside my mother, ignoring these abuses, and manipulating others just like her. Heso saved my life."

Melbon's eyes welled up, and she held Piper's hand.

"Tell me, please. When she died… was it… quick? Did she suffer?"

Piper drew her close, and they hugged. She whispered in Melbon's ear, "She didn't suffer at all, Mel. Her death was instant."

They pulled apart. Melbon's lip quivered. "In our culture, we don't struggle for meaning like you Asterians do. A death is a death. It is sad but not the end. Nevertheless, it hurts knowing I could not protect her."

"You were the older sister."

Melbon nodded. "Do something for me, Piper?"

"Of course."

"Thudorans may not strive for abstract meaning in our lives, but we hold value in high regard. Assure me, then, that what you do with your life honours her memory. As I try to do the same every day."

She straightened. The stone sent her Melbon's inner thoughts. Her pain. Her hope. And the unnerving fear she held for Piper's well-being. "I'll try to make mine a worthy life, Mel. I promise."

They returned to the lab where they said their goodbyes. Piper marched across the bullpen, past the work stations, toward her old supervisor's office. As she did, keeping her head down, the whisper stone vibrated in her pocket and, given the degree of distrust, she vowed not to tell a soul about it.

EIGHT

"PIPER MADISON, IT IS YOU!"

Bornham's voice carried across the entire research area. She greeted the thin man at his office door by shaking his hand, and he invited her to take a stool by the window overlooking an adjacent park.

"I tried contacting you on that dark planet, but for whatever reason, you didn't respond to my comms."

"Not just yours, Dr. Bornham. Communications are sketchy at best at the Olavus lab on Hauntor."

"You weren't simply ignoring me, then," he asked with a mildly sarcastic tone.

"Not at all." She glared at the man with a sudden and deep suspicion. His academic background was astrophysics and planetary geosciences. She'd known him since she was a student in the Institute herself. A pleasant fellow, but not much of a scientist. Too often, he used his preliminary findings for political gain, rather than for pursuing knowledge. Regardless, his current role as a manager in the

Space Research Division was predictable. And unfortunate.

He broke eye contact first. "What's been keeping you occupied on Hauntor without any interruption until now?"

She fingered the stone in her pocket. It triggered no more insights. "Oh, geological and geochem surveys, mostly. Nothing fancy. Suffice to say that after the events of my mother's fall from the Chancellor's office, I needed time away from Capital City, and the work kept me busy."

"Of course, I understand," he said, pouring them both glasses of Kurusian tree-water. He handed her one, and she sipped the cool, sweet liquid. "Despite the isolation, you're looking well. Now, what brings you here this morning?"

She cleared her throat. "Honestly, I don't know. I want to resume my science projects. Do some research on the geological specimens I found. But it seems like a lot has changed here. New people. Work reassigned."

"Yes, true. I replaced Dr. Flann about two weeks after your mother... resigned. That period proved difficult; the violence impacted many researchers. I mean, none of us likes to be threatened. Is that not so?"

Piper's internal alarm sounded. She couldn't trust him, and she was smart to keep her thoughts to herself. So she borrowed a line that she'd often heard her mother exclaim. "Everyone wants peace, Dr. Bornham. After all, this is the Torfinn Galaxy."

"Yes, it is. But let's not get sidetracked. You're here now because you'd like to return to work?"

"Well, not today, but I plan to soon. If you can fill me in on my previous projects and perhaps others I could lead, I'd appreciate that a lot."

He placed his glass on the side table by the window and stared at the lush scenery. "Piper, it's not that simple."

"Oh, I understand you can't give me projects today without thinking through the resource implications. I get that."

"No, not that," he said, crossing his legs.

"Then... what?"

Bornham adjusted his shirt. He pointed out the window at some kids playing in the park. "Looks like they're having a good time, hm?"

Piper recalled Ariel's initial desire to teach the Hand children at the Moaning Bones mine site. They ran around without a worry in the world. "Carefree fun."

"I agree. But they're the exception, Piper."

"How so?"

"The last two months proved difficult following your irresponsible actions."

She faced him, mouth agape. "Seriously? Dr. Bornham, I've been off-planet all that time. Incommunicado. Whatever you feel I've done or influenced, you're gravely mistaken."

"I appreciate how you feel that way," he said, "but your shadow continues to spread over the planet. You may not have been here in person, but your lingering presence was. See all the fresh faces in here?"

"Yes."

"After the Chancellor was relieved of her duties and thrown in jail, a lot of Asterians were upset. She had many followers, many loyalists. Still does. But I don't think anyone expected the immediate impact it had on us at the ATI."

Piper scratched her head. "What are you trying to say, Doctor?"

He pursed his lips and continued. "The Chancellor's loyalists demanded her release. Obviously, she remained in prison, but the ensuing debate about what the Council should do with her, the Ethical Protocol, the problems on Robos 7 and Borta, and the destruction of Erus created a schism of epic proportions among the people. It's more difficult than ever to trust."

"Doctor, we're scientists, not politicians. Our only driving force is the pursuit of truth. Who cares about anything else?"

"The truth is not so simple. It comprises many shades of grey."

"Stop speaking around the issue, sir. When can I return to work?"

He lowered his gaze, exhaled, then looked straight at her. "There's no coming back here, Piper. I ended your employment a month ago."

The news hit her like a sledgehammer. She placed her hand against the window. "But... why?"

"Look at these." He grabbed the tablet from his desk, tabbed through, and handed it to her.

Piper read the various messages, and her heart sank. "No... not this..."

"I have a young family," he said. "These threats are real. Scroll down, Piper."

The menacing missives continued *ad nauseum* for page after page. She stopped before hitting the end. "Do they all say the same thing?"

"More or less. The prevailing theme is: if I keep you in Space Research, they will harm my family. It's why I've been trying to contact you, to find out your plans, and talk about these threats." He collected his thoughts before continuing. "Rest assured, nothing about your work was subpar. Far from it. But I can't risk my family's lives. You understand."

Defiance and rage boiled through her. Somehow, her mother remained in control of these loyal followers even though she sat rotting in a jail cell. Her removal as Chancellor, hailed by many Asterians as liberating, was obviously viewed by others as misguided. They blamed her for that, too.

If she had any hope of returning to a normal life, she'd

have to confront her mother again and work something out.

"I'm sorry, Piper."

"Thank you, Dr. Bornham. No need to apologize. The current situation is clearly untenable." She stood and marched toward the office door with deep resolve.

Only one destination consumed Piper's thoughts while she stepped through the ATI lobby.

She had to find her mother.

THE PROTORAN RUNABOUT CIRCLED THE GOVERNOR'S mansion in Edenfall where interim leader Feryn Graves and his senior ministers awaited the arrival of their guests. Scyther scrutinized the city. The once pristine capital had fallen into complete disrepair. Hand rebels, during the overthrow of the government in the uprising, damaged the city's air scrubbers and domed protection against harsh, polluted Robosian industrialization. The mansion itself—home to the traditional seat of political power—remained intact. Soldiers and battle equipment surrounded the area.

After the ship with the diplomatic team landed, Feryn Graves met Scyther on the steps of the grand main building. The young man appeared shorter than Scyther had envisioned, but already hardened from his days in the resistance and subsequent fallout.

"Welcome to Edenfall, Scyther, and to Robos 7," Graves said, with no hint of warmth. "Come. Join us in the Great Hall for some refreshments."

Scyther introduced the two diplomats and Sheilor to the Interim Governor, then followed him up the impressive stone staircase to the mansion. Inside, the stately foyer rose to the ceiling. Several people, Hands he presumed, lingered, awaiting their instructions. They were as unnoticeable as the utilitarian furniture.

Graves escorted the Protorans down a long corridor to a chamber that opened into a grand salon. A dozen men and women sat and hovered around a large table. The group stood as one when the two planetary leaders entered and the others appeared.

"Allow me to introduce my ministers," Graves said.

"If you agree, Governor, I'd rather get directly to the business at hand. Time, you see, is of the essence." Scyther grunted and remained standing.

Graves pursed his lips and glanced at his ministers. "All right. We'll handle the formal introductions later. Please... have a seat."

The Protoran team settled into the high-backed chairs. Hands appeared from the shadows, distributing water to the guests.

"So tell me, Scyther. What's on your mind?"

Scyther cleared his throat, scanning the audience, reading their life signs, evaluating their organics. Their healthy bodies were... enticing.

"Governor Graves... ministers... I know these are trying times not only for Robos 7 but also for the entire Torfinn Cluster of Planets. We have not seen this degree of political and social upheaval for a generation. Yet, here we are." He pushed the glass of water away, as did the other Protorans.

"That is true," Graves said. "Change is inevitable, and often messy, but we welcome all discussions to explore stabilizing the Fairfield Sector." He leaned across the table. "However, we remain somewhat in the dark regarding your urgent request to meet for... how did you phrase it... *mutually beneficial* discussions? So... what precisely are you looking for?"

Scyther preoccupied his mind by scanning the chamber, measuring its dimensions, analyzing the composition of the air. He shifted his attention to attending ministers. "Robos 7 has a problem," he stated plainly. "Intelligence suggests you are fighting against various factions of renegade Hands and assorted sympathizers. Some supporters might even be here around this table.

He flashed his orb throughout the room, scanning each individual for sudden shifts in biometrics. Two stood out. One of those caught his immediate attention.

"Would you like me to identify them?"

Graves' face reddened, and he seethed. "That won't be necessary. Let's cut to the chase."

"Very well. You need protection, and I can supply trained security forces to complement your myrmidons, along with several battle-class cruisers and viper gunships. You also require significant help to rebuild your air exchangers, infrastructure and such. I will provide you with our formidable engineering corps and construction crews."

Graves glanced around. Several of his ministers bowed their heads. The young man focused again on Scyther. "We have some interest in getting all the help we can, if it brings stability to our planet and helps us restore law and order. But this is an overly generous offer. What do you want in exchange?"

Scyther said, "Only one thing. The reproduction facilities… do they remain operational?"

"The farms?" Graves asked. "Where the Hands were bred like cattle?" His demeanour took on a cautious tone. "The programs are not operating at the moment, given recent events. But I—"

"Understood, Governor, but they remain functional?"

"Yes. Why?"

"The Protoran race relies on organics to survive. As transhumans, we combine both machine and man together for our existence. As you can see, the visible face is primarily biological; its underlying structure, however, is artificial. My world has exhausted its supply of raw indigenous material, and despite several attempts to find a solution through the Torfinn Council, those other so-called civilized planets want nothing to do with helping us." He lowered his voice. "But Robos 7, Governor, is in a unique position. You are already in the Hand manufacturing business. And to that end, we would like to exchange our military support for full access to your reproduction facilities. The diplomats here are willing and able to negotiate the finer details, but if you agree in principle, I will send my security crews here immediately."

Several ministers cleared their throats. Scyther monitored Graves' biometrics, noting his hands clenching, the rise in adrenaline and shallow breathing. He'd hit a nerve in the inexperienced man. *Perfect.*

"I sympathize with your predicament, Scyther. Machine and humanoid interdependence is something we understand, although not as intimately as you. And I forgive you for suggesting a trade involving human capital, since our goals here may not have been well articulated." He swallowed hard and his face turned to stone. "So let me be abundantly clear. The Hands are not resources like the minerals we mine. Despite their historical breeding for servitude, we have freed them. They are humanoid beings. They have rights. Our current difficulties aim to settle this matter, enabling a more just society where all individuals are equal partners, cooperating for collective success.

"So there is nothing to negotiate here, Scyther. My answer to your request is a loud and clear No."

Sudden rage coursed through Scyther's body. He glanced at Sheilor and wondered what she thought about this. As if on cue, she broke the tension between the two leaders by saying, "Forgive us, Governor. We do not appreciate the subtlety surrounding the conflict here. Perhaps you or your ministers are aware of other potential solutions. We need humanoid organics to survive, and we are becoming... desperate."

Graves exhaled, leaned back, and his biometric readings

returned to within normal range. He said, "Conferring with our medical specialists could help. Despite our historic isolation from other cluster planets, our resources supply much of the wealth generated in Torfinn. We are knowledgeable about many research activities throughout the member worlds. May I suggest, therefore, that I call them in on a priority basis to work with you on a solution? I'm confident there must be one that doesn't involve harvesting other people."

Scyther growled to himself, allowing Sheilor to take the lead while he observed the Robosian reactions.

"That is most welcome, Governor," she said.

"Then let's not waste a minute more." He introduced his team of ministers, beginning with those responsible for research, industrialization, and manufacturing. Sheilor stood and shook their hands. The diplomats circled around the interior officials tasked with infrastructure and security. Soon thereafter, the meeting broke up into smaller, informal talks. Several non-essential ministers exited.

Scyther refused to meet Graves' eye. He remained seated, processing what had transpired. The Governor said something meaningless to him that he ignored before Graves departed.

After several hours of discussions, Sheilor sat beside him and said, "It appears the Governor has more faith in his medical team than is warranted. They have no solutions that we have not already attempted. Sympathetic, of course, but unhelpful. Although they suggested we reach out to the Governing Council for assistance."

Scyther scoffed. "Sheilor, we have been to the Council many times. I have spoken with the former Chancellor, Tephera Madison, about our plight. While she seemed the most sympathetic and, indeed, I thought she might support us in our need for acquiring organics, her own constituents overthrew her before anything could happen."

The doctor massaged her organic chin. "I recall those talks. You appreciate that I am not a supporter of harvesting people, but that has been our way, and our survival always trumps whatever personal objections I possess."

He stared at her. "I admire how you have been able to separate yourself from those moral questions. We all like to think we're civilized... different from the animals. But that is a mistake. When the time comes and our very existence is at risk, we will revert to our brutish nature."

Sheilor studied him in silence, then bowed her head.

"You need regeneration, too." He reached over and touched her forearm. Sheilor winced, pulling it away.

"What else, beside this arm?"

"Both legs," she said, not looking up.

Scyther's anger kindled again. "How much time do you have?"

"Maybe a few days. I shall reduce my energy consumption."

The room eventually emptied. Protoran diplomats hovered around their leader, although not close enough to be intrusive. He fumed as the organics spoke in low voices with each other, vacating the chamber. One of the Heads, a junior economic minister he identified earlier as a sympathizer, smiled politely and strode toward the foyer.

She is the right height. And strong.

Scyther learned many years ago that his sole purpose was to lead his kind to prosperity and long term health. Protor had emerged as a formidable producer of technology, and its designs and equipment were found across the Torfinn cluster. Under the Ethical Protocol, those planets ignored Protor's exploitation of the indigenous people to service their need for organics. Life was much simpler when Tephera Madison ruled the Council. And now? He was reduced to begging for bodies at the feet of some *boy* who could barely hold on to power.

This would end.

He stood, signaling to the junior minister to wait. She brushed the hair from her face and lingered in the foyer.

Scyther leaned over and whispered, "Come, Sheilor. Let us depart." He evaluated the firm Robosian awaiting him. "I have a better idea for getting what we need long term. But first," he said, helping her stand, "let's get you repaired."

NINE

PIPER SWIRLED THE CUP OF COFFEE IN HER HAND AS SHE sat on the stone steps outside the Asterian Technical Institute's west wing, a quiet area shaded by large trees and full of aromatic gardens. She often came here before all the troubles, to collect her thoughts or to tackle a stubborn physics problem. Now, she kept her head down, staring at her feet over the rim of her cup, waiting for the call.

Despite several attempts since returning to Asteria, Piper could not connect with either Ariel or Feryn on Robos 7. The conflict there continued unabated, and communications overall were patchy at best. Still, her premonition or hallucination involving her half-sister had frightened her on Hauntor, and she needed to discover the purpose behind it.

The ping from her comms device startled her. On the other end of the transmission was Ambassador Welkin. She got straight to the point.

"Your request is difficult, Piper. True, you have

every… noot… right to visit your mother, but you must understand the inherent danger associated with that and the required logistics."

"Yes, Ambassador. Is there anything you can do?"

The Erusian's face on the vid screen tightened. *"I am sympathetic. What I ask is that a security team takes you to the holding cells to ensure your safety. If you agree, they will meet you at the ATI and go from there."*

The last thing Piper wanted was to draw more attention to herself with some armed escort following her around. Since everyone in the Space Research Division knew she'd been there, word would quickly spread, and who knows what kind of trouble that might present. But, if she insisted on seeing her mother, she had no choice.

"Alright, Ambassador. How soon can your officers meet me?"

"Send me your… noot… coordinates, and I'll dispatch them immediately." She clicked her tongue and added, *"There's something I'd like you to do for me, Piper."*

"Sure," she said, "what's up?"

"I have a clandestine mission to Robos 7 for you… to be my contact on the ground. The communications remain unreliable, and we hear all kinds of rumours about the social upheaval there. I need someone I can trust. Under the radar, you understand. Assess the situation and report to me."

Piper licked her lips and kicked the dirt. Getting pulled back into the fray when everyone viewed her as the primary problem made little sense. No, the answer was the exact opposite: flee Asterian politics as quickly as possible.

"Sorry, Ambassador, but I can't get involved."

Welkin dropped her head. *"Very well. I hoped since Ariel and Feryn are your siblings, you may want to help them out more directly. I suppose I… noot… thought wrong."*

Despite the Ambassador's plea, Piper refused to be

drawn in. She ended the call and, no sooner had she finished, a squad of four officers arrived in a small hover vehicle and whisked her away.

THE ASTERIAN MAXIMUM SECURITY PRISON SQUATTED like a bunker on the northern edge of Capital City. The surrounding land had been cleared of all vegetation, and for a moment, the scene reminded Piper of the toxic, barren mining lands on Robos 7.

The craft approached at high speed, and landed in an outer staging area where a line of armed soldiers met them, scanned them for hidden weapons, and cleared the group to enter a secondary zone behind thick steel walls.

Another escort appeared and guided them through a maze of corridors and reinforced doors deep into the heart of the building. Piper noted the complete lack of natural light in the facility and concluded this design feature kept the inmates disoriented.

The group stopped in front of a massive entrance guarded by two soldiers. "This is it," the man groused. He presented his face at the scanner and the door clacked and unlocked.

Piper peered into the gloom. Hard, sporadic ceiling lights illuminated a long, dark corridor.

"She's at the end, straight ahead," the man said, and stepped aside. Piper gulped and stared at the group of security officers with her. "Can they come with me?"

"I insist they do, ma'am."

Piper took a few steps, noticed the others weren't following, and spun around. The lead officer muttered in a low voice, "Just wanted to give you a bit of privacy, Ms. Madison."

"Definitely not needed, Officer."

The man sprang to join her, drew their weapons and held them at the ready.

Piper continued along the harsh corridor until she arrived at the central cage. She peered in, and discerned nothing but the outlines of odd shapes. Perhaps that one was a bed. A toilet. The whisper stone in her pocket shrieked with the darkest, most vile thoughts imaginable. She pushed them away, stopped several meters from the cell bars and cleared her throat.

"Mother?" Her voice sounded tinny and weak. Tentative.

An ethereal response floated across the murk. "I wondered when you might show up, Piper."

This voice belonged to her mother. That odd lilt she had. The touch of a rough edge. But something had changed it. Her words rang hard and beaten.

"Where are you?"

The whisper stone responded first. *I hate you... if I had a knife I'd gut you from the—*

Then her mother said, "What, you can't see me? I'm over here in the corner. Come closer."

Piper threw a cursory look at the security officer, who now stood beside her.

"Be careful, Ms. Madison," he whispered. "She's in here for a reason."

Piper swallowed hard and inched toward the cell. She squinted, looking into the deep shadows. Darkness bathed the area, but Piper detected movement and then saw Tephera Madison pull herself up from the stone floor. She was stark naked and covered in sores.

Chains rattled as she rose. Shackles covering her arms and legs were fastened to a thick metal post in the centre of the cell. A leash. Piper shuddered at seeing the once powerful Chancellor of the Torfinn Cluster Governing Council reduced to this. Her heart broke and she had to remind herself that this person tried to kill her and, worse, invited that sadistic monster Zadicus Verman to have his way with her.

She reached down and rubbed that spot on her thigh where the Bortan electrocuted her with a firestick.

"Why are you here?" Tephera croaked.

"To see you, Mother."

"Well, here I am." She slunk forward toward the bars. A thin light from the ceiling in the corridor cast hard shadows across the former Chancellor's body. She tried straightening, but had lost much of her physical strength. Regardless, defiance scarred her face, and her eyes shone like glass as she stared at Piper.

"What do you think? Are you proud of what you did to me?"

You did this to me! Why don't you love me?... the stone screamed a confused mix of emotions to her.

Piper's fear and trepidation receded under the woman's glare. "I'm not here to argue with you."

"Here to gloat, then?" the elder Madison spat. "I hope this is what you wanted."

"Mother," she whispered, "I didn't want any of this. You brought it on yourself with..." she stopped. She hadn't come to fight. "Nevermind all that. I have something to ask."

Tephera Madison gripped the bars. "Well go ahead, then."

Piper inhaled and took two more steps toward the cell. She stopped about a meter away. At this distance, her mother's wrinkled face showed more age than she anticipated. Worse, a foul-smelling stench floated off her pasty white body.

"Don't worry, I'm beyond any more shame. Once the humiliation was complete, I gave up caring." She lifted her chin. "This is who I am, thanks to you and that flyboy Carstairs."

Piper clenched her teeth, ignoring the bait. "Mother,

you seem to have a hold on many Asterians. It's made the planet a dangerous place. You prided yourself on keeping the peace, on giving the people a reason to live and enjoy their lives. But now, they distrust each other because of you. Is there anything you can do to change that?"

Tephera snorted. "What can I influence from this jail cell? You're wrong, Piper. If the Torfinn citizens aren't happy, it's their own doing." Her eyes sparkled. "But there is something, Piper. Yes, a task only you can do."

"What are you talking about?"

"Listen. That Erusian bitch, Welkin, listens to you. Use that to set me free." She lowered her head. "I've learned my lesson, Piper. I know what I allowed to happen was monstrous." Tephera moved closer. "But I've changed. Now, convince the lizard to let me go, so I can resume my work." She rattled the shackles on her thin arms. "Please, won't you do this for me?"

You damn well better do as I say, you little puke. If you love me...

Piper froze. A part of her ached for her mother's self-respect to be restored, and she wondered how a conversation with the Ambassador might proceed.

The security officer behind her cleared his throat, and she remembered the pain her mother inflicted not only on her, but on the millions of Erusians who perished under her violence.

"Sorry, I won't help you with that."

"Then why did you come here?" Tephera croaked.

"I suppose out of curiosity... I wondered if you might do something to bring peace to the planet. Or maybe I came out of pity."

She rattled the bars. "Get the hell out of here. And by the way, I never wanted you in the first place. That goddamn animal father of yours laughed at me when I told him. Didn't matter. I was prepared to flush you down the chute like a stain."

Piper fought to prevent tears from spilling across her cheeks. She turned and marched toward the corridor exit, followed by the security officers. A thin whisper floated down the corridor to her.

"But I didn't, Piper, because you made me so happy. I love you."

Tephera Madison's madness continued, and she launched into another spiteful rant under her breath. Even after the prison escort locked the heavy door behind them, the hateful, confused voice echoed in her head. The thoughts emanating from the stone were too ugly, too bestial to acknowledge.

Except for one thing rising above her personal devastation.

She loved me.

The Hillsborg Hollows formed part of a geologically curious range of rocky hills and valleys a couple hundred kilometers east of Capital City. Few Asterians ever traveled there because, other than a multitude of deep, narrow caves, little else remained in the barren district. Scientists had long ago surveyed the caverns, mapping them as they went, but since the area contained no economic minerals, industrialization never took hold.

Carstairs knew the region well. He'd hidden out there in the past when raiders or irate customers chased after him. The labyrinthian caves were popular with smugglers and black market traders, too.

Asteria's two moons glowed on the horizon, bathing the area in thin light. Across the valleys and along the ridge, however, the world sat in shadowy darkness. The *Dauntless* approached the Hollows at low altitude, skimming the tops of craggy bluffs and settling on a flat clearing near the designated coordinates.

"Any other lifeforms around, Quirp?"

"Negative," the ship mind chirped. "Of course, there may be some in the tunnels themselves that my sensors cannot detect."

Carstairs scanned the area, first with the ship's instrumentation and then visually through the main viewer. He couldn't see beyond the range of the vessel's external lights. Night vision revealed nothing, either.

"Shut off the spots."

"As you wish."

The captain leaned back in his command chair and waited. He'd already strapped a thermal flux gun to his waist, hidden beneath a jacket. Within moments, headlights from a ground vehicle approached out of nowhere.

"I'm guessing that's the reception party. I'll head out to meet our hosts. If there's any sign of trouble, Quirp, get the ship out of here. Don't wait for me, got it?"

"Understood, Captain."

The portal cycled open and Carstairs marched down the ramp to the hard stone just as the ground vehicle pulled up. A uniformed man dropped to the surface, scanned him, and removed his flux gun.

"You'll get it back after you meet with Dhollot," he grumbled.

The captain hopped on a seat and they churned away from the *Dauntless* toward the caves.

The Hollows were a maze of twists and turns, caverns, and bluffs. Carstairs knew how easily a man could get disoriented here, so he noted some key features en route to the meeting with Dhollot just in case.

Outside a gloomy opening, the rover stopped and the two men waited. The familiar merchant lumbered from the gloom and raised a hand.

"I suppose that's my cue," Carstairs muttered.

He jumped out and approached the trader.

Dhollot's face was impossible to see in the dark shadows, but his eyes flashed like fiery diamonds. "I wasn't sure you'd show up, Captain. Again, you surprise me."

"What can I say? You kindled my curiosity with this Black Bond cartel business. So let's get right to it, shall we?"

"Very well. Follow me."

Dhollot led him into the gloomy cave. Carstairs squinted, trying to see ahead of him, but the gloom filled the entire area. He heard whispers off to the side. Dhollot's men, no doubt. They stopped at a rock ledge and the man fired up a lantern. Carstairs peered around. The cave was empty except for some shadowy figures lurking just out of the lantern's brilliance.

"We share a problem," the trader began. "We are all suffering under the increased pressure of those Asterian patrols and the Battle Fleet monitoring the chaos on Robos 7. Truth is, we need them to go away."

"Sure, but that won't happen until the entire Fairfield Sector is stable, not to mention the Cluster leadership. That could take years."

He grunted. "True, but planets and politicians are not the issue. Keeping those patrols and fighters out of our trading space is." Dhollot pulled a comms device from his coat pocket. "The contract is straightforward. Remove these ships from our space so we can resume our profitable operations."

"You make it sound like doing laundry."

He chuckled. "As I said, it's simple. But not easy. We're looking at hundreds of ships with various capabilities, and at least a dozen known patrols occupying our trade routes. To move them will require a permanent diversion of considerable magnitude."

Carstairs reflected on the requirement and shivered. *This is a lot more challenging than I thought.*

As if sensing the pilot's hesitation, Dhollot said,

"You're not getting cold feet, are you, Captain?"

"How do you define *diversion*, Dhollot? It sounds like the cartel wants an old school conflict to draw the Fleet away for good."

"It does, doesn't it? That's only one of several potential options."

Carstairs chewed his lip.

"If you agree to take this job, do whatever you like as long as the Fleet abandons our routes. The sooner, the better. And because it's a challenging task, and given the importance of achieving success, the cartel is offering one million credits. They'll give you a third upon acceptance; the rest when the trade routes are restored."

"I see. And what's in it for you?"

"Me?" Dhollot grinned innocently. "Why, I am a simple trader, Carstairs. All I'm concerned about is getting back to my business. Now, if I find a suitable candidate like you for the cartel, they are known to be generous..." He stared at him, stone-faced.

Carstairs considered the job for a moment. A quick diversion would have to be sustained for the Fleet to pull its ships back. Opening the routes would help everyone, especially him and the other pilots who relied on them for a living. Besides, Piper had talked about restoring the Torfinn Cluster, and this could be a critical first step. Fix the trade. Life returns to normal, and they'd no longer be vilified. A big win.

He spent the next several minutes reviewing the contract. Dhollot was right: the requirement proved straightforward, and the reward unlike anything he'd ever seen before.

If the cartel's end game was to remove the Asterian Fleet, the *Dauntless* could get an entire overhaul and then some with that kind of dough.

"Well, Captain?"

Carstairs handed the comms device back to the trader and said, "Count me in. I can start in the morning."

TEN

PIPER POWERED DOWN HER PUBLIC ONE-SEAT SCOOTER as she approached the Pilot's Lounge at the industrial Northern Airfield situated on the outskirts of Capital City. The mid-afternoon sun warmed her bare shoulders, in stark contrast to the cold, blustery conditions on Hauntor.

She grounded the flier in the paddock and wandered up to the nondescript building where off-duty freelance pilots hung out... the same place she'd first met Jay Carstairs.

When she entered, the darkness and musty odour of the room caught her by surprise. After her vision adjusted, she ignored the curious stares and headed toward the bar.

A local, grey-bearded man with long hair stumbled through a rear entrance, a box of bottles in hand. He saw her and placed the carton down, wiped his hands on his pants, and approached.

"Something I can do for you, miss?"

"Yes. I'm looking for a pilot named Jay Carstairs. He

captains the *Dauntless*. Used to hang around here."

The man grunted. "Maybe I've seen him. Who wants to know?"

Piper grabbed a stool. "I'm Piper Madison. I flew with him a few months ago and—"

"Ah," he said, raising his eyebrows. "I thought I recognized you." He leaned toward her, close enough that she could smell his sour breath. "I'm not sure it's safe for you here, miss. Many of these guys have been jobless since the troubles started. They blame you and Carstairs."

Piper shook her head. "Figures. But never mind all that. I won't stay long."

"That'd be wise."

She glanced around the lounge, noticed several patrons watching her and speaking in hushed tones.

"Listen," she said, "I don't want any trouble. Have you seen him? Do you know where he might be?"

The bartender spread his large palms apart and chewed his lip. "No," he finally replied. "Not lately. He hasn't been around since he left the planet a couple months back, when the Chancellor..." he stopped talking and studied her face for a reaction. She gave him none. "When she got arrested. Sorry."

Piper clenched her jaw. The stone in her pocket vibrated, and she sensed danger.

"Heads up there, missy."

She snapped to attention and turned, her hand instinctively reaching for a thermal flux gun that wasn't there. Three pilots approached her from behind. The one holding a chipped mug wiped his crooked mouth and said, "Is there a problem with this customer, Cullin?"

"Relax, Gaz, we're good here."

The unshaven man stumbled up beside her. "Hey, Cull, I's just tellin' the boys here that I's not flown for 63 days now. Sixty-three days! That's the longest I ever been out of a cockpit." He turned to Piper. "And this here witch is responsible for that." He glanced at his friends. "Isn't that right?"

The others muttered and shuffled their feet.

Cullin straightened, reaching behind the bar. "I'll have no trouble here, Gazzer. The lady was just asking about Jay Carstairs, then she'll be on her way."

Piper stood, clenching her fists as adrenaline pumped through her blood. "You seen the old man?"

"What's it to you?" Gazzer scowled.

"He's a… a friend of mine."

"Hmph," he chided. "Hear that, folks? She's lookin' for a friend. Any of youse want to befriend her?"

Piper faced Gazzer and raised her chin. She'd learned from her mother as a youngster that if she stood up to bullies, they most often backed down. And judging by the man's bloodshot eyes and uneasy gait, he was in no shape to fight, anyway. "If you want to go," she spat, "then let's dance. But I'm warning you. Take a swing at me, and you'll never fly again."

The lounge exploded in raucous laughter. Except for Gazzer. A hint of fear and adventure flashed across his ruddy face. He scrutinized her up and down, and said, "I ain't a-gonna fight no woman. 'Specially one as nice-lookin' as you." He drained his mug. "But if I help ya, what's in it for me?"

Piper studied the collection of misfit pilots representing various species. They all gawked at her and Gazzer. Not with any expectation of conflict, she remarked; rather, their faces spilled over with an odd mix of hope and despair. "Listen, I messed up big time. I'm aiming to restore the cluster to the way it was. But I need Carstairs. Tell me where he is, and you'll be helping us return life to normal, including freighter traffic and other flying jobs."

He frowned at her. "Buy me an ale, and I'll tells ya

what I got."

The room quickly settled down as Gazzer hauled another stool beside her. Cullin placed a fresh mug in front of him and said, "Compliments of the lady." Piper noticed he stayed close by, ignoring the box he'd brought in, scanning the lounge like a bodyguard.

The burly, drunk pilot took a sip, burped, and muttered, "I's not seen Carstairs or his old bucket of a ship since you ruined the galaxy, Piper Madison. But he's done this before, eh?"

"Done what?"

"Disappeared into thin air." The man waved his arm with a flourish. "You've flown with him. You know what he's like."

Piper reflected on her time aboard the *Dauntless*. Under fire, the captain was the coolest man she'd ever seen, but he had a streak of insecurity and frustration that often appeared without warning. And oh, so many secrets.

"Try the outer planets," Gazzer muttered, taking another swig. "He's been known to isolate out there. Don't care for people much."

"There are literally hundreds of known dark worlds in the galaxy. A thousand we haven't even charted yet. Any idea which ones he likes?"

"Well, I doubts he'd go too far. Nothin' too unfamiliar... too unknown. Nah, he prefers them uninhabited rocks. Like I said, he don't like others. 'Specially Kurusians." He gulped a mouthful of ale.

That explained the man's accent and speech patterns. Kurus had been a long-time member of the Torfinn Cluster, but always felt inferior compared to the others. Her people often carried grudges of unknown origin, and this man was no exception.

"Here," he said, reaching into his pocket and pulling out an old-fashioned paper booklet the pilots preferred using. He grabbed a stylus from Cullin and scribbled, then ripped the page out and handed it to her. "It's a list of planets where I knows he's been before. Well, up to a point anyways. Survey them for the ship's transponder. You may get lucky. He mighta forgot to turn it off."

Piper glanced at the names on the paper. Takton, Varth, Coatus, Berrin 1 and 2... She knew little about them except for the last planet on the list: Izillon.

"When was he last on Izillon?"

"That would be when youse all got exiled by the Council for the mess youse left on Robos 7, 'member?"

Could he have returned there? It had plenty of food sources and the climate was good. The beasts were a problem, unless... She stood and swiped her card across Cullin's reader to pay for the Kurusian's drink. "Thank you, Gazzer. You've been a great help. I bought you and your pals a couple more ales for your trouble."

She pocketed the list and headed for the door.

"Hey, Madison," he growled.

Piper hesitated.

"Don't come back here."

She bristled at the man and his lingering cronies. Blood boiled in her gut. *No one tells me what to do.* But she had enough good sense to quash it and exit the lounge.

Outside, the sun's glare blinded her momentarily. She mounted the scooter, wondering how to find Carstairs on these outer planets, when her comms device pinged with an urgent message from Ambassador Welkin. The whisper stone crashed her mind with the sudden name of her half-sister.

Piper answered. "Ambassador, this is a surprise. What can I—"

"Sorry, Ms. Madison, I do not wish to... noot... be rude, but I must tell you the news."

"What is it? Something happen to Ariel?"

Welkin hesitated. *"I ordered that your mother receive regular hygiene and clothing. It makes me feel... small, hearing the guards humiliated her that way."*

Piper furrowed her brow, scanning the airfield as a solitary freighter settled for landing. "Okay, I appreciate that, Ambassador, but that's not why you called."

"No, there's more," the Erusian muttered in a throaty voice.

And she knew.

Piper stiffened. The stone sent visions of her sister being dragged away in the dust and shadows. "Something's happened on Robos 7."

"Yes... I bring disturbing news from that planet. We succeeded in establishing contact. It's about your half-siblings."

Piper frowned. "Ariel *and* Feryn? What's going on? Are they safe?"

The ambassador clicked her tongue before saying, *"How can I tell you this? I will simply say the words. There has been an uprising at the Governor's mansion where senior cabinet members gathered to manage the conflict. A series of explosions destroyed much of the complex. Your half-sister Ariel is missing. And your half-brother Feryn is dead."*

ELEVEN

PIPER'S JAW DROPPED. THE AMBASSADOR'S MONOTONE voice faded into the background as her arm fell to her side. She ended the call. Meanwhile, the whisper stone vibrated in her pocket. When she overcame the initial shock of the news concerning her half-siblings, she trained her mind on the animated stone. Somehow, she thought, Ariel's familial connection had to be linked to the strange whispers and cries for help she heard on Hauntor. *As if this stone opened a mental pathway between us.*

Welkin's news changed everything. Piper's heart pounded in her chest as she composed herself outside the Pilot's Lounge. Nothing would prevent her traveling to Robos 7 now, finding Ariel, and helping her restore order any way possible.

So Carstairs' whereabouts must wait. That Kurusian, Gazzer, said he may even have gone to Izillon. In an odd, circular fashion, that made complete sense to her. Returning to the exile planet where the simian creatures almost killed them served as a counterintuitive place to hide.

A pair of cajoling pilots stumbled out of the lounge and interrupted her thoughts. They stopped when they saw her. Piper ignored them and, full of a newfound resolve, punched up the Ambassador's office. One of Welkin's underlings connected with her.

"It's Piper Madison. Is the Ambassador available to speak?" Heat shimmered over the airfield under the hot Asterian sky, disrupting her efforts to spot unwelcome movement, no matter how slight.

"Oh, Ms. Madison, I regret hearing about your family. Please stand by," the young male voice responded. Within seconds, Welkin's voice broke over the channel.

"Piper... noot... *thank you for calling me back. I know you are close to Ariel Graves and understand the politics on Robos 7 better than most. Again, I'm sorry to...* noot... *share this news when you're going through your own difficulties."*

"Never mind that, Ambassador," she said, watching the two drunk pilots stagger away, clinging to each other. "Is the Robos 7 mission still open?"

The Ambassador made that odd Erusian clicking sound with her mouth and tongue, pausing long enough for Piper to think something else had distracted her. Finally, she said, *"Yes, the offer stands. Now that the interim government has been attacked, I wonder if it is...* noot... *prudent to travel there under these current conditions."*

Piper clenched her teeth. "Is the Battle Fleet in orbit around the planet?"

"Yes."

"And they haven't been drawn into the conflict?"

"Not yet. They embrace the Ethical Protocol of Non-Interference."

"Then I don't see a problem. Besides, I must find Ariel and make sure she's okay. I've created enough trouble there and perhaps I can do something about it. Any news of her husband, Dolian?"

The Ambassador grunted. *"Dolian's whereabouts are a mystery, Piper. But, there is another factor to... noot... consider."*

"What's that?"

"Our reports show an armada of warships from Protor heading toward Robos 7. The purpose of such action is unknown, but prior to the fall, the Protoran leader Scyther met with Feryn Graves at the Governor's mansion. Perhaps... noot... with so much instability in the Fairfield Sector, the Protorans see an opportunity to expand their influence."

Piper wracked her brain. Protor was another industrial planet in that sector, but she couldn't remember what they produced, or what they even looked like.

"Can you tell me more about them, Ambassador? I'm drawing a blank."

"My team will prepare a dossier on the planet and Lord Scyther and forward it to your comms device. But a more pressing issue is preparing you for the voyage to Robos 7. I think it best to... noot... meet in person to discuss the logistics. We cannot be seen as interfering in their internal affairs, you understand."

Piper fired up the scooter. "Oh, all too well, Ambassador. I can be at your office in a matter of minutes." She prepared to end the call when an idea struck her. "There is one other thing. You have resources you can tap to find missing people, to track down others who've disappeared, right?"

The Erusian fussed. *"I have some powers, while respecting the privacy laws. Is there someone you wish to contact?"*

"Yes, there is. Captain Carstairs."

The Ambassador clicked anew, with more enthusiasm

than before. *"I figured if anyone knew his whereabouts, it would be you, Piper."*

"Not this time, unfortunately, and I must speak to that idiot right away."

"In this circumstance, I am uncertain whether I can breach the privacy protocols for a... noot... personal matter. But leave it with me. I'll get an answer for you soon."

They finished the call and Piper flew from the airfield toward the Torfinn Galaxy Governing Council buildings downtown. As she merged with traffic in the skylanes above the city streets, she thought of the captain. *What are you up to, Carstairs? And why are you hiding?*

The Council administration buildings were all too familiar to Piper, since she practically grew up there when her mother ruled as Chancellor. She parked the scooter and turned to run up the steps to the entrance when two hulking security guards beelined directly to her.

"Ms. Madison?"

"Yes?"

"We're here to escort you to Ambassador Welkin's chambers."

"That's fine," she said, "but I know my way around the building, and I can manage on my own, thanks." She stepped away.

The other officer cleared his throat and stood in front of her. "Understood, ma'am, but this is for your own safety."

"I beg your pardon?"

His head turned, observing the platform's comings and goings. She noticed his hand on the flux gun.

"The Ambassador will explain all that better than I can, Ms. Madison. Unfortunately, you have some enemies here on the Council. We must be cautious.

Piper tugged on her jacket and gazed around the square. Initially, everything appeared normal. Then she spotted the trio of men milling at a street coffee kiosk, staring at her from the shade. A chill coursed through her body.

"Lead the way, Officers."

The escorts marched her through the main entrance and whisked her past security. They rode the lavish elevator to the Ambassador's office on the fourth floor where two more armed guards stood at attention outside the Erusian's door. They spot scanned her before showing her and the guards inside.

Ambassador Welkin's ante-room, in contrast to her mother's, had modest and clean lines and minimal accessories. Some of the furniture had shortened legs to accommodate the Ambassador's small stature compared to humanoids; other chairs and tables remained normal size. Her aide greeted Piper and dismissed the escorts. He invited her to sit.

"The Ambassador will be finished shortly," the man said. "May I offer you something to drink?"

"No, I'm good, thanks."

"Very well." He took the chair across from her. "I must apologize for the security officers. I take it you didn't expect that."

Piper shrugged. "No, but I suppose it isn't surprising. My mother had many loyalists and likely still does. Ferreting them out, I imagine, is a full-time occupation."

"Trust is a volatile commodity these days, Ms. Madison." His personal comms device pinged. "Ah, she's ready for you now."

He stood and showed her into the Ambassador's office. Two other senior people flanked the diminutive Erusian. Welkin rose and greeted her with her outstretched arms, and they embraced awkwardly, given the Erusian's stature.

She introduced her grim-faced advisors, Ostas and Tinala.

The other aide bowed and exited, closing the door.

"Ms. Madison... *noot*... it is indeed a pleasure to see you again. My advisors will join us. Whatever we say is safe with them."

Piper glanced at the two, detected nothing from the whisper stone in her pocket, then followed the Ambassador to her sofa.

"I cannot tell you how relieved I am that you changed your mind about traveling to Robos 7. I wish... *noot*... it could have been under better circumstances, but we must adjust to the present conditions. I need you to determine which planetary groups support the Council. We need an assessment of our ground strength there before we can determine options for a course of action." Her tongue darted over her thin, black lips.

"How soon can I leave?"

Welkin blinked at her senior advisor, Ostas, who immediately outlined the logistics of the secretive flight path, the fact she'd be traveling alone, and that she could in no way be linked back to the Ambassador.

"Yes, I understand all that," Piper said, dismissing their concern. "I won't sell you out if things go bad. But tell me, what ship will I be using? I'm not licensed to fly anything larger than a two-seater."

"We have taken care of that, Ms. Madison," the underling continued in a quiet voice. "I have commissioned one such vessel from the Asterian Technical Institute's modest fleet. The mechs are outfitting her now with additional power and defensive weaponry."

"The ATI?"

Ambassador Welkin said, "Yes, we often use their ships for Council business when the need arises, and they are less recognizable than the battle cruisers. I believe you are already familiar with this vessel. She's the *Penny Rose*."

Piper recalled the last time she flew the *Penny*. A problem with the ship's power distributors caused her to crash on Robos 7, setting in motion the series of events that led to Governor Graves' death, her discovery of her half-sister Ariel, her mother's imprisonment, and the increasing turmoil that now gripped the Torfinn Cluster.

"Oh yes, I know that ship well. I trust she's still flight worthy?"

"No doubt about that," Tinala chimed in. "The Robosian workers repaired her back to original specifications, and she'll be ready to go once the last checks are complete."

"When's that?"

Ostas glanced at his comms device. "Within the hour. We need to remove all her markings and transponder codes."

The Ambassador sipped from a cup of tea. Sadness poured over her face, and she remained silent for several minutes. The Erusians were a sensitive species, and Piper surmised that between the loss of her own people under Zadicus Verman's ruthless attack and the stresses of holding the Cluster planets together, she must be struggling under the pressures, both internal and external.

Piper cleared her throat. "Perhaps I'll take my leave and head over to the ATI mech shop." She rose, but the Ambassador held her back.

"Please stay a moment." Turning to her advisors, she added, "Gentlemen, wait for me in my... *noot*... private meeting room, please."

The two men disappeared.

Ambassador Welkin approached Piper. "You wanted help to find Captain Carstairs."

She'd almost forgotten about the request.

"Privacy matters as much as ethics to member planets. I'm sure you realize that."

Piper didn't respond, and followed the Ambassador's lead by sitting again.

"These statutes may be overruled solely when Cluster health and safety is threatened. An example of this might be a... *noot*... threat from an intruding intergalactic force."

"I understand," Piper whispered. "Well, I won't push my luck by challenging that. I've learned my lesson."

The Ambassador's face remained unchanged, except for her thin lips tightening in a line. "Regarding the captain, I made an exception and requested my network's assistance in gathering information."

Piper straightened her back and leaned forward. "I don't want you to get into any trouble for my sake, Ambassador. Please tell me you didn't."

"My actions, or inactions, are solely my burden. If problems arise, I am accountable and shall abide by whatever the will of the Council dictates."

The Ambassador rose and gazed out the large picture window overlooking the Asterian capital. Piper joined her by her side.

"Want to know your captain friend's location?"

"Ambassador, I don't think you should tell me. If breeching the privacy laws brings another whirlwind down on the galaxy, I'd rather remain in the dark."

"Perhaps your concern may be assuaged knowing that, if I am found at fault, it will not matter who told you."

Piper studied the Erusian's scaled face, and what struck her was a sudden internal conflict between wanting to know Carstairs location, and the ugly possibility that someone else might be with him.

As if reading her mind, the Ambassador continued. "He is alone, Piper. After we met in the hospital where you recovered, he scrambled his transponder signal and left Asteria, but with some time and effort, my... *noot*... analysts determined he landed on Izillon."

So the old Kurusian in the bar was right. "Izillon?" she said. "We almost died on that grim planet. What would compel him to return there?"

"It seems the captain has launched a fish distribution enterprise from there. Travels across the galaxy, doing business... *noot*... with the unaligned planets." Welkin continued peering out the window. "By all accounts, he is successful in his endeavour."

"Is it possible to contact him?"

"Not directly. Izillon is outside reliable communications range."

Piper's emotions wrestled in her gut. Of all the vocations she could envision for Carstairs, being a fishmonger was not one of them, and this new occupation of his mystified her. She would have preferred taking the *Dauntless* under his command to Robos 7, but unfortunately, that couldn't happen. Besides, what could she say to the man after he bolted from her life in favour of going *fishing*?

She exhaled and squeezed the Ambassador's stiff hand. "Thanks for this. I'll keep it all to myself, but at least I know."

Ambassador Welkin continued with dispassion. "Ostas will brief you on the way out about the chaos in Edenfall. Piper," she added, lowering her voice, "the Robosian society is highly unstable at the moment, and many others in the Cluster are watching to see if we can resolve this conflict... *noot*... whether there may be opportunities for them to... benefit."

Piper searched the Ambassador's golden eyes. They showed the immense concern and stress weighing on her shoulders. "I'll keep you apprised, somehow, of what's happening on the ground there, Ambassador."

She marched toward the heavy door, flinched as fresh pain suddenly shot up her leg from her healing knee and asked, "If you hear from Captain Carstairs, will you let me know?"

Welkin nodded, and Piper left to meet Ostas in the corridor.

TWELVE

A MIST HUNG OVER THE VERDANT VALLEY THAT stretched away from Scyther's private residence. The shimmering orange sun dipped in the sky, and he became lost in thought about how to keep his people alive in the absence of fresh organics. He narrowed the ways down to three: persuade the Robosians to change their minds about their farms; find other flesh on one of the conquerable dark planets, or take the Robosian reproduction facilities by force. Whichever option he chose, he had to act soon, since the daily reports continued to show an exponential increase in the number of Protoran deaths.

A gentle knock at the door interrupted him.

"Come," he said.

"Lord Scyther?"

He turned away from the picture window and marvelled at Sheilor standing upright and tall in the open doorway. The rays of the setting sun caught her form just so, casting a warm glow across her partly-mechanized body.

Long hair flowed over her shoulders. The sheer, plunging top ended at her thighs, showing off her young, new legs.

"You look beautiful, Sheilor," he growled in a low voice. "The minister's organics are satisfactory?"

"Indeed, they are, my Liege, although I am still getting used to them."

"Please," he said, approaching her and stroking her cheek. "Let us dispense with the formalities in my home."

The door *whooshed* behind her and she stretched up to kiss him. "I haven't felt well enough to be here in a long time," she purred. "And I have yet to dine."

Scyther took her hand and led her toward his bedroom, but on the way, his comms station pinged with an urgent, incoming message. He hesitated, then marched to the communications desk. The origin of the coded missive was Robos 7... Edenfall. "Ah, Doctor, perhaps our friends have reconsidered."

She sat on an oversized sofa. "Or they're missing a pretty minister," she mused.

The transmission, sent on a secure line, crackled with static. A man's face appeared, one that Scyther recognized from the meeting.

"I remember you," he said, scanning his database for a name. "You are Larrin, the minister of regional development."

"You have an excellent memory, Scyther. I apologize for the interruption, but as you appreciate, these are desperate days on Robos 7, and my people need help." The man pursed his lips. *"Specifically, your help."*

The big Protoran glanced at Sheilor. She leaned forward.

"I'm not sure I follow, Larrin. When we met yesterday, Feryn Graves made it clear there was nothing he could share with us, despite our crisis. Neither the farms, nor any of the lowly Hands. Are you saying he's changed his mind?"

"No, he has not. But it may interest you that a group of friendly supporters here attacked the cabinet, and the Interim Governor unfortunately lost his life."

Sheilor gasped, but Scyther showed no emotion.

"Regardless, many of us around the table do not share his idealistic views about the Hands and their role in our society. They are bred for servitude. Nothing more. And yet, we are supposed to treat them as equals? For decades, we have—"

Scyther, feeling the tug in his loins, cleared his throat. "Larrin, I am a busy man. Please get to the point. You said you needed my help. What precisely are you looking for?"

The Robosian inhaled. *"There is a way to secure the breeding farms and raw materials for your people, Scyther. Back me and my group. Send us weapons. Help me secure the government here, and you will have unfettered access to the facilities for as long as you wish, including an immediate shipment of adult Hands."*

When she heard this, Sheilor stood and moved closer to him. "A word, my Liege," she whispered into his aural sensor.

Scyther muted the conversation and turned to face her.

"As your confidant and friend, as well as a member of your senior staff, I urge you not to rush into anything. We do not know this man, or what his ambitions are beyond taking power."

"I have no fear of this organic puke."

"You are the most courageous man on Protor, my Lord. All I'm suggesting is caution. Tell him to prepare a more substantive proposal for your review. Find out what support he already has from the other factions in Edenfall. That will give us time to check out his group. Remember, the Asterian Battle Fleet remains in the Fairfield Sector. We would be wise to avoid drawing them into any conflict."

The Protoran leader accessed the latest visuals around

Robos 7 in his mind, noted the Fleet maintaining an aggressive posture near the planet. "Very well, Sheilor. You make a good point."

He unmuted the comms and said, "Larrin, your verbal musings interest us, but I require more information before I consider a decision of this magnitude. My primary goal is to negotiate with whoever now leads the government. If that isn't you..." The minister protested, but Scyther cut him off. "I'm not saying you and I can't work together. Only that I need to know more about your group, its size and strength, its goals."

"I understand," the Head said with a serious countenance. *"I'll have one of my men contact your office with our manifesto and make himself available to answer questions you may have. However, the situation here is fluid, Scyther. Things change minute to minute. The governor's seat is open, so I ask that you decide quickly."*

Scyther stood. "Rest assured, Larrin. Have your man contact my chief medical advisor with that information. I commit to reviewing it in short order."

The minister licked his lips, clearly pleased. Scyther ended the transmission and turned to his confidant. "What do you make of that?"

She folded an arm behind her head, complementing her mechano-organic physique. "Encouraging, to be sure. But I am cautious, especially with the leadership vacuum there."

"Normally I would share your caution, Sheil, but not this time." He pulled up a screen on the comms monitor showing a table of data. "Have you seen the latest mortality numbers? Across the entire planet, our people are dying. Once in a while, we stumble on some lone indigenous organic, but these events are rare. Do you see the projections here?" He pointed to the model. "Our world faces widespread decay within months."

Concern spread over Sheilor's face. "I understand. As soon as this fellow's information comes in, I'll review it for you."

"Thank you," he uttered.

In his mind, he had already accepted to work with Larrin, barring any serious problems, but he would not second guess his lover. Allowing Sheilor to do her homework not only assuaged any fears she may have but also ensured that he didn't act too impulsively. He had no choice but to prepare for anything.

He fired a private message to Commander Wesling, one of his trusted bridge officers aboard the flagship *Volantis.*

Ready the Primary Attack Squadron and 10,000 ground troops. Stand by to depart for Robos 7 at dawn.

Wesling acknowledged the order immediately.

"Now where were we?" Scyther embraced Sheilor, felt the warmth of her organics touching his. He loaded a new subroutine, developed especially for this occasion, and took her hand.

"Before we stir it up with the Fleet, I want to grab more provisions, Quirp. How's the Northern Airfield in Capital City look?"

"Captain, their supply depot is overstocked, according to the latest inventories, because of a reduction in flights over the last several months."

Carstairs grabbed a gel pack and slumped into his command chair. "Perfect. Maybe I can get a deal." He slurped the liquid. "You want anything, Quirp?"

"I am a non-sentient machine, Captain. I require nothing but power and my memory crystal."

"All right. Lay in a course to the airfield, but monitor the surrounding traffic for any ship without transponder ID. We'll spend the night there and take care of business in the morning."

The flight from the Holborg Hills to the city took less than twenty minutes. During that time, Carstairs retired to his quarters to catch up on all the correspondence that didn't reach him on Izillon. He scanned over missives from disgruntled pilots threatening to kill him for destroying their trade routes and deleted those immediately. Then several pieces related to new, state-of-the-art equipment he might be interested in. He saved those in a separate folder. When he checked his credit account, he couldn't believe the profit he'd made from his fish supply business—*I guess there wasn't much to spend it on in the middle of nowhere*—and as he reviewed the invoices from various customers, the first payment from the Black Bond cartel winked in.

Carstairs whistled. "Quirp, did you hear anything from Dhollot?"

"I have not, Captain. Would you like me to follow up with him about the contract?"

"Not necessary, my nerdy little friend. The cartel already paid us."

"Then I shall send him an acknowledgement."

The captain leaned back in his cabin chair and reviewed the other pieces of correspondence. Buried in the noise of death threats, several messages caused him to hold his breath. They came from Piper.

He grimaced and opened one of them.

…can't believe you would up and leave like that. You didn't even say goodbye. Jay, what's going on? I thought—

He deleted the message, then trashed all the others from her before breathing a guilt-riddled sigh of relief.

The *Dauntless* settled at the end of the airfield and powered down. Quirp scheduled a maintenance session with the mech shop for the morning when Carstairs searched for more supplies. He hoped for a pre-noon departure from the planet to reconnoiter Fleet operations in the Fairfield Sector, praying like hell to devise a plan somewhere en route.

But tonight, he sought relaxation, and the Pilot's Lounge would be ideal. Despite many years of sobriety, he continued socializing with drinkers. Not so subtle reminders of his past life, and what awaited him if he yielded to temptation.

He grabbed his jacket and said, "I'm heading to the watering hole, Quirp. Don't wait up for me."

"As you wish, Captain. Since numerous pilots hold you responsible for their unemployment, shall I keep the engines warm just in case?"

"Nah," he said, tucking a thermal flux gun inside his coat. "This isn't Tilley's. I'll be careful."

He strolled down the ship's ramp and walked a few hundred meters to the lounge. Laughter and loud voices greeted him as he pushed through the door and found an empty table near the back. He drew a few stares, but tonight, no one wanted a fight.

Delma, a server from the old days, brought a bottle of non-alcoholic Kurusian tree-water in a brown bag. She placed it in front of him and winked.

"Thanks, Del. How're you doing?"

She tugged her ear. "Seven years now."

"Great," he said, "keep it up, eh?"

"Yeah, I will. Say, someone come in here yesterday lookin' for you."

Carstairs sipped from the bag. "Oh? Someone else wanting a piece of me for wrecking their livelihood?"

She giggled, placed her tray on the table, and sat beside him. "Nothin' like that, handsome. Although, look around here. Quiet now, but plenty of clowns spoilin' for a wrestle, if you're not careful and all."

The gloomy bar was about half-full. Carstairs recognized a few of the old regulars, but many were unfamiliar. Drifters, most likely, coming into Capital City trying to find work that wasn't there.

"So you wanna know who, or what?"

"Hm? Oh, sure. Who's looking for me now?"

Delma shrugged. "Some young thing. Pretty. Blond hair. Half your age, I reckon."

His heart sank, and he choked on the tree-water. He instantly regretted deleting all her messages.

"What did she want?"

"No idear. Cullin took care of her at the bar. She chatted with some Kurusian fellow for a few minutes, then disappeared. Not sure what they talked about, but Cull told me afterwards that if I see you, I'm to let him know."

Carstairs glanced toward the bar. The bartender acknowledged him with a slight bow.

"I guess there's no need for that now, huh?" Delma stood and cinched her waistband. "Gotta run, darlin'."

The captain grabbed his bag and strolled toward the bar, ignoring the stares. Cullin finished taking a fellow's order and said, "Hey, Carstairs. The Chancellor's daughter was in here looking for you. She and Gazzer chatted it up. No one knew where you'd gone."

"I see. Did she say why she wanted to find me?"

"No. I figured it was some kind of unfinished business related to her mother's downfall. And I don't like to pry. Bad for my health."

Carstairs took a stool and leaned on the bar.

"Planning on sticking around town for a bit?"

He shook his head. "I'm loading some supplies and getting a quick maintenance check. Heading out after that."

"To Izillon?"

The man's question could not be ignored, and he studied him with deep suspicion. "What do you know about that?"

"Nothing, until just now." Cullin grinned. "Listen, can

I give you some free advice, Captain?"

"By all means. Everyone else does."

He lowered his voice. "Call her," he said. "She's in a bad way."

"How so?"

"Banged up knee. Bruises. Crazies gunning for her. Hearing voices, apparently. She could use a friend."

Carstairs downed the last of his drink. "What makes you so sure?"

"Oh, I hear things. Part of the job."

"Well, I'll think about it, Cull. Thanks."

He hoped to spend a few hours relaxing in the warm confines of the lounge, maybe listening to some music or chatting with strangers. But this news about Piper soured him. He slipped from the bar and maundered across the airfield to a lone, scraggly tree where he sank to the ground and stared at the stars.

THIRTEEN

THE ATI MECHANICAL SHOP AND STORAGE HANGAR ON the other side of town hummed with activity when Piper arrived on a scooter. She pulled to a stop by the shop entrance and hobbled into the office on her increasingly wonky knee.

"Piper Madison! You're a sight for these sore eyes of mine!" The Chief Engineer cleaned his hands on a tattered rag, then emerged from behind the counter.

"Hey, Paulie. It's been a while." She said sheepishly, hugging the man.

"It sure has, but never you mind. You got a ship to fly." He lowered his voice. "Maddie, you won't recognize the old gal any more. Same basic foundation, but all kitted out like a complete new build. Runs like a charm. New defensive systems. Improved stealth. There's nothing close to her around these parts, not even in the Fleet." He hopped on his feet, barely able to contain his excitement.

Piper raised her eyebrows. "Sure you're not

exaggerating a wee bit there, Chief?"

His jaw dropped in mock innocence. "Me? Never. Come on, I'll show you."

They marched toward the storage hangar, and Piper downed a painkiller when Paulie turned his head. The whispers from the stone in her pocket returned like a low-level white noise. She fished it out and noticed a thin blue glow coming off its surface. *A trick of the light in here.*

As they rounded a corner beside a tiny flier crawling with mechs, the *Penny Rose* gleamed ahead of them under a parade of lights, not 20 meters away.

This machine is the best thing I've ever worked on. Love this ship!

Somehow, the stone picked up the chief's thoughts. Or maybe they came from another mechanic's mind? Either way, she grew more comfortable with her emerging second sight and viewed it as a powerful advantage.

"I love this ship!" Paulie said, approaching the vessel with great veneration.

Definitely his thoughts. She plunged the stone deep into her pocket again and followed the engineer around and through the revitalized ship, noting all the upgrades and mods he and the crew had made.

The cockpit rivaled those on the most sophisticated vessels she'd seen. She sat in the command chair and the *Penny* sprang to life.

"We just put a brand new Xanthalite crystal in her this morning. Model QRO-5000."

Piper pulled a face. "Serious? That's some kind of power."

"I know, right?" the engineer's face beamed. "But look, you can get acquainted with the ship mind en route to wherever you're supposed to be going on behalf of Ambassador Welkin." The stocky mechanic furrowed his brow. "Listen Piper, I was sorry to hear about your mother.

I hope you're okay."

"Thank you, Chief. I'll be fine. Just need to get this leg healed, and I'll get to that as soon as I return." She stood. "Anything else to know before I go?"

"Nothing you can't figure out on the way." He chased a couple of mechs from the vessel and headed for the exit. "Have a safe flight, Ms. Madison."

"Will do, Paulie, and thanks again."

He hopped out, gathered his workers like an old mother duck, and retreated to a respectable distance.

"I am pleased to make your acquaintance, Ms. Madison," the ship mind said in a pleasant, male voice. "Please call me Ro, if you wish."

"Ro... very well." She leaned forward and reviewed the controls. Her ship's console mirrored the others she'd flown, and she relinquished control to the Xanthalite. "Let's see what this new bird can do. Engage thrusters, Ro, and take us up 200 meters. Then set a course for Robos 7. I'll provide more details once we're out of orbit."

"As you wish, Ms. Madison."

The *Penny Rose* lifted in a vertical line off the surface, hovered a moment at 200 meters, then eased into the afternoon sky.

"HEY RO, SINCE WE HAVE SOME TIME TO KILL ON THE WAY to the Fairfield Sector, I'd like to ask you a few questions."

Piper leaned back, gazing at the main viewer over the console as the painkillers dulled her senses. She just completed reviewing all the fancy new systems and equipment that Paulie installed, and her mind turned to Neris. She wished she'd had the whisper stone to read his mind back when he abandoned her for the Valley... to know his true thoughts. And yet, would she want her most private thoughts available to previous lovers?

"As you wish, Ms. Madison. How may I assist you?"

She straightened up. "The subject is whisper stones. Do you have all the science packs installed?"

"Affirmative."

"Great. What can you tell me about how they work for reading thoughts and images over great distances?"

The ship veered on a course change—part of the stealth flight path Welkin's aide gave her prior to leaving.

"This is a highly irregular question, Ms. Madison, since whisper stones are a myth."

She exhaled long and slow. "Pretend they do exist, Ro. Treat my question like a thought experiment."

The ship mind adjusted its approach and provided her with a suite of assumptions and hypotheticals that could, in theory, explain a person's abilities to read someone else's thoughts. Ro began with a discussion on energy, then thought-energy equivalencies, and finally quantum entanglement as a mechanism for transcending space-time.

Piper concluded from this treatise that second sight—if real—remained unpredictable and dependent on both the user's and the subject's specific mind.

"Perhaps the larger question, Ms. Madison, is not so much the mechanism of the stones, but the moral and ethical dilemma they would present."

Piper leaned on the back of the command chair, mesmerized by the smear of stars screaming by on the main viewer. "Not sure I follow."

"If my understanding of humanoid philosophy is sound, the invasion of someone else's private thoughts could be considered as an emotional violation... a breach of trust. And if the person being targeted is unaware of such an act, the attack would be even worse."

Kitto more or less said the same thing back on Hauntor. She could have turned the stone over to Bornham at the ATI, or to Welkin. But she didn't. Why? Perhaps the stone's insight could prove useful to her in the current conflict. Or maybe she simply liked the ability to see the truth in someone else's mind.

She ached to know the real reason why Neris rejected her... if it was something she did or said.

And why Carstairs abandoned her in the hospital without a word. Did her find her that unattractive?

The whisper stone gave her that power... the ability to finally know the whole truth without the deceit of words.

"You raise a good point, Ro. I suppose it's a good thing these whisper stones don't exist, hm?" She pulled the stone from her pocket and stretched, allowing the medication to flood her body. When she brought the gem to her eyes, it glowed and pulsed in her fingers, like the heart of a tiny sparrow.

Where are you, Neris? Where are you, Jay? Why can't you be honest with me?

Scyther admired the tranquil view from his private balcony the following morning, sipping a cup of sweetgrass tea, languishing in the gentle breeze, and waiting for Sheilor to arise.

During the previous hour, he recharged in a regeneration pod, servicing his assorted servo-mechanics and cleaning out the debris from his computational databases. His mind was sharp, his new limb felt strong, and he'd already heard from Commander Wesling that the attack squadron and troops had assembled and were standing by to launch.

The soft padding of organic feet behind him interrupted his private moment. Sheilor appeared carrying a comms device and wearing one of his ceremonial tunics. The unbuttoned garment fell from her thin shoulders like a short blanket, hiding little and, although much of her torso was mechanical, her chest was primarily flesh. Scyther raised his eyebrows with admiration.

"Apologies, Liege, it was the only thing I could find," she shrugged.

He kissed her on the forehead and offered her some tea from a nearby tray. She sat on soft banquet, placing the comms device on her lap.

"During the night, I ordered our security group to run a background check on this fellow, Larrin. This is a preliminary report." She touched the screen and hesitated.

"Do we have any cause for concern?" he asked, returning his gaze to the lush countryside surrounding the balcony.

"No. Minister Larrin is exactly what he says he is. A solid functionary in the old Robosian government under Morden Graves. Holds a couple of portfolios in the interim regime, at least until the latest rebel attack. Nothing criminal on his personal record. By all accounts, my Lord, he is a legitimate and effective public servant."

The big Protoran grinned. "Shall we open talks with him right away?"

"Yes. Whether he has sufficient support from his colleagues to pull off a coup remains unknown, and the absence of information concerning affiliated militias presents an ongoing risk; however, I do not view that as problematic."

"Understood," Scyther said. "No doubt that's why he's sounding us out for help." He joined Sheilor on the banquet and took her hand in his. "I'll contact Larrin straight away and inform him that a squadron is ready to assist with his plans." Then, scanning her with his ocular eye, he added, "Join me on the *Volantis*, Sheilor. It will be like old times again, when our world was a lot more hostile and volatile, and we forged from it a splendid society."

She beamed at him with a distant look. "Those were heady years, my love. But we are not the same anymore. Neither of us." She glanced around anxiously. "But those were beautiful days, and I am full of fond memories."

He stood and they moved inside to the comms station. After a few moments, Larrin appeared on the main viewscreen. Scyther noticed the chamber in the Governor's mansion behind the man, now empty except for a few Robosians moving cautiously by the far wall, navigating with care around a pile of debris.

"Lord Scyther, thank you for contacting me. Have you had a chance to consider my offer?"

The Protoran leader fidgeted with the comms control and said, "We have, Larrin. At this moment, I'm ordering an attack squadron of fighters to Robos 7, along with a troopship full of experienced soldiers. I'll join them as well, and we'll contact you while en route soon. Your colleagues may wonder at the presence of Protoran fighters approaching the planet. You must be ready to address this and, if possible, keep your own fledgling Robosian fleet grounded." He leaned closer to the screen. "Will this pose any sort of problem for you and your supporters?"

Larrin shook his head. *"We have been prepared to do whatever it takes to preserve our traditional way of life. And with your help, Lord Scyther, we will not only achieve our goals, but our two planets will also be in a splendid position to enjoy a long-lasting relationship. I look—"*

"Do not get too far ahead of yourself, Larrin, my friend. There are no guarantees of anything. And do not underestimate the resolve of the young Graves girl, Ariel. I understand she remains missing, and therefore, possibly alive. She proved her worth in the battles with the Bortans, remember?"

The Robosian minister concurred.

"Make your preparations, Larrin. May the winds be at our backs."

Scyther cut the transmission and turned to face Sheilor, who pressed against his side. A concerned look swept over her face. "Loss of life is sometimes inevitable with these actions, my Liege, and I know you kill only to preserve our survival. But what about those soldiers? Will they show the same respect to others as you do?"

He brushed the hair from her face. "This squadron commander, Wesling, is a rule follower. He'll keep them in line and focused on the task at hand. To be honest, I could not care less about who governs that polluted planet of theirs. But we must have those reproduction farms. Securing them is my only desire."

Sheilor opened her mouth to respond when an alert interrupted her. They faced the main viewer. A communications official appeared on the screen.

"My Lord," he said. *"We have intercepted a transmission from Asteria that may interest you."*

Scyther scowled. "Report."

"We tracked Piper Madison arriving on Asteria a few days ago. Apparently, she's been undertaking research on a dark planet. Something to do with—"

"Get on with it, man. What about the girl?"

"Well, our spies inform me she left that planet in a scientific runabout a short time ago... not the same one she arrived in... some altered craft. My agent on the ground thought little of it until he recognized the vessel was equipped with transponder scramblers and other stealth equipment. Weapons systems, too. When he tried tracking her position, the ship disappeared without a trace."

Scyther glanced at Sheilor. A worried look crossed her face. She moved in front of the screen and the communications official turned away.

"Do you have any idea where she's going?" she said. "Is it possible she's returning to that planet to continue working and wants to keep her course confidential for scientific purposes?"

"Anything is conceivable, Doctor," the man replied,

staring at his boots. *"But we believe she may be heading to Robos 7."*

"Robos 7?" Scyther bristled. "Why her sudden appearance in this sector? I doubt it's a coincidence."

"It's impossible to be certain, my Lord, but she has been there before, and the former Governor is, or was, her biological father. Perhaps she's been in contact with her half-siblings. If that's the case, then I—"

"Yes," Scyther interrupted, "I understand the potential ramifications. Listen. Focus your attention on any chatter around Robosian space and keep me apprised the moment her ship surfaces. I also want you to watch the Asterian Battle Fleet for any new movement." He cut the link. "Sheilor, I must prepare to join the armada. Will you come with me?"

"I'll meet you on the *Volantis* in twenty minutes." She downed the last of her tea and departed.

Scyther flexed his fingers. He ordered Commander Wesling to launch his ships and wait for him in orbit, then changed into his battle dress and admired himself in the full-length mirror in his bedroom.

He did not fear the uppity Madison girl. Not one bit. But he respected her resourcefulness and ability to fall into trouble and then emerge unscathed. He would not take her for granted like those fools on Robos 7. Indeed, she and that flyboy sidekick Carstairs had not only taken out a formidable planetary leader, but they'd also altered Torfinn history forever by removing Tephera Madison from power.

As he adjusted his battle tackle, he muttered, "I wonder what happened to the old Chancellor?"

And if her problematic daughter showed up on Robos 7 or anywhere near his operations, he would not hesitate to remove her if she got in his way.

FOURTEEN

PIPER'S KNEE THROBBED WITH AN ACHE SHE HADN'T FELT since the cave-in on Hauntor, as she piloted the juiced-up *Penny Rose* toward Robos 7. The reconstructive surgery at the community hospital on Second Point had gone well at the time, and she enjoyed a few pain-free days. But something now prohibited the healing. Piper worried she may have overdone it, but she only understood one speed, and that was full throttle. Regardless, she would have to find a doctor to check it out soon. Kitto's warning about the risk of permanent damage echoed in her mind.

"What's our ETA to the planet, Ro?" The dark, polluted orb blended with the blackness of the surrounding space, rendering it almost invisible to the naked eye.

The ship mind chirped, "Twenty-four minutes to achieve standard orbit above Robos 7, Ms. Madison."

She bit her bottom lip, then hobbled aft to the stores to find the medical supplies. Between the bandages and braces sat a container filled with painkillers. She snapped open the seal and chewed two of the tablets. The stabilizing effect on her knee was instantaneous.

Her testing of the ship's equipment and functionality of the runabout had gone off without a hitch. The only systems she hadn't evaluated—other than in simulations— were the weapons, and she hoped she wouldn't have to.

A warning tone filled the cockpit.

"Ms. Madison, I am detecting a squadron of twelve attack fighters, a battle cruiser, and a troop carrier en route to Robos 7," the ship mind droned. "I am monitoring the Asterian Battle Fleet's movements and communications, but they appear to have no interest in this armada."

Piper took the command chair and leaned forward over the helm. Ro had marked the viewscreen with icons showing the Asterian Fleet and these new attack ships. "What's their origin?"

"Their design is Protoran, Ms. Madison."

She hadn't read the dossier that Welkin's underling provided, so she still knew little about that planet or its people, other than they supplied technological components to the Torfinn Cluster and were a junior player in the Fairfield Industrial Sector. Piper tried recalling if she'd ever met a Protoran during her mother's reign as Chancellor, but nothing came to mind.

"Perhaps these ships are helping to keep the peace for the Robosian leaders. They don't appear to be making any hostile moves." She studied their flight path, noting that the Asterian Battle Fleet apparently had no issue with them, since they maintained their positions. "What do we know about the Protorans, Ro?"

The ship mind stated, "They are a transhumanist people, Ms. Madison. Part machine, part organic. Dependent on both for survival. They settled on Protor over a century ago and have established themselves as first-rate technology providers and innovators. However, because of their transhuman nature, they decimated the local indigenous population in order to ensure their own existence. It is unclear how many of the native life forms remain on the planet."

"Why do they require organics?"

"Despite several attempts and ongoing research, the Protorans could not survive as machine beings only. They rely on flesh for proper functioning. This symbiosis remains poorly understood."

Piper frowned. "Another of these closed societies, eh?"

"Yes, Ms. Madison, much like the Robosians and Bortans. It seems to be a common trait among the industrial planets in this sector. However, they are a peaceful people historically, keeping to themselves and engaging in honest trade."

Piper winced with a wry expression. The Fairfield Sector held many secrets... nasty social behaviours that only came to light when she exposed them to the rest of the Cluster. She wondered what mysteries the Protorans might have.

The *Penny Rose* hurtled toward the planet, and Piper checked the ship's stealth transponder to ensure they remained invisible to scanners.

"Shall I establish contact with the Planetary Communications Unit?" the ship mind asked.

She shook her head. "Let's stay quiet for now, Ro. I don't want them or anyone else to know we're here." Piper touched the comms controls and brought the ship's long range scanner to focus on the area surrounding the capital city of Edenfall. Given the distance from the planet, the image resolution appeared pixelated, but clear enough to show pockets of destruction throughout the urban centre, and the polluted atmosphere encroaching on it.

"It used to be beautiful when I first arrived there," she said. "Ro, we must choose our landing spot wisely. Find a suitable location to hide the *Penny Rose* that's not too far from the city."

"As you wish," the ship mind replied.

A klaxon pierced the quiet air in the runabout. Two Protoran attackers peeled off from the armada, targetting the ship.

"What's happening, Ro? Are we no longer invisible?"

"We remain in stealth mode, Ms. Madison. Perhaps the Protorans have superior technology that enables them to detect us."

She buckled in. "Apparently, they do."

"Their weapons are online and warmed. May I suggest we—"

"Yes, get us out of here. Let's not engage these freaks. We'll fly close to the Robosian surface and see if they follow."

"As you wish, Ms. Madison."

The *Penny Rose* increased velocity and nosed into the atmosphere above the planet. The ship mind attempted to shake the chasing attack fighters with a variety of evasive maneuvers, but without success.

"They're anticipating our every move," Piper said in a measured voice. "I think it's time we tested the *Penny's* defensive capabilities, Ro."

"Weapons systems are online and armed, Ms. Madison."

The runabout screamed over the planet's surface, less than 100 meters above the toxic lands. The Protorans, oblivious to her attempts to outrun them, gained distance and fired warning shots over her ship.

"I've had enough of this crap," she said. "Ro, maintain defensive shields and life support at all costs. Time to find out what these fools want."

Piper grabbed the steering shaft and pulled hard to starboard. She launched several covering salvos, and the two

Protoran attack ships split up. One continued pursuing her on a line, gaining ground and targeting her engines. The second flew high and circled around to flank her.

The *Penny Rose* was far more maneuverable with the refit. Piper appreciated the refined and nuanced movements, and her speed had improved over the clunky, previous model. But the weaponry impressed her the most. She zipped between hills and over polluted river valleys, maneuvering the ship with abrupt, unpredictable turns. She fired covering shots to deter the attack ships.

But it was no use. She couldn't shake them. As she approached a massive granite ridge, she decelerated, allowing the one pursuing attacker to gain more distance on her. Then, with proximity alarms screaming through the cabin, she pulled hard on the stick, gaining altitude, then looped around, falling in behind the startled Protoran.

With weapons at the ready, she fired a volley of torpedoes. The first two missed the target, but the third one slammed into the attack vessel, searing it in half and sending it to the ground in a shower of smoke and flames.

The second ship, however, was not fooled by Piper's maneuver. From a higher altitude, it launched several short range torpedoes toward the *Penny Rose*, smashing into the ship's fuselage.

"Ms. Madison, our defensive shields are gone," Ro reported in a dull voice. "The ship will not survive another attack. I suggest we land while I attempt to repair the damaged circuitry."

Piper swore under her breath. This wasn't the way she'd hoped to arrive on Robos 7. "So much for stealth," she muttered. "All right, take us down to the surface."

The ship mind piloted the *Penny* to a level patch near a blackened copse of poisoned trees. The Protoran vessel followed, hovered a moment, and landed beside her. For several minutes, the two ships remained quiet as the dust settled around them. Ro assessed the damage to the ship's systems while Piper stared at her adversary through the main viewscreen.

"Attention unidentified runabout." A metallic male voice filled the cockpit. *"You will abandon your ship immediately, or be destroyed."*

Piper snorted in disdain, but realized she had little choice.

"Very well." She grabbed an air filter and limped from the *Penny's* port side opening.

The stench and heat of the planet seized her as she limped cautiously toward the Protoran vessel. About ten meters from the *Penny*, she stopped and admired the attack fighter. Its sleek lines indicated she was clearly built for atmospheric travel and deep space. Rail guns, protected by heavy shielding, lined the attack ship laterally. Massive torpedo bays hung from its belly. *If they wanted to destroy me, they easily could have*, she thought. *So what do they want?*

An iris doorway opened and a strange man dressed in a black protective suit descended the short ramp. He marched toward her, carrying no obvious weapon. Piper reached for her thermal flux gun, only to realize she'd forgotten to strap it on in all the excitement.

He halted before her. His entire head seemed enveloped in a rubberized substance.

"Do not be afraid, Piper Madison," he said. "I am Commander Keelin, from Protor. My orders are to bring you unharmed to the Governor's mansion in Edenfall."

"What if I don't want to go?"

"That would be unwise."

She eyed the *Penny Rose*. The crippling attack left scorch marks across the vessel's fuselage and stern, and she wouldn't be flying away in it anytime soon.

"Okay," she said, "and why are we going to Edenfall?"

"Patience," Keelin responded. "You will see."

"IF YOU DON'T MIND MY SAYING, CAPTAIN, YOU SEEM TO be quieter than usual this morning. Are you having second thoughts about the contract with the cartel?"

Jay Carstairs shifted in the pilot's seat, staring at the main viewer. The *Dauntless* sat in a hangar reserved for maintenance at the Northern Airfield. Mechs scurried about the space, gathering tools, crawling over the ship like insects.

"Don't know, Quirp. I've been looking into the state of affairs in the cluster since I left, and it's pretty grim. Ambassador Welkin tries her best to keep the Council together, but maintaining her position is increasingly difficult."

The ship mind acknowledged the goings on, agreeing with the Captain that life in the Torfinn Galaxy had become far more challenging. "However," Quirp said, "is this not the normal pattern in times of social upheaval?"

A couple of mechs entered the cockpit, and Carstairs showed them to the control panels. They unbuckled the covers and went to work.

"I suppose you're right, but that doesn't make it any easier. Of greater concern to me at the moment is the Battle Fleet."

"How so, Captain?" Quirp sing-songed.

"Because they have more firepower than any other group in the galaxy, yet they're married to that damn Ethical Protocol, so all they do is watch planets destroy themselves. They rarely intervene." He shook his head and wrenched a coffee from the sidebar.

This lack of Council support and the toothless fleet in particular also drove Piper nuts. On this matter, she and Carstairs shared the same opinion.

"What this means for us, Quirp, is that provoking those

ships to return to Asteria and leave the Fairfield Sector—and the trade routes—is next to impossible." He brought the cup to his lips.

"Perhaps that's why Dhollot couldn't find an appropriate supplier for the cartel."

Carstairs smirked. "Sure. You know, I figured we could approach the fleet like a mosquito and create some havoc that would send them running home. I hadn't worked out all the details, but that was my overall strategy." He sipped his coffee, watching the mechs in the hangar.

"And now?" Quirp queried.

"Well, I'm wondering what the hell I got myself into."

"Before you ask, Captain, I have reviewed the fine print in that contract. It is fully binding. There is no escape clause. As such, you are on the hook."

"I figured as much," he said matter-of-factly. "And as long as the Cluster remains in complete chaos, nothing's going to change soon."

The two mechs finished their diagnostic on the cockpit consoles and left. The entire maintenance package would take several more hours, leaving Carstairs with enough time to travel downtown and wander around some of his old haunts. Maybe even look for Piper.

"Quirp, I need to clear my head. Didn't have a great sleep last night. So I'm going into town for a while. Mind the ship while I'm gone, will you?"

"As you wish," Quirp said. "I shall contact you when the repairs are complete."

CAPITAL CITY HAD CHANGED LITTLE SINCE HE LEFT A FEW months ago. Except for the people. He wasn't used to being recognized on the street, but after his encounter with Zadicus Verman, and the subsequent arrest and jailing of Piper's mother, everyone knew his face and name and entire history, it seemed.

This unnerved him, so rather than stopping in at his favourite places, he bypassed them altogether and stuck to the less populated areas.

Beside an under-used park, he discovered a bank of public comm screens, and logged in to read the news. Most of it, he was already aware of: troubles on Robos 7... Borta under martial law with an interim leader... divisions within the Torfinn Governing Council... He scowled at how quickly these peace-abiding planets fell into distrust and conflict. It hadn't been this way when Tephera Madison ruled the cluster, and when any planet tried to operate outside the rules, she brought the hammer down on them, hard.

There was something to be said for that kind of rule.

When he scanned the reports for news about Piper, the number of written articles about her in the past couple of days alone surprised him. She arrived in Capital City, spent some time visiting the ATI and the Northern Airfield, and wound up in the Governing Council building. He wondered if his movements were being tracked as well, concluded they were, and reminded himself to stick close to the shadows with his elbows up.

Additional reports showed she stopped at the Institute's hangar, where she secured some decked-out ship and disappeared into space. *So much for finding Piper.*

He peered up. On this sunny morning, a couple of young families arrived in the park, kicking a ball around and laughing. Behind him, a pair of men stood chatting by a scooter paddock, glancing inconspicuously toward him.

Danger and insecurity were hallmarks of his career prior to the onset of galactic madness. Regardless, Carstairs now yearned for his previous rollercoaster life. Before the fall of Robos 7 and the mayhem on Borta. Before Piper almost died and her mother got turfed out of power. *In those days*, he reflected, *at least you knew where you stood, and abundant peace and order filled the galaxy.*

Not anymore.

And in that instant, between the families playing in the park and the pair of toughs lurking behind him, the beautiful seed of an awful idea germinated in his brain.

His contract with the cartel didn't specify *how* he was to liberate the trade lanes. And if the Asterian Battle Fleet refused to get involved in anything—useless as they were—then he needed to find a different tack than needling them.

A proven alternative.

Something, or *someone*, who could restore order and put an end to the multiple conflicts, thus sending the Fleet home.

Someone like Tephera Madison.

Yes, the former Chancellor was the key. He found her jail location in the news articles and abandoned the kiosk, walked to the park and sat on an isolated bench. From his vantage point, he caught glimpses of the building where Tephera used to rule with an iron fist. She still maintained a healthy grip on many in the Council, not to mention across the land, if the reports were correct. Why, some of the prison guards were likely sympathetic to her plight, so maybe it wouldn't take much to...

Carstairs chuckled. "What am I thinking?" he laughed aloud. "This is crazy talk."

Still, within seconds, he raced to the public scooters, ignored the toughs, hopped on a vehicle and screamed away. On the scooter's navigation screen, he punched in the coordinates for the Asterian Maximum Security Prison.

FIFTEEN

LORD SCYTHER STOOD ON THE BRIDGE OF THE BATTLE cruiser *Volantis*, mesmerized by the dogfight he just witnessed between Piper Madison's runabout and his well-trained attack squad. He replayed the chase on his personal viewer. *She is a formidable pilot. Most unconventional. Unfortunately, she neutralized one viper, but Commander Keelin's experience showed, and he brought Madison's ship down without harming her.*

Dr. Sheilor sidled up. "Two of the crew are suffering from significant organic decay," she whispered. "We must find more flesh quickly, Liege. Perhaps there are bodies on the planet's surface that…"

The Protoran leader turned from the viewscreen and said, "I know this all too well. However, a plain solution already exists. If the agreement with Larrin holds and he keeps his end of the bargain, then we shall enjoy unfettered access to adult Hands immediately, along with the reproduction farms on Robos 7. Our need for flesh will be addressed, Sheilor, and I don't want to jeopardize that. Indeed," he schemed, "we may even begin reproducing our own people again."

Her thin, tight mouth betrayed the hopeful strain on her face. Although his confidence knew no bounds, he acknowledged her concerns around the use of organics for their own benefit alone. *Harvesting*, she called it.

"Sir," the Navigator interrupted, "Commander Keelin is en route to Edenfall with Piper Madison. Do you wish to speak with him?"

Scyther shook his head. "I want to chat with Tephera Madison's daughter, Mr. Derrah. But I'm a patient man. Once I arrive at the Governor's mansion, we shall talk then."

"Yes, Liege."

"Sheilor?" he said. "Join me on the runabout and we'll travel to the planet's surface. On the way, perhaps you can review these production figures that Larrin sent."

The two Protorans left the bridge and marched in silence toward the shuttle deck. His personal vehicle had been prepped, and its engines hummed, warming as they entered the hold.

Once they departed the *Volantis* for Robos 7, Scyther engaged the ship mind, and unbuttoned the top of his tunic. He offered Sheilor a drink, which she refused. Instead, she leaned over a map on the comms panel, studying the Robosian reproduction facilities and reviewing the numbers.

"What do you think, Doctor?"

She shook her head. "The production estimates are so much greater than I ever expected." She blinked rapidly, calculating various scenarios in her head. "You are right, my Lord. With these farms, we will perpetuate our species for as long as we desire."

"That won't be easy," he said, standing beside her and

studying the data. "There is much chaos in this industrial world, and civil war between the Heads and the Hands is a distinct possibility." He checked the main viewscreen. Grey and black clouds covered Robos 7. At the edge of the monitor, Edenfall glimmered like a bright green smudge.

Scyther grunted. "We may have insufficient soldiers to dissuade these Robosians from tearing each other to pieces. Ten thousand troops should be enough to secure and protect Edenfall and the breeding farms, but Larrin says there are pockets of Hand militias throughout the lands. Not to mention the political factions who all want power." He turned to face her. "This mission will test us, Sheilor. The men are not experienced in guerilla tactics. But our need is great, and my resolve is true."

She stood tall on her new, sturdy legs. Her overall physical improvement was remarkable, and he ached to provide his entire world with fresh, ripe organics like hers. Larrin had assured him that as long as he ascended to power on Robos 7, the Protorans would enjoy everything they needed. So far, he'd proven a man of his word.

The doctor glanced at the approaching planet on the viewscreen. "What are you going to do with Piper Madison? The girl could be a problem, my Lord, and has already taken down one of our ships. Let us not underestimate her like others have."

Scyther clenched his jaw. "Honestly, I'm not sure. We will keep her under guard, for she has shown an ability to fight like few others in the galaxy." He paced around the cramped cabin. "But I wonder if we might use her to gain more influence with the Torfinn Governing Council."

"How so?" Sheilor asked. "Intelligence suggests she is no longer in good standing on Asteria because of her involvement in destabilizing the entire cluster. Unless there has been a change of heart among her people, I fail to—"

"I've read the reports of her predicament. Welkin likes

her, and I bet that lizard queen is behind her clandestine romp into Robosian space. But the other common folk on Asteria feel the opposite. Many blame her for disrupting their peaceful lives." He sat on the edge of the pilot seat. "But she may help us convince the Council leadership of our need for organics once she sees how the people suffer."

"Perhaps," Sheilor said in a soft voice.

He reached out and pulled her close. "Doctor... Sheil... what eats at you so?"

She licked her flesh lips. "I see how much our citizens suffer, Liege, and it breaks my heart that I cannot help them given our lack of organics on Protor." She brushed the matted hair from his temple.

"This agreement is of crucial importance to our future."

"Don't misunderstand, my Lord. I am conflicted. In order to save our people, we must harvest others. I never thought much of it back home with our own indigenous organics. They could barely organize themselves into social groups. No better than common animals." She searched for the words. "But these Hands are intelligent. Competent. Deserving of respect like any other creative beings, and—"

He dropped her hand and stood agape. "I can't believe I'm hearing this. Are you suggesting we forsake this agreement and simply die off?"

"No. I mean yes. Oh, I don't know, Scyther. Something feels amiss. Are we sure another solution is impossible? Have we truly explored all possibilities with the Cluster? Perhaps there are creatures on one of the dark planets we could harvest instead of these humanoids. Or maybe the Torfinn scientists developed a synthetic organic lattice like we've been talking about."

Scyther stormed away, marching back and forth in the confined cabin with long, powerful strides. He stopped in front of her. "You have missed most of the discussions with

Council researchers and policy advisors over how many years. And every time, Sheilor… every single time they flick their fingers at us and say *tut tut now* and show us the door." He held her shoulders. "Believe me, love, I tried everything. The only person who ever showed the courtesy of taking our need to others was Tephera Madison. She seemed to understand our predicament and sympathize." He frowned, allowing his deepset anger to surface. "But now she's in shackles and that Erusian reptile has too many other priorities to even give us the time of day."

Sheilor whispered. "I never knew."

"We are not monsters, Doctor," he said. "We are only trying to look after each other. To survive. Would you not do anything to protect your family?"

"Of course. I'd give my life so that you may live."

"And I the same. All Protorans are my kin. Each one, Doctor. And there is nothing I won't do to save them."

A comms alert filled the cabin.

"Lord Scyther, Commander Keelin's ship landed at the mansion. Larrin and his people escorted our guest inside."

"Acknowledged," Scyther bellowed. "I'll meet with her and Keelin soon. We shall arrive in Edenfall within a few minutes."

Sheilor took her seat beside him and kept her head down.

"I cannot do any of this without you, Sheil."

She took his hand. "When we work together, love, there is nothing we can't accomplish."

"Come." He squeezed her mechanical hand. "Let us meet our Asterian guest." He grabbed the flight stick and screamed through the polluted atmosphere toward Edenfall.

SEVERAL ARMED PROTORANS, WITH COMMANDER Keelin in the lead, escorted Piper through the bomb-ravaged mansion toward a narrow staircase off a meeting room. On the way, dozens of Hands and soldiers cleared rubble and repaired the fallen beams and wrecked walls caused by the recent attack.

Hard to believe so much has changed so quickly, she thought. Several months ago, when her ship first crash-landed, the Governor's mansion glistened like a diamond in the pristine city of Edenfall. Before she wrought immeasurable trouble, that is. Before the uprising.

They marched single-file down the winding staircase, with Piper in the middle. She did not appear to be under arrest—they didn't bind her hands—yet their presence suggested her freedom was restricted. And, as she'd learned from Carstairs, it's often prudent to go along with the captors in order to determine their plans and their weaknesses. Then fight back from a position of knowledge.

The staircase descended forever, dropping into the bowels of the building, straining her injured knee. When they reached the bottom, the guards took her down a long, dark corridor to what looked like an old storage area they'd cleared for a makeshift holding cell. The group stopped, and the men ushered her inside before remaining at the entrance.

Commander Keelin removed his black head covering, revealing a shocking mix of organic face and machine metal. He frowned awkwardly. "Piper Madison, you will remain here until Lord Scyther calls for you. I apologize for the conditions, but I trust you'll find this accommodation comfortable. The security guards," he thrust his chin toward the open door, "won't harm you as long as you cooperate. Observe, there is no lock since you are our guest. But these are dangerous times and we must be extremely careful."

Keelin turned on his heel to leave.

"Commander," she said, "why are you here on Robos 7?"

The Protoran stiffened. His body language suggested

he struggled with whatever responses floated in his software.

"We will answer all your questions in due course, Piper Madison." His ocular orb flashed at her. "What is that item in your pocket?"

Piper gulped. She'd forgotten about the whisper stone. Deciding to play it cool and upbeat, she said, "Oh, this?" She pulled out the gem. "Just a memento from my work on Hauntor. A good luck charm. Want to see it?"

Keelin shook his head stiffly. "This concept of luck is illogical, Piper Madison. Keep your trinket, if it helps you sleep at night."

After he departed, she shoved the stone away and surveyed the entrance. The silent sentries kept their hands close to their girded weapons. She returned to the cot and flopped down, waiting for this Scyther fellow to summon her.

She didn't have to wait long.

A few minutes passed when the guards began moving about. Piper heard nothing spoken between them, and presumed wireless communication. One entered the cell and said in an artificial voice, "Lord Scyther will see you now." She jumped up and followed the pair down the corridor to a different staircase.

When she limped into the old Governor's study, several Protorans looked up from their work around a large table. Other Heads lurked in the background—one of whom seemed familiar.

A tall man confronted her. His glance at the guards sent them fleeing into the hallway. This Protoran's face, like many of the others, was primarily organic. Much of his skull, however, was covered in the same protective skin Keelin used. The rest of his uniform resembled battle coverings: thick leather, heavy metal boots. He studied her. "So this is the famous Piper Madison."

"And you must be Lord Scyther."

"Indeed." He waved his arm around the room, introducing the other key members in the gathering, including Larrin, the Head she recognized. Except, with Feryn now dead, others referred to this fellow as *Governor.* No *Interim* moniker attached to his name, she noted. The truth of the situation became clear.

"Come, join me in the sitting area."

Scyther headed for the large couch and comfortable chairs surrounding a utilitarian coffee table.

"I always imagined you as being taller, Ms. Madison. Funny how our minds conjure these false images, isn't it?"

Piper shrugged. They sat across from each other. A Hand appeared from nowhere with a tray of assorted beverages and food, and she helped herself to some water and a meal stick.

"You're not having anything, Lord Scyther?" she asked.

His dark face scrunched up. "I will dine later."

The cool liquid, that she recognized as Bone Sip, refreshed her sore throat. "So, what would you like to discuss? Must be important if your pilots crashed my runabout."

"Ah, a woman who gets right to the point. Good... good. Ms. Madison, my first question should be obvious. Why have you come to Robos 7?"

"I could ask you the same thing."

The Protoran scanned her body. "Once you've satisfied me, I will answer your questions," he said. "Obviously, you're not here for the weather or the beautiful scenery. Is it to mourn your half-brother? To see your half-sister? Perhaps you seek to cause more trouble?"

Piper leaned forward on her elbows. "Of course, I'd like to find Ariel and make sure she's okay. And to pay my respects to Feryn."

Scyther scrutinized her with deep suspicion. "But I

understand the Torfinn Galaxy Council has restricted all travel to this dung heap. And we found you en route under stealth conditions. I can't decide whether you're a spy for that lizard queen, or simply wanting to keep a low profile because of your notoriety."

"Like I said, my only concern is finding Ariel. Anything else you're doing here is not my business."

Scyther made a guttural, mechanical sound Piper assumed was a type of Protoran laughter. "And fate saw fit to put you in an upgraded shuttle, armed to the teeth with state-of-the-art weaponry, defensive shields, engines... Come now, Ms. Madison. Am I to believe you secured this *runabout* for a search and rescue mission?"

Heat crept up her body. She couldn't trust this stranger at all, but she had to toss him a bone if she hoped to be freed. "Well," she began, "the Ambassador requested a report on the rival factions in this region. For example, that Larrin fellow becoming Governor... I never realized he had sufficient support to take on the position. So, I doubt she knows much about that."

"Finally, we're getting somewhere," Scyther mused. "The Robosian bootlick approached me, looking for backing. I listened to his proposal and agreed it made sense. That's why my people are here. To help establish a stable government on the planet, and quell the uprisings. It will take time, of course, but establishing proper relations with Larrin and Robos 7 pleases us. In the Fairfield Sector, we must work more cooperatively given the current chaos."

His story was compelling; however, those at his level are always driven by self-interest first and foremost. More favourable trade conditions? A stronger voice at the Council?

"I'd like to repair my ship and be on my way," she said, rising from the chair. "Can someone shuttle me to the *Penny Rose*?"

Scyther stood and approached her. He rubbed his bare organic arm, and a chilling thought slammed into her.

"That's quite impossible, Ms. Madison. I cannot allow you to return to Asteria, or roam free in the streets of Edenfall. You see, you represent far too much of a risk to the new government. Besides posing a threat to my own world."

She stepped back. "What are you saying?"

Several Protoran soldiers appeared as if by silent command.

"You will remain locked up. At least until the current emergency is under control." He turned to a guard. "Take her to the Robosian cells in Edenfall."

As the guards cuffed her and escorted her outside toward an awaiting shuttle, the only thought consuming Piper now was escaping, finding Ariel, then determining the truth behind this Protoran presence.

THE LOW-ALTITUDE VESSEL SKIMMED THE CITY ROOFTOPS on its journey from the Governor's mansion to the central core of Edenfall. When she last visited months ago, the city rested peacefully, protected from the industrial pollution by a massive dome. Enormous purifiers stationed throughout the downtown scrubbed the polluted air clean, and the resident engineering crews fashioned a false sun that gave the impression that Edenfall was as pretty as any other centre in the known galaxy.

But that had all changed. The cracked covering no longer protected the citizens from the ghastly poisons caused by extensive mining operations on this industrial planet. And because of the vacuum in stable leadership, that wouldn't likely change soon.

She wrapped the air filter closer over her mouth and nose.

The shuttle settled on a pad close to a non-descript,

two-story grey building. Everything about Edenfall was utilitarian, including the architecture. Part of the planet's philosophy under her father's rule. Hard to imagine the Heads would tolerate this chaos much longer.

"Follow me," Commander Keelin said once they'd landed. Piper had no choice, but at the instant where she stepped from the shuttle onto the docking pad, the smallest of gaps appeared between the guards ahead and the men following behind. She bolted for the narrow streets around the buildings.

She didn't get far.

The Commander jumped, landing on her back and slamming her into the pavement. Keelin dragged her back to the others.

"That was a poor decision, Piper Madison," he said. "Both my legs are machine. You could never outrun me."

She struggled against his vise-like grip. Even though the hand grasping her was organic, his strength was formidable. Piper relented and allowed Keelin to take her into the building.

From the outside, the edifice resembled any other drab government facility on other planets. Cold, few windows, grey, dead. But inside, once they'd moved past the facade of a lobby, she encountered an extensive collection of jail cells and numerous Head security guards—as well as Protorans—occupying the space.

Keelin marched her down a long, spotless corridor.

"Do you communicate through an internal comms device?" she asked.

He refused to answer.

"My specialty is deep space comms," she said, attempting to make small talk and stay on the Commander's good side. "That's why I ask."

"Yes," her captor relented.

"What range do you get with that? The device I use

has its limitations. Mostly groundwave transmissions, unless the atmosphere's messed up. But it seems—"

"Silence, Piper Madison. You ask too many questions." They stopped in front of a cell and the gate opened automatically.

The tech built into their machine bodies is for communications and remote operations, like opening this door, she thought.

Keelin pushed her through and removed the cuffs. "Remain here until further notice," he said. "No funny stuff, understand?" The Protoran Commander shone his ocular scanner at her, then continued on with a trio of security guards behind him.

Darkness covered the jail cell, and it took Piper a minute to realize she wasn't alone. Someone sat against the stone wall in the far corner of the cell, deep in the shadows. She discerned the slightest of movements... a tilt of the head... a shift in the shoulder. The whisper stone warmed in her pocket and a myriad of visions peppered her mind. Not words or voices like she'd experienced before.

Impressions.

"Who's there?" Piper took a step toward the body. "I guess we're both stuck in this place, eh?"

"I am... Rennok Zero-Nine," the low voice croaked from the deep.

The stilted speech and nomenclature of his name told her that Rennok was a Hand, bred for labour and servitude by the ruling Hands. Not a hybrid like Dolian.

"Piper Madison," she said. "I'm a... friend of Ariel Graves. How'd you end up here, Rennok?"

The creature stirred, arching his back against the wall. "You know Ms. Graves?"

Piper inched forward. Now the outline of the Hand's features became apparent. Hard to tell his height while he sat, but his arms were thick; his head large.

"Ariel is my half-sister."

"Ah!"

"The former Governor was my father, but I never knew him. I've lived in Asteria my whole life."

Rennok splayed his fingers against the wall and eased himself to a standing position. She now appreciated his immense size. He towered a full foot taller than her.

"There used to be a light in here," he grunted, pointing to the ceiling, "but I broke it. An accident."

The stone continued flashing images through her mind. In them, this Hand appeared conducting various tasks: lifting wooden beams, digging at a mine face, being flogged by a Head.

"Could you step closer to the door, Rennok? The corridor light will help us see each other better."

The man struggled to move and hobbled to join her at the cell door.

"They shattered your bones," she said, images whirling across her thoughts.

"In my feet, yes, so I can still walk, but it's very painful and difficult."

Rage bubbled inside her. This was her mother's legacy. Ignoring abuses on these planets to maintain peace at the Council. And she saw Rennok in the vision, fighting with several Hand security personnel before succumbing to their will.

"You stole some bread," she said, "and they beat you and threw you in here."

Rennok cocked his head, confused. "H-How did you know that?"

Piper wondered momentarily if he could be a spy, tasked with uncovering her plans in exchange for reduced punishment. The whisper stone revealed nothing to suggest that the man was anything more than a poor servant struggling to avoid starvation during the social turmoil.

"A good guess," she said.

They moved to the lower cot on the double bunks and sat.

"Do you know what brings the strange machine men here?" he asked.

Piper said, "Something about stabilizing the government, I think."

"Hm. Not exactly."

"Then why?" She touched the man's broad shoulder. "You can trust me, Rennok."

He licked his cracked lips and glanced around, eyes darting. Then he leaned in close. "The machines need actual flesh to survive. They are both machine and meat."

"I saw that."

"Their soft parts are... sick. They die. The machines have no more flesh on their planet, so they come here to take our people... to run the farms. So they can live again. They tried to catch me, but Rennok Zero-Nine is strong." He shook with excitement in the faint light, exposing more than one missing tooth.

The impact of this revelation floored Piper. She suspected Scyther's altruism extended beyond neighbourly assistance, and now the ugly truth appeared. *Rennok must be referring to the reproduction facility out on the land*, she thought. *Bad enough breeding Hands for a lifetime of servitude, but something entirely different to breed them for their body parts.* The very idea sickened her.

Rennok spoke again out of the blue. "I liked Ariel Graves. She was always kind to the Hands. We have much respect for her." He turned to face Piper. "I know where she is being held."

"She's still alive?"

The Hand raised his thick eyebrows.

"Who took her? Where is she?"

Clipped footsteps marched along the corridor, growing

louder.

"Quiet," Rennok said. "Someone's coming."

SIXTEEN

CARSTAIRS SETTLED THE SCOOTER BEHIND A BROKEN LINE of trees a few kilometers from the Asterian Maximum Security Prison. Without question, this entire area would be under constant surveillance, so finding a way onto the grounds and then into the massive building itself would prove extremely challenging.

Regardless, he wanted to speak with her and gauge how much support she actually had. If the Council ever reinstated her as Chancellor, could she restore order in short measure? Increased security and oversight could easily assuage concerns about her behaviour.

But he needed to see her first.

The Asterian sun beat down on his shoulders as he hiked along the dirt road toward the institution, mulling over how to get inside. He rounded a sharp curve and discovered a cargo craft grounded in a nearby field. A fellow wearing a corporate uniform had opened the ship's access panel for repairs.

Carstairs seized the opportunity and approached him. "Need a hand?"

The man shielded his face, turning from the sun. "Know anything about Heinrich engines, mister?"

"Oh, a bit. Practically grew up with my hands inside those babies. What's wrong with this one?"

The fellow explained how, on his way to the prison with a load of food supplies, he lost power and ditched the machine in this meadow. Carstairs peeked at the engine hold and recognized the problem. He set to work with a wrench.

"This shouldn't take long," he said. "Name's Jay, by the way."

"Salba," the man replied, extending his arm.

"Heading to the jail, eh? Perhaps I could ride with you?"

"Sure."

Carstairs flared a slipperhead tool at the combustion chamber to weld the crack closed. "Heard they got Chancellor Madison in there. That true?"

Salba exhaled. "Sure is," he groused. "Damn shame what they done to her, too."

"Agreed." He faced the man, and they shared a knowing glance. "Truth is, I'm hoping to chat in private with her if the guards will let me." He returned his attention to the engine.

"Good luck with that. Pick the wrong bossman and they'll chuck you in there, too."

Carstairs finished and secured the covering panel. "That ought to do it. Fire it up and see how she sounds."

Salba hopped into the pilot seat and engaged the thruster. It sprang to life, and the vessel rumbled with power. He set the engines on standby and returned to Carstairs.

"Look, I can't thank you enough, Jay. You saved my

job, no doubt about it. If there's anything you need in return, just say the word."

"Well," the captain said, "since you're already taking me up there, I won't ask for more, except…"

Salba cocked his head. "What is it?"

"I need to find a guard who sympathizes with the Chancellor."

The man frowned. "That's a tall order."

"I'll make it worth your while. Would ten thousand credits help?"

"Sure, but what you're asking is life-threatening. If they discover I smuggled you in, I'd never see my family again."

Carstairs clenched his jaw. "Of course. I wouldn't want to jeopardize your life. Look, I can go as high as twenty. You put me in one of those uniforms, take me inside, point me toward a friendly guard. I'll speak with the Chancellor and meet you back at the ship before you leave."

Salba removed his cap and scratched his head, turned toward the prison shimmering in the distance, and said, "Twenty thousand?"

"Yes, sir."

"All right. Hop in. There's an extra uniform in the side panel."

CARSTAIRS AND THE PILOT HOVERED BY THE FIRST GATE, waiting for the guard to approach. The thick-set woman of Thudoran ancestry held her weapon across her chest and grunted, "You're late, Salba."

"Couldn't be helped. Engine troubles. But my new assistant is plenty handy with a toolbox and got us going again, so better late than never."

She studied Carstairs sitting in the passenger seat. He kept his head low, gazing forward.

"Need your ID, Mister…?"

"Jay, and… well, er…"

Salba interrupted. "The fellow's new with the company, Bergo. Been with us a week and still don't have no tags. You know how slow those admin types are."

The Thudoran rolled her eyes. "Sure do. Okay, hurry up and get unloaded. The men are waiting for you at the dock."

The man thanked her and eased forward. "That gets your heart pumping, don't it?"

"Yeah, a bit too much."

The cargo craft settled at the open dock and within moments, several guards began unloading the supplies. Salba peered around and fixed his gaze. Carstairs followed it toward a large, solitary figure stacking a dozen smaller boxes onto a dolly. "That's your fellow there, Scrauts."

Carstairs raised his door. Salba grabbed his arm before he stepped outside. "You got about twenty minutes before she's unloaded. I'm not waiting."

The captain pulled his cap lower, took a small carton from the cargo hold, and marched toward the man.

"New guy, huh?" Scrauts said, coming to greet him. He stood over six feet tall, with massive shoulders and a sour countenance.

"Yeah. My name is Carstairs. And I'm guessing you're Scrauts. Word is you're a sympathizer."

Scrauts froze, dropped the cargo and grimaced. "I got no clue what you're talking about."

"Oh, I think you do. Listen, I must speak with the Chancellor. We all feel bad about how she was treated, and I have an idea that might change that."

He gathered up the box and began loading again as the other guards brought their cargo to him.

"It's a disgrace what they did to her," he muttered under his breath. "An absolute shame." He flung a container against the others. "Many of us think the same."

Carstairs grabbed a carton from one of the workers and handed it to him. "Can you take me to her now?"

Scrauts surveyed the room and found a worker nearby. "Hey Smith," he shouted. "Spot me for a few, will you?"

The man approached and continued stacking. Scrauts pushed Carstairs toward an unmarked exit. They quick-marched along a corridor, around a series of offices and meeting rooms, and then onto the Dangerous Offenders ward. On the way, he tossed a box into the captain's arms and grabbed one himself.

The stench of rotting flesh and waste smacked him, and his stomach rebelled. They approached a pair of guards in front of a thick, grey door.

"Johnson, we got these fresh clothes for the Chancellor."

The man buzzed them through without saying a word.

Tephera's cage stood at the end of another corridor. A thin light struggled against the heavy shadows. Carstairs followed Scrauts to the cell bars.

Madison rose from a filthy cot and approached the pair. Her thin face sagged, and she smelled of feces and urine.

"Better be quick," Scrauts said.

He cleared his throat. "Chancellor, it's me. Carstairs."

She craned her neck and eyed him. "You!" she screeched. "What the hell are—"

"Quiet," he said in a low voice. "I'm here to ask if you want to resume leading the Council."

Tephera glared at him. "Is this a joke, Carstairs? You're the one who put me here, and now you tease me about a return to power? Forget it. Whatever game you're playing, I'm not interested." She turned and dragged herself toward the cot.

"The galaxy is a complete disaster, Chancellor. Planets at war. The Council's divided. As much as I hate to admit it, they need your leadership. Someone to take over and restore order. They need you, Tephera."

She froze and said without turning, "That makes no sense. My people tell me this already. I have better intel in here than you do out there. But if things are truly that bad, why hasn't the Ambassador approached me with an offer?"

One of Carstairs' questions appeared to be answered. She still had many supporters, and they remained loyal. That could only benefit him.

"I can't speak for the politicians, Tephera. I have my own motivation to see you restored to power."

"Naturally," she derided. "So tell me, handsome, what's in it for you? And don't lie."

Carstairs worried about how much to share with her about his contract with the Black Bond and determined she had probably worked with them herself over the years. He lowered his voice. "I'm doing a job with the cartel, Chancellor. We all want trade to return to normal. Meaning, the Battle Fleet needs to stop patrolling the black market routes and stay out of our business."

She approached him, narrowing her gaze. "Does this have something to do with Piper?"

"No," he said, lowering his head. "She and I are... well, we've gone our separate ways." He returned to the subject at hand. "I must leave now, but if you agree, I'll put an escape plan together and get you out of here in exchange for opening up the trade routes. In a matter of days, you could be leading the Council again. What do you say?"

The former Chancellor remained silent, sizing him up. "If I find out you're lying, Carstairs, my sympathizers will slit your throat in the public square and hang you there for the flies and maggots to eat."

"I'm not playing around," he said, shuddering. The game was real now. "I understand your hesitation, Chancellor. Say the words and I'll disappear... no harm done. But if you wish to regain power, tell your supporters to let me know. I'm at the Northern Airfield."

"All right," she said from the shadows. "I shall consider your offer."

He turned to leave.

"Carstairs," she cooed with a wry smirk on her face. "I always knew you'd come around. Like a dog returning to its own vomit, eh?"

He pulled away and marched along the corridor toward the cell entrance, Scrauts in tow.

A TRIO OF ARMED ROBOSIAN MYRMIDONS HALTED BESIDE Piper's cell. Without saying a word, two men entered, grabbed her, and pulled her into the corridor.

"What do you want now?" she spat. "More interrogation?"

The whisper stone hummed to life in her pocket, but she read nothing.

"Silence!" the one in command said. "You will come with me." He raised a thermal flux gun and motioned for her to follow.

The other two myrmidons trailed behind them.

Piper fumed, but cooperated. She aimed to uncover more about the Protorans' plans and reasons for backing Larrin. But the primary objective now was to escape and free fellow prisoners as a way to destabilize the new regime. Then, to find Ariel.

The stone proved useless at reading the machine men's thoughts due to the amount of technology in them. All she envisioned was a jumble of incoherent ideas and computer language. But if the Protorans shared their plans with others, like these Head myrmidons, she might be successful hearing those.

Moreover, the stone's properties might also transmit and receive both ways, and if that turned out to be the case, she could use it to her advantage. So far, she had no reason to believe that was the case, but she also hadn't tested it.

Before sending an innocent trial thought to the myrmidons, they stopped at an intersecting corridor to allow several more troops and security guards to pass. After resuming their march, she fixated on the stone, murmuring, "Master cell key location?" repeatedly. Unlike the machine men, the Robosian soldiers relied on old technology to keep the jail cells locked.

Her first attempts proved unsuccessful. However, after repeating the mantra many times, a faint message appeared in her consciousness: *belt chain... belt chain...*

She noticed a magstick hanging from the leader's webbing.

That must be it.

Piper waited until the corridor cleared out, then she feigned tripping, causing the trailing myrmidon to reach out for her. The leader whirled around at the commotion. Piper lunged forward, ramming her shoulder into the commander. His flux gun skittered across the smooth, concrete floor. She pushed him off-balance into the wall and grabbed for the magstick.

She learned from Carstairs and some of the Hand fighters at the Moaning Bones mine site that a microsecond of hesitation could be the difference between living and dying. When Piper failed to remove the magstick fast enough, the trailing soldier slammed the butt end of his gun into her kidneys, sending her toppling to the floor with a burning pain.

The leader gathered his weapon, and the soldiers hoisted her to her feet. His pretense of civility dissipated. They pulled her arms behind her back as she doubled over, and placed the cuffs on her wrists.

"It didn't have to be this way, Madison," the commander said, clutching his side, mirroring her.

In the confusion and screaming pain of her own gut,

the myrmidon seemed to experience phantom discomfort.

"W-Where are you taking me?" she coughed.

The man refused to answer. Instead, he pushed her forward, and the two myrmidons dragged her the rest of the way down the hall.

Moments later, they stopped beside an unmarked door and slammed her face first into the adjoining brick wall. A series of tones and clicks followed, and the door *whooshed* open. The soldiers dragged her inside, throwing her onto a chair.

Someone moved in the shadows, approaching her through the dim light... a Protoran.

"Leave us," she ordered the men, in an unmistakable female voice.

They exited and the door latched behind them.

Piper shook the stinging cobwebs from her head and studied the Protoran. "I've seen you before," she mumbled.

"I am Dr. Sheilor, the Chief Medical Advisor on Protor, and one of Lord Scyther's senior staff. You saw me in the Operations Centre at the Governor's mansion."

The doctor increased the lighting, revealing a suite of empty hospital beds and various diagnostic machines. The back wall held lines of cabinets with transparent doors.

"Is this a... a regeneration room?" Piper asked, squirming in her seat and pulling at her cuffs.

"This barbaric clinic? Not even close." Sheilor scraped a chair over and sat across from her, crossing her legs. "Ms. Madison, I wanted to talk with you—alone—about our people and our urgent needs. I'd like you to understand the level of desperation that brought us here. That's why I had those men bring you to me."

Piper winced at the pain in her kidney. Her knee flared up again and she grit her teeth.

"I can give you a painkiller for that." She stood and fished a package from a small cabinet. "Here," she said, placing a couple of pills in her mouth.

Piper did not object. After she swallowed them, she said, "I understand you plan to use the Hands as... as replacement parts to keep your people alive."

Sheilor sat again. "That is true. But we don't do this without having tried everything else. Listen, our kind have lived on Protor since before the colonists arrived in the galaxy. No one recalls how we first came here... I suppose that doesn't matter, anyway." Sheilor leaned forward. "Regardless, we shared the planet with a type of proto-humanoid, organic population that we came to rely on for our survival."

Piper scowled.

Sheilor's lukewarm smile implied a different interpretation. "These creatures were unlike other indigenous populations in the sector. They could not speak. They could barely gather sufficient food for their needs. We studied them for many years and determined they were more aligned with animals than sentient humanoids."

"You used them for their body parts," Piper said. The painkillers had kicked in and she no longer felt the searing fire in her gut. Her tongue stuck to her dry mouth, but she still added, "And even if they were animals, you had no right to harvest them."

Sheilor frowned, rose, and began pacing behind her chair. "Again, this is moot. We have depleted the population across Protor, and my people are dying. Scyther and his advisors struggled to find alternatives. We contacted the Governing Council and sent exploration ships to the dark planets. We begged others for help. None of them did. Some members even mocked us. Called us robots and washing machines."

"And now you're backing this Larrin fellow in exchange for access to the reproduction facilities and all the people created there."

"Yes. Ms. Madison, don't you see?" Sheilor approached her and bent down.

The whisper stone remained silent.

"Robos 7 provides the only viable option. If the leadership here refused to help, that would sentence us to death. They're giving us the farms and have promised a supply of these adult Hands for immediate use."

Piper struggled to maintain focus under the heavy cloud of the drugs. "You cannot take the lives of other people, even if it means you must die." When she said the words, she immediately questioned her own wisdom. *Would I not kill to survive?*

Sheilor raised her voice, ordering the myrmidons to re-enter. They pulled Piper from the chair. "Ms. Madison," Sheilor said, "I hoped you'd be more open to understanding our operations here. I've looked into your past actions on this dung heap and elsewhere, and we know you're here on the Ambassador's behalf. You carry a lot of influence both on Asteria and throughout the galaxy. That sway would help restore order to the Fairfield Sector and ensure we Protorans could continue as a viable people." The doctor lifted Piper's face by the chin, examining the lacerations. "I suppose I was wrong."

She glanced at the myrmidons, and they dragged her from the room.

Piper fought to stay on her feet, but the painkillers she received were more potent than her own. The fight had all but abandoned her. As they dragged her to the jail cell, she repeated the thought in her mind, hoping the stone would speak again.

Where is Ariel?
Where is Ariel?

She received no answer.

SEVENTEEN

"DON'T LOOK SO DISAPPOINTED, SHEILOR," SCYTHER said after she debriefed him on her chat with Piper Madison. They huddled together near the window overlooking the neglected grounds of the Governor's mansion from Scyther's Operations Centre. A pair of Robosian myrmidons stood guard at the main entrance. Larrin and various other strategists continued to develop their governance structure.

"I felt as if it wouldn't matter what I said, my Lord. She refused to budge from this stubborn attitude of hers."

A Hand approached with a tray of water, and they both took a glass.

"The girl will come around. Remember, her focus is on finding that half-sister. Once we have Ariel Graves in custody, Madison will understand how wrong she and others have been."

A Protoran aide, limping, entered and kept his distance. When Scyther looked up, the man said, "Time for the link,

Liege."

"Excellent." He motioned to the doctor. "Come, let us present our case to the lizard queen."

Leaving the centre, they marched down a carpeted hallway to a converted communications salon. Scyther stood in front of a large viewer. Sheilor watched from behind.

The screen blinked and crackled, followed by the Torfinn Galaxy insignia.

"Connection established, my Lord, and awaiting the feed from Asteria."

Within moments, Welkin appeared from a private comms room. No one else joined her.

"Lord Scyther," the Erusian spoke, *"it is good to see you again."*

"And you, too, Ambassador. You seem well. Governing must agree with you." Scyther said his words only as a courtesy. In fact, he despised the scaled, cold-blooded creature.

Welkin grimaced, ignoring the comment. *"I understand your intentions on Robos 7 involve backing one of the factions in order to bring stability to the planet, despite the—*noot—*the Ethical Protocol and what we are all required to do under its authority."*

"The Protocol is useless now," Scyther spat. "Only you Asterians and your toothless Fleet continue adhering to it."

Sheilor cleared her throat. Noticing her cautionary expression, he adjusted his tone to be more diplomatic. "Ambassador, my apologies. I'm glad you agreed to establish contact with us and provide me an opportunity to explain the delicate situation here, and why my people feel compelled to bring order to Robos 7."

"By all means. I'm ready to listen."

For the following ten minutes, Scyther reviewed the existential threat on his home planet and outlined the many efforts he and others had made to the Governing Council for an appropriate solution to their life-threatening problem. He referred to various scientific endeavours, exploratory voyages to the dark planets, and even considered synthetic organic material to protect their existence—all of which failed.

After summarizing the predicament, he said, "I trust you have a clearer understanding of why we must now take desperate measures to ensure our ongoing survival."

Sadness covered the Ambassador's face. *"Lord Scyther, we always knew about your challenges, but I did not appreciate the depth of your needs. I am sorry for that, both personally and on behalf of the Council."* She leaned toward the screen and narrowed her black eyes. *"But your problems do not give you permission to invade another sovereign planet. These actions are illegal, and we cannot allow them to continue."*

Scyther used his optical scanner to try reading her face for telltale signs of weakness. There were none.

"Listen, Welkin, even if you choose to send the Battle Fleet after us, we will fight rather than die ugly deaths from organic disintegration." He cleared his throat. "So I have a proposal for you... one that ensures peace, stability, and Protoran longevity in this sector."

The Ambassador stated, *"Good, let's hear this plan."*

Scyther allowed a moment of silence to fill the space between them. He peered at her and said, "Protor is backing the interim Robosian government headed by Minister Larrin. We shall remain here until peace and order are restored on Robos 7. As for the many factions on the land and other groups that insist on creating chaos and violence, we shall only intervene if Minister Larrin makes a formal request."

Welkin stared at him without moving.

He continued. "In exchange for providing security,

Larrin agrees to allow Protor unfettered access to the Robosian Reproduction Facilities, where we will address both our short- and long-term survival. We will develop a robust, respectful protocol for the breeders and the farms, taking only what we need and no more. Therefore, I am asking for Council approval to proceed."

Scyther stared at the screen, awaiting the lizard queen's response.

The Ambassador's reaction seemed measured, and he could not discern whether the creature was upset, or simply non-committal. *"I prefer to negotiate in person, Lord Scyther. Come to Asteria, and we'll have a fulsome discussion about this."*

He glanced at Sheilor and her voice pierced his internal sensors. *"Do not be fooled, Liege."*

"That's impossible, given the state of affairs here. I'm sure you understand. And make no mistake, Ambassador. We shall have our organic solution with or without the Council's approval. Naturally, we'd prefer your support in this matter, but we will act alone, if necessary. Remember, our existence is at stake."

Welkin moved her thin lips and hung her head. *"With so few details, it is impossible for me to decide unilaterally. I shall—noot—take your proposal in principle to the Council for a full discussion. That's the best I can do."*

"Very well, Ambassador. I ask for nothing more." He toyed with cutting the transmission when another thought struck him... one he had not discussed with anyone else. Not even Sheilor. "While we're both here, there is a second item I'd like you to consider..."

THE MYRMIDONS RELEASED PIPER'S CUFFS AND THREW her into the cell like a bag of meat. She fell on the cold, concrete floor, and realized that, despite the fog of the painkillers, her cell-mate had disappeared.

Leveraging the side of the cot, she hoisted herself up and turned to face the soldiers. "Where's Rennok?" Her voice sounded distant and disembodied.

"He's been taken for questioning. Then he'll likely end up in one of those Protoran regeneration rooms." The lead guard snickered. "See what happens when you don't cooperate, Madison? And for what it's worth, I wouldn't hesitate to end you for the harm you caused our planet and way of life. These machine people, however, want to keep you alive for some odd reason." He swiped the cell door locked. "But whatever," he continued, "I may yet get my chance. Remember that." The myrmidons trudged away.

Piper collapsed on the cot and rubbed her temples. She fingered the whisper stone out of her pocket and squeezed it in her palm.

Where is Rennok?
Where is Ariel?

The stone responded with an incoherent jumble of words and images. A group of Protorans smeared through her mind. The backs of Robosian Heads, marching through tunnels. Groups of Hand miners out on the land, fighting the hostile winds. She discerned nothing from the mess. Unable to do anything, she lay down, exhausted.

PIPER DID NOT KNOW HOW LONG SHE'D BEEN ASLEEP when the click-clack of many stomping boots awakened her. She heard numerous guards and soldiers passing by her cell, yet this sound was unique. Louder. Larger. She knew they came for her.

She sat up, peering through the dark cell for something she could use as a weapon. The place was spotless. Anything loose had been removed. The cot, sink and shit tube were bolted to the floor.

A squad of eight heavily armed Protorans halted at the cell's entrance. They must have been transmitting messages with wireless tech, for they moved as one without speaking to face her, raising their weapons. The leader's height exceeded six feet—a powerfully built man whose muscles strained against a uniform that clinged to his body. Their faces remained hidden under the battle garb she'd seen on that pilot Keelin who shot her down over the Edenfall hills.

The tall one swiped the jail cell open and entered. "Piper Madison, you are coming with us." His artificial voice reminded her of a hollowed-out grinder. He towered over her. When he reached for her arm, she recoiled back on the cot.

"The hell I am!" She slammed her boot into the leader's midsection, sending him stumbling backward. Other soldiers surrounded her in a flash and grabbed her limbs. Before she could say another word, they gagged her mouth and wrenched a hood over her head. It smelled of the polluted land and Piper choked in the muffle.

They yanked her arms behind her, cuffed them, and forced her to move from the jail cell with the business end of a weapon pressing into her back.

Piper's senses floated in the hood's stifling darkness. She soon lost track of the turns they'd made, the many corridors they marched along. At one point, the entire group stopped. She couldn't make out the voices, but it sounded like a discussion with Robosian guards.

Moments later, a loud metallic door clanged open. They were outside now. The cool night permeated her clothing and polluted gusts swirled around.

Then, without warning, a soldier pushed her to the ground. Hard. With her arms cuffed behind her back, she couldn't break her fall and smashed down on her chest, knocking the wind from her. The familiar *brrrackkk* of thermal flux gunfire filled the air. She guessed a rogue band of rebels attacked the Protoran squad. In the distance, an attacker screamed.

Someone knelt beside her and rolled her onto her back. "We must run."

Piper, unable to say a word with the gag, groaned instead.

The man heaved her to a standing position, grabbed her arm—almost tearing it from the socket—and raced across the ground. More footsteps joined them. Someone nearby opened fire, and ozone permeated the hood covering her head.

"There are two steps coming up. I'll tell you when," a Protoran growled.

They ran along solid stones, slowed, and the man poked her. She lifted her leg and lowered it gently until she found purchase. Then the other. Despite the deep-seated throbbing in her knee, she held her weight and balance.

"Lower your head," the voice said.

A hand pushed down on her. *Something definitely isn't right.* She tried speaking, but the gag across her mouth dug into her cheeks and squeezed her words into useless, pathetic utterances.

Someone grabbed her jacket and heaved her the rest of the way off the stairs.

The wind stopped howling.

The polluted air dissipated.

The firefight continued, now heavily dampened.

Piper imagined they took her to a secure warehouse... perhaps even a makeshift regeneration room. She struggled to break free. The guards held her fast, but to her surprise, did not harm her. Scyther's edict about keeping her alive shone on full display.

One man slammed her onto a flight seat and strapped her down. And all this time, the quickened stone continued sending mixed signals and bizarre, baffling images to her.

Not a warehouse. A shuttle of some sort.

Perhaps they planned to take her to the mothership.

After a moment, engines whined to life.

"Wait," the metallic-voiced soldier said.

Chatter among the Protorans increased. A wave of cool wind filled the craft and others clambered onboard. Piper felt her ears pop as the cabin pressurized, and within moments, the vessel screamed into the air, acceleration forces pinning her back in the seat.

After several minutes of flight, someone unfastened the hood and pulled it off her head. She blinked in the harsh sting of the cabin lights. Then the soldier unlocked her cuffs and walked away. When Piper's vision stabilized, she glanced around. The Protorans occupied their own seats in silence. One fighter held his dangling arm, sucking his teeth under his dark facial protection.

A blast must have punctured his organics, she concluded.

The tall leader approached from the back of the shuttle and stopped beside her. "You are courageous," he said. "Welcome aboard." The man unclasped several fasteners from his rubberized battle mask and eased it away.

Piper froze in disbelief.

This was no Protoran… no half-machine with organic parts.

This was a Robosian *Hand.*

Her jaw dropped as she stared into the man's large, familiar face.

At the front of the aisle wearing a huge, toothy grin stood Ariel's husband, Dolian.

EIGHTEEN

PIPER GRABBED THE ARMREST AND HAULED HERSELF UP from the shuttle's flight seat. She approached Dolian and hugged him warmly. "How are you, my friend?" she said, fighting back tears of joy.

Dolian continued removing his Protoran battle garments. "Good, now that we found you, Piper. Were you… mistreated?"

She shook her head. "Most of my injuries came from a cave-in on a dark planet. But never mind that. Is Ariel with you?"

The big Hand frowned. "I have not seen my wife for several months. The war separated us, and now she is stolen and could be anywhere."

The other soldiers removed their battle tackle. The group consisted of Hands, Heads, and a Bortan medic tending to the injured soldier's arm.

"First," he said, "we get you to safety. That firefight with the real Protorans on the surface… they know we have you and they won't be happy. We must prepare for retaliation. Rest now. It is a long flight, the way we go."

Piper fell into her seat and Dolian took the one opposite. She stared out the shuttle window at the gloomy landscape below. Edenfall shone like a dim light in the distance as they criss-crossed through the dark hills.

"We are heading to the Moaning Bones, Piper."

That old mine site represented the beginning of Piper's troubles. Many of the Hands escaped into tunnels there after Governor Graves' death. Feryn had joined the resistance and organized tactical strikes from deep within those caves. She warmed at the memory of Ariel surrounded by Hand children, all wanting to play with her.

"How safe is the mine?" she asked.

Dolian grunted. "There is danger everywhere. No place is completely secure. But we guard the tunnels, and the warning system is effective. You will see."

A soldier trudged by with a dusty bag of food and drinks. Mostly protein bars and unleavened bread. Piper couldn't remember the last time she ate, so she grabbed a small loaf and a water pack.

She took a bite of a stale crust and washed it down. "Dolian, we have to find Ariel."

"Yes. Robos 7 has only one legitimate leader, and it is her. That weasel Larrin is not a friend to the Hands. And we do not know what the Protorans are doing backing him. Maybe they want our mineral resources for their technology."

"More than minerals," Piper said. "It's the Reproduction Facilities. They need organic body parts to survive."

Shock covered Dolian's face. "Of course," he muttered. "We shall fight them, but we must keep you safe in the tunnels. Healers will look after your wounds while me and my squad continue searching for Ariel. We have many friends throughout Edenfall who are looking."

Piper studied the man's rugged face, awash in sadness. Dolian had been a skilled mechanic and measured thinker before the unrest. And he had proven his worth as a fighter and member of Carstairs' crew aboard the *Dauntless*. Now, he led this group of rebels trying to restore peace and order to the planet, without the company of his wife. Not an enviable task.

Piper stretched across the aisle for his hand. "I want to help find her. Promise me you'll take me with you."

The man shook his head. "Too dangerous." She protested, but he cut her off. "You are what the Heads call an *asset*, Piper. When others discover you are with us, they'll come after you. Some want to kill you. Others will use you for negotiating with Ambassador Welkin, or make you part of a new Robosian government." He clenched his fists. "No, you are too important and will draw much attention. We must operate in the shadows, like Hands have always done."

Piper bit into the bread and stared out the window. The shuttle careened through valleys and river gorges, snaking low to the ground along the scorched landscape. No ship—Protoran or otherwise—followed them, but the pilot took no risks, weaving through stone canyons and zig-zagging along the fracture zones.

She dozed for several minutes before waking, startled, and faced Dolian. "Ariel is my half-sister and I won't be left behind on the sidelines."

"Where is the captain of the *Dauntless*?" Dolian asked, refusing to address her demand.

"Who knows," she snapped, then quickly added, "we're not together anymore."

The big man shifted his weight in the seat, leaning toward her. "I am saddened by this. You and the Captain love each other."

His honest assessment of her affair with Carstairs surprised her. Piper frowned and said, "It wasn't for lack of trying, Dolian. He simply disappeared. Word is, he's on Izillon, biding his time until the galaxy stabilizes. But who knows?"

A Hand fighter approached and whispered in his ear.

"Piper," he said, "we arrive in twenty minutes. I must warn you... the landing will be bumpy because of the big winds. Remember them?"

She recalled the unrelenting gales around the mine site, and how it got its name when the wind blew through the tunnels, creating a haunting, ghostly wail. Turning to Dolian, she insisted, "I'm joining the search."

"I know," he replied, buckling in.

Without notice, wind gusts hurled the shuttle back and forth, almost crushing it onto the surface. Piper gripped the arm rests and concentrated her thoughts.

Where are you, Ariel?

Where are you, Carstairs?

The whisper stone remained silent in her pocket.

THE *DAUNTLESS* SAT AT THE END OF THE NORTHERN Airfield, gleaming in the afternoon Asterian sun. Jay Carstairs and Quirp completed their own review of all the upgrades, maintenance, and modifications undertaken in the repair hangar over the past couple days. The work took longer than expected, but the results were worth it.

The captain inspected the ship's hull. "Most impressive, don't you think, Quirp?"

The ship mind communicated with him through his remote radio unit. *"Indeed. These new functions exceed those found in most light cruisers. Only the Asterian Battle Fleet has similar operational features."*

Carstairs popped open a side panel near the engine hubs and peered inside. "It cost a lot more than I wanted to pay, but since it's the cartel's dough, I'm happy to spend it."

He pulled his head out and closed the covering. Sudden movement at the far end of the airfield caught his attention. "Quirp, your sensors picking up anything we need to know about?"

"There is a high velocity scooter with one pilot heading in our direction, Captain."

Carstairs reached for his thermal flux gun. "Anyone we know?"

"Negative, but there are no markers indicating any possible threat."

The one-seater approached in a cloud of dust, slowing as it neared the *Dauntless*. Carstairs took a few steps forward and awaited its arrival with hands on hips.

The female pilot grounded the vessel several meters away and dismounted. She unbuckled and removed a flight helmet, allowing a flow of dark hair to tumble across her shoulders. She wore no weapon that he could see, but her striking looks alone were dangerous enough.

And that made him nervous.

"Captain Carstairs?" she asked, approaching him with her arms held at her sides.

"Who wants to know?" he demanded, unmoving.

The pilot smirked. "I appreciate the caution, Captain. Have your ship scan me, if you want."

"Quirp," he said, "will you do the honours?

A thin light emanating from the *Dauntless* bathed the rider.

The ship mind transmitted in his ear. *"Our guest is a genetic Asterian, Captain. Thirty-two years old. No weapons. No chronic diseases. She broke her leg in three places as an adolescent. Fractured wrist, likely suffered as a child."*

Carstairs relaxed and greeted her with a handshake. "What can I do for you?"

"My name's Leda," she said in a matter-of-fact voice. "I bring you a message from a mutual acquaintance."

"Oh?" He figured this woman must be a Tephera Madison foot soldier, but could easily be one of Dhollot's lackeys or a cartel bootlick. "Does she have a response to my offer?" Her reply would show who she represented.

The pilot stood almost at his same height. She moved in close. "She says to go ahead with the plan, and to make it fast. When you're ready to move, you are to contact me." Leda handed him a mag card. "My information is all on there."

"Very well," he said, turning it over in his fingers. "Tell her I'll set to work on the project immediately."

"Splendid." She hesitated a moment and then added, "There's one more message from her."

"What's that?"

Leda grabbed his face in both hands, pressed her body into him, and delivered a long, seductive kiss. He pulled away in shock and embarrassment.

"The hell was that?" he asked.

"She says, 'Welcome back'."

With that, the pilot returned to her scooter, donned the helmet, and raced toward the airfield entrance.

Quirp interrupted his thoughts. *"Captain, I do not understand the significance of this meeting. Will you share what this was about? It may assist me with my ship operations."*

Carstairs ignored the computer, clanked up the portal ramp, and entered the *Dauntless*. He strode to the cockpit and slammed Leda's mag card into an input slot. Her contact information blinked on the main viewer. Along with her personal data, a list of 20 key allies also downloaded. The names remained hidden, but their backgrounds were visible. A video recording showed at the bottom of the screen.

"Quirp, play the vid."

On the message, Leda strolled toward the camera. She introduced herself and said, "Captain, feel free to contact any of these allies. They are aware of your intention and are putting their own operations on standby. Reach out to them if you require help." The recording finished with her spewing political slogans.

"Captain," Quirp sing-songed, "I do not wish to be a pest, but since you are not sharing your intentions with me, I caution you against getting involved with internal Asterian affairs. The last time you did, the—"

"I'm aware of that, Quirp. But this is different. It's about bringing stability to the Torfinn Galaxy, as is required under my contract with the Black Bond, remember?"

"So you are planning a diversion for the Fleet?"

"Never you mind. Just focus on keeping the *Dauntless* ready, scanning for uglies, and generally doing as I command. Got it?"

"Yes... Captain."

Carstairs noted a momentary hesitation in the ship's response. This unit's personality exceeded those of most ship computers, and he and Piper spent much time learning its quirkiness.

He sat in the pilot's seat and pinched the bridge of his nose. *She would not approve of this one bit.* If he refused to stay with her because he felt incomplete and unworthy as a man, then his current actions would make his self-esteem even worse. He exhaled deeply, wrestling with the gathering demons.

Maybe Tephera was right. Perhaps he was as predictable as a dog returning to its own puke. He never quite understood why he did what he did. Possibly, this behavior grew out of his DNA and was unavoidable.

Regardless, now the tough work really began. He needed to figure out how to free the former Chancellor from the most secure penitentiary on the planet without alerting anyone to his ultimate goal.

He let his mind wander and imagined various scenarios, from using the ship to blast her out, to a more subtle attempt by infiltrating the institution. But after several minutes of blue sky speculation, his thoughts refused to focus. Piper's imagined disappointment in him consumed his consciousness.

"Quirp," he announced, "isolate which of Leda's pals works in the prison system and send their names to me."

"As you wish, Captain."

"Say, you're a smart little ship mind, Quirp. I need a plan to breach the Asterian Maximum Security Prison.

"Pardon?"

"Consider it a thought experiment, Quirp, in case one of us got stuck there." He stood and stretched. "I'm heading aft to my cabin for a rest. You know the drill about disturbing me."

"Yes, Captain. I shall only wake you in case of an emergency."

He trundled off the bridge toward the cabins, trying to refocus on the suddenly unbearable task at hand. He planned to free the most tyrannical leader the galaxy had ever known. And yet, the most effective at keeping the peace between disparate planets.

And what did Tephera mean by "Welcome back"?

NINETEEN

SCYTHER PACED THROUGH THE OPERATIONS CENTRE IN the Governor's mansion. Larrin briefed him on his government's latest successes bringing the rogue gangs running the city under control. The man spoke with enthusiasm, thanking him for Protor's military backing and support dealing with the rebels.

Scyther appreciated the report, but his mind remained elsewhere. His fresh arm appeared to be satisfactory, but odd sensations pulsed in his organic leg and through his face.

He needed to see Sheilor.

"Larrin," he said, "I'm glad you're pleased with the partnership to date." He scanned the Robosian and detected minute variations in the man's biometrics. "But so far, I have seen nothing in return. The reproduction farms remain under rebel control, and I've received no plan from you about supplying fully grown Hand organics."

The Governor shifted his weight. "I concede, Lord Scyther, that the farms are a challenge. But I assure you, we will prevail. As more factions come to realize our resolve, they will succumb and join us. Then we'll simply overpower the land fighters."

Scyther folded his arms. He didn't care for this Larrin fellow, but the man seemed confident in his abilities and in delivering his end of the agreement. "Very well, but understand this: my people are dying as we speak. I want to know how many adults you can deliver to me before daybreak. Understand?"

"Yes, my Liege. I'll have a full plan for you soon. In the meantime, we have detained several hundred Hands and Hybrids in a holding pen west of the city. They're available whenever you need them. Right now, if you wish."

Scyther's mood changed in an instant. "This is good news, Larrin. I'll send transport ships and troops to this cage for immediate relocation to Protor."

The Governor exited and Scyther resumed pacing. Yes, something had definitely shifted in his own organics. Despite his self-diagnostic, he could not determine the problem. He called for Sheilor to meet him in the temporary medical clinic they'd constructed at the mansion.

"THIS IS AN ARTIFACT OF THE ORGANIC LEG'S INFERIOR quality, my Lord," Sheilor said, waving a scanner across his leg and torso.

Scyther lay on a meta table in what used to be an art salon featuring industrial photographs and historical mechanical memorabilia. The doctor and her team of medical specialists had converted it into a makeshift clinic, complete with portable regeneration surgical equipment.

"It has given you several years of service, Lord Scyther, but appears to be approaching its fail point. Unexpected this early, but these poor quality organics are unpredictable that way. We will need to replace it as soon as possible."

Scyther grunted. If Larrin was correct about the

hundreds of flesh units in the holding pens, he could pick and choose an appropriate animal.

Sheilor continued, scanning his new arm and the patchwork of flesh around his face. "Any word yet from the Council about your proposal?"

"They scheduled an emergency session for this evening, Asterian time. It will be several hours, if not days, before we hear the outcome. Either way, we'll move forward, but I prefer having the Council's public approval."

Sheilor held the scanner over the side of his face and frowned. "My Lord, your facial skin shows signs of deterioration. We should replace those grafts, too."

"Very well."

"I say that with some urgency, my Liege. I can have one of my team inspect the animals and identify a youngling for these organics if you wish."

Scyther considered her offer. Normally, he would agree with her advice, but he wanted something different. Someone young, yes. But more personal. He brushed her scanner aside and swung his legs over the examination table. "No, Sheilor. I have a better idea. That Piper Madison's skin seemed... delicious. Young and pliable. Healthy, despite the recent lacerations. I suspect it would last for many decades."

Sheilor returned the device to its proper place alongside the other instruments before answering. "It would, my Liege. But I must caution you, as well. Ms. Madison is a valuable asset in the galaxy, and attached to the Ambassador's inner circle. Using her skin for your facial reconstruction carries political risks, especially since we're attempting to gain the Council's favor with your proposal. Although some might love to see her disfigured, others may not be so inclined."

Scyther had already made his decision. "Noted. Can we perform the surgery now, Doctor?"

"Why, yes. Of course."

"Good. Send a message to the jail that I want Piper Madison brought here immediately."

"Right away, my Lord."

Before Sheilor could summon a comms officer, a runner with different sized legs hobbled into the room.

"Lord Scyther!" he gasped. "There's been an incident in the jails."

"What? Speak, man!"

"A gang of rebels disguised as Protoran soldiers entered the jail, broke into her cell, and fought their way to an awaiting shuttle. They destroyed the comms hub there and escaped, Liege."

"They broke into *who's* cell, grunt!" He feared the man's answer would drive him mad.

"Piper Madison's, Liege. Whoever they were, they took her. She's gone. Last we tracked them, their vessel headed toward the western lands. That's when we lost all contact with the ship."

Scyther ran several risk modeling programs through his internal systems, attempting to determine where Madison may have been taken, by whom, and what their next move might be. However, he lacked sufficient input data to find anything within reasonable predictability.

"Very well. Return to your duties."

"Yes, Liege."

"Oh, but take a few minutes with the doctor before you go. We need to get proper legs for you, son."

The runner stood in shock. His fully organic face—save his one ocular implant—froze. Dr. Sheilor led the fellow to a second examination table and began scanning his torso.

Scyther stepped toward her and whispered in her ear. "A moment, Doctor."

They retreated, leaving the runner alone with his

thoughts.

"I don't feel secure on this planet, Sheil. If a band of rebels infiltrated our troops so easily, kidnapped Piper Madison and disappeared into the night, who knows what they're planning next?"

Sheilor agreed. "It would be wise for you to return to the *Volantis*. Shall I choose another suitable candidate for your skin? I could operate on board the ship."

"The surgery can wait, Doctor, until we find the girl. I'll depart immediately with a cohort of armed guards."

Sheilor fiddled with her scanning device. "You know I don't recommend delaying the operation, Scyther. The risks are far too great. We must no longer avoid it."

"Understood, my love," he said, dropping all formality. "I'll attend to the facial organics soon."

"CAPTAIN, ANOTHER HIGH-VELOCITY SCOOTER approaches from across the airfield. Same codes as those of Ms. Leda."

Carstairs' shoulders slumped. Hardly 24 hours had passed since she'd planted a Tephera kiss on him. Piper's face from the time she recovered in the hospital plagued him, and he struggled more and more to bury it under the flotsam of his muddled thoughts. "Very well, Quirp." *No more turning back now.*

He rose from the flight seat and slipped a thermal flux gun through his webbing, then pulled a jacket over his battle tackle. "I'll wait for her outside. Watch the *Dauntless*. Any sign of trouble, get off the ground and head for *Luna Majoris*."

"As you wish, Captain."

Carstairs lingered, for he knew this ship mind a little too well. "What is it, Quirp?"

"Captain, I have discovered that Ms. Madison is on a mission to Robos 7 on behalf of the Ambassador. There is still time to reconsider your decision about liberating the former Chancellor. Clearly, you do not wish to take this action. Perhaps you should abandon the experiment and see if Piper requires assistance. Biometric scans suggest—"

"Too late for that now, Quirp. I'm committed. Besides, the money is too good to pass up. The Council will put some constraints on the Chancellor so she won't have as much power as before. That should keep the more skittish member planets satisfied." He pulled on his jacket. "But we need her to make things safe and stable again. Once that happens, the members can figure out what to do with her. That's not my problem."

He glanced at the viewer, noted the scooter decelerating as it neared the *Dauntless*. For his plan to work, he needed the cover of a major storm system. The forecast showed just such a front moving in from the northeast. He studied the growing cloud bank. "If all goes smoothly, I'll be back in a few hours." He pushed the manual opener and stepped out into the cool evening breeze.

Leda eased the scooter to the ground.

"Your people all set?" he asked, approaching her.

"Yes. Once you free the Chancellor, we'll put her into a secure hideaway until she's ready to assume power. Our inside man Scrauts at the prison is standing by for your arrival." She tossed him a bucket for his head and motioned for him to hop on behind her. He wrapped his arms around her tiny waist and held on awkwardly as she screamed into the oncoming storm.

THE RAINS BEGAN FALLING, GENTLY AT FIRST, AND THEN with a more powerful stroke. At the edge of the industrial quarter, Leda turned off the scooter lights. They flew a few meters off the ground, nosing through valleys and scrub land until, several minutes later, they slowed at the crest of a wooded hill overlooking the institution. The maximum security prison glowed in the distance under its own massive lighting grid, and Carstairs recognized the road where he helped the delivery man. Thunder rumbled and lightning cracked the air. *A perfect night.*

She grounded the scooter, and they dismounted. He checked his webbing again and reviewed the plan in his head. Scrauts would take part of the electrified outer fence offline for only five minutes during the storm. He could then use that time to cut through it and reach the interior stone wall. He'd have to climb over that unseen, and find the third security door, where he'd meet the guard and gain access to the prison. From there, he'd rely on Scrauts to help him break the Chancellor out of her cell, exit through an old water conduit, and uncover the awaiting two-seater that Leda and her people had cached in the woods.

Timing was critical. If he missed the five-minute window where the power flickered, he'd lose the opportunity to execute the plan. He had one chance, and one chance only for success.

"Shuttle's ready?"

"Yes," Leda said. "Evasive route pre-programmed as you instructed. Our people will meet you at the designated drop off location." She handed him various tools.

He zipped his jacket and thanked her.

Leda hopped on the scooter and, before she left him, she hesitated. "Hey, Carstairs."

He wiped the rain from his face. "Yeah?"

"You're doing the galaxy a great service here."

More *true believer* rubbish. He was a coward and a failure. And at this moment, if he had an opportunity, he'd be slamming a shot down his throat at the Pilot's Lounge to assuage his pain and guilt.

Leda beetled away into the darkness, and Carstairs found himself alone with nothing but the driving rain pounding off the foliage to keep him focused.

He checked his bio-marker masking tech, and it showed a full charge and activation. The handy device allowed him to snake through the long, drenched grasses to the corner of the prison compound near the outer electrified fence without detection.

The cage rose ten meters into the night sky, according to the plans given him by Scrauts, so scrambling over the top would be impossible. He'd have to cut through it once the power outage hit, and do it the old-fashioned way with heavy-duty wire cutters, since lasers would telegraph his position.

Carstairs knelt behind a spit of shrubs several meters from the gleaming fence. The prison lights shone with intense ferocity. Thunder crashed and lightning sizzled across the land, and the unyielding rain fell in great swaths.

There!

The roof top lights flickered once, then twice. The signal to stand by.

Adrenaline coursed through his body. He held the industrial wire cutters Leda supplied by the long handle.

And he waited.

They flickered again. The compound suddenly sank into complete darkness.

He set the countdown on his timer. He had five minutes maximum to get inside the building before full power returned.

Carstairs raced to the fence, listened for the sound of electricity humming through the wires. Nothing. He began cutting the wire patchwork just enough for him to squeeze through. The thick gauge made the operation challenging, and in his haste, the cut chain snagged his jacket. He fought to free himself and remembered not to panic. *Focus on the problem. Work the problem.* Carstairs took several precious seconds to unravel the snag. He needed to wrangle a section of stiff fencing away before the opening allowed him to push through.

Once inside, he ducked into the shadows and approached the interior wall. He checked his timer and had fallen behind his schedule already.

This second barrier was built from stone and steel. He ditched the cutters and unfolded his grappling hook. Under any other circumstances, he would have used his jet boots to ascend, but he couldn't afford to be spotted, and the exhaust trails would surely give him away. Through the rain, men's voices rose somewhere in the night as teams of guards organized themselves on the grounds.

The power remained off. Carstairs's success hinged on getting this right. He stood a few meters from the wall, swung the hook in a couple of circles, and released it at the best angle to latch onto the top of the barrier.

He tugged the rope. The hook tumbled down, landing beside him. Voices grew louder. *Did they notice me coming through the fence?*

With increased desperation, Carstairs launched the grappling hook again, sending it over the wall. He steadily pulled the rope until the hook reached the top and snagged. Then he put his body weight on it and pulled hard. The hook latched on.

He reclined, feet braced against the wall, then quickly scaled the slick, damp stones. Half way up, his footing slipped, and he dangled there momentarily with the rain teeming over him. With no minor effort, he righted himself and, with long strides, made it to the summit and gathered up the rope just as a squad of soldiers ran across the compound toward the outer fence.

Carstairs examined the imposing building ahead of him. He had enormous difficulty identifying the door where Scrauts was supposed to meet him. But a flash of lightning filled the sky and in that moment, he spotted the right one. The readout on his timer showed less than a minute.

Crap.

He tossed the rope down, turned to face the wall, and bounced to the ground, leaving the gear where it was. He heard no voices here. Saw no other soldiers or guards. So he raced to the building and assumed a prone position against the wall. Crawling onward, he reached the designated door and prayed to a nameless god that Scrauts wasn't in the business of double-crossing him.

Too late to worry about that now.

Carstairs stood, pulled the thermal flux gun from his belt, and tapped on the door with the butt end of the weapon.

Someone opened it.

At that moment, lights flooded the area. In one swift motion, the door swung wide and a powerful hand grabbed him by the jacket and hauled him inside.

"I thought they got you," Scrauts said in a low voice. "Follow me."

The burly security guard jogged down a dusty old corridor, with Carstairs shaking the water from his head right behind. In the muted light of this old supply area, a tangle of pipes circulated above them, running throughout the ceiling. Scrauts halted at a dark entranceway. "The abandoned tube is there," he said, pointing to the floor. "Workers missed this conduit during past renovations years ago."

"How do you know it isn't full of water?"

"I followed it once. A tight fit for me, but should be fine for you and the Chancellor. Took me right out past the outer fence."

Carstairs was thankful for a chance to catch his breath. "No one else knows about it?"

"Not a soul." He grabbed his arm. "Listen, I won't be around to help you through the pipe. You'll need to do this part yourself. Understand?"

The captain glanced at the tube cover and nodded.

"Good. Then let's free Chancellor Madison and restore justice to the Council."

TWENTY

WHEN CARSTAIRS HATCHED HIS ESCAPE PLAN FOR THE former Chancellor, he knew he'd have to trust others he didn't know. So when Scrauts introduced him to half a dozen other so-called sympathetic guards at the end of a long corridor, his senses burned on full alert.

"You didn't tell me about these other men," he said. "This was for you and me only. When we enter the Chancellor's cellblock, we can't attract any attention to ourselves with this circus."

"Listen, Carstairs," the thickset guard said, "I had to make a snap decision. The soldiers found your point of entry in the outer perimeter. The entire prison's on lockdown." He pointed to the guards. "I'd stake my life on these fellows, and you'd be wise to do the same."

The captain studied them, noting the resolve ingrained in their faces. "Very well." Turning to Scrauts, he added, "Anything else I should know about?"

"Yes," he said, drawing his weapon. "Fortunately, my

squad and I have orders to move the Chancellor to a deep cell lockup for safekeeping." He cocked his head. "Funny how that works sometimes." A short guard tossed a backpack at Carstairs. "Put that on so you blend in."

He rifled through the pack and found a pair of pants, jacket, and cap. He threw them on. "Okay, you lead. I'll be right behind you."

The squad lined up single file and Scrauts pulled the heavy steel door open. On the other side, they picked their way through a storage area covered in dust and old furniture, then exited into one of the pristine hallways Carstairs remembered from his earlier visit. They marched toward Tephera Madison's cellblock.

"It's about time you got here, Scrauts," the gatekeeper grumbled, running through the procedure to unlock the Chancellor's cage. "And hurry."

The captain clenched his jaw. He'd been in jams too numerous to mention, and developed a sixth sense about right and wrong. He grimaced. Gaining entry to the block was too easy.

"Hold up," he said.

The guard turned.

"It's a trap, Scrauts. They've got us all boxed in."

Without warning, the hall leading to Madison's cell flashed in brilliant light. A voice echoed through the corridor. "Halt! You have nowhere to go and nowhere to hide. Place your weapons against the wall and back up ten paces. Failure to comply will result in your immediate execution."

Dammit!

Carstairs grabbed him by the arm. "Make like you're complying. I'm getting the Chancellor."

"Then what?

Scrauts obviously hadn't seen this degree of action before.

"Then we bust out of this hellhole, guns humming. Got it?"

The guard failed to respond.

Carstairs left him and raced toward the cage. The voice shouted its warning again. When he reached her cell, Madison stood in silence at the centre of her room, smiling.

"So this is how you're going to rescue me, Captain? I'm more inclined to stay put."

He ignored her chiding remark and yelled, "Move back!" His thermal flux gun would never crack the lock on the cell gate, but it might be effective on the stabilizing hinges and supports attached to the concrete pillars. He aimed at them and fired.

The first shots damaged the stone, but the hardware held. He shot again, and the bottom beams crumbled. The cell door hung precariously from the ceiling by a pair of bolts. Shouts arose from down the hall. Then several more shots rang out.

Carstairs bent the gate back, creating enough space for the Chancellor's thin body to squeeze through. And, for the first time since he met this woman over 25 years ago, he no longer saw the confidence, aloofness he'd known. Instead, fear filled her dark eyes.

Her eyes.

The night he confessed his betrayal.

A beam from a flux gun smashed into the stone above his head, showering them with dust and debris. Carstairs grabbed her bony wrist. "Stay low and follow me close behind."

The squad was pinned down, unable to move. Only Scrauts had his weapon raised. He provided covering fire, but his men could not retrieve the guns they'd dropped. The captain fired at the overhead lights and blasted the hallway into almost complete darkness.

The echo of scrambling boots filled the spaces and,

within a moment, Scraut's gang shot back toward the cellblock door.

Carstairs tugged Madison's arm, forcing her to keep up as he ran along the corridor and joined the others.

"Chancellor!" Scrauts shouted.

"Loyal Scrauts," she said. "Good to see you."

Carstairs interrupted them. "Are your men capable of killing their own?"

"What?"

"There's only one way out of here, Scrauts, and that's the front door. We'll need to blast through, and those others are standing in the way."

The burly guard caught his breath and nodded.

"Then you'll follow me through the old water tube."

He agreed, gripping his weapon, and the captain shouted commands to the other guards.

Given the amount of flux fire in the corridor, Carstairs estimated only a handful of soldiers protected the opening. That wouldn't last long. Once word got out, more would descend from all corners of the compound. He had to act.

"You know what to do, men!" he shouted above the din. "And where to go once we're through!"

He stood and fired a volley into the ceiling above the entrance. Chunks of concrete and plumes of dust rained down.

"Now!"

The others blasted at random into the doorway. Several groans floated through the air. One of Scraut's men took a hit in the gut, splattering viscera across the floor.

"Move!"

They ran toward the expanding light. Two guards low. Two high. When Carstairs saw they were ready, he shouted, "Go!"

The fighters wheeled around the corners, flux guns humming with energy. A laser blast slashed into another man, and he keeled over. The Chancellor gripped Carstairs by the waist, finding an inner strength he hadn't counted on.

A guard at the entrance hollered, "Clear!"

"Come on, Tephera," he said. "Time to get you to safety."

Klaxons shrieked through the corridors. Scrauts took point, with Carstairs and Madison close behind. The remaining guards covered the rear. Shouts rang through the hallways, and the captain wondered if they'd make it to the tube without being seen.

They crashed through the dusty storage room. Two guards stayed back, blasting down the corridor to buy them some time against an approaching army of prison fighters. But the others were organized now. They knew how to handle riots and breakouts. Someone shot the pair of rearguard allies in quick succession just as Carstairs and the Chancellor reached the thick steel door.

The soldiers had massive weaponry. No more flux guns for these brutes. From the sound curdling through the humid air, Carstairs recognized the whine of plasma equalizers powering up.

After Scrauts' last man entered, the captain slammed the door.

Within moments, an enormous dent in the steel appeared from the plasma equalizer discharging its volley.

"Come on, there's still time to reach the pipe," Carstairs insisted.

But Scrauts glanced at his men and shook his head. "You take the Chancellor and get her to safety. We'll hold them off as long as we can."

"Forget it! You're coming with us."

"No," the big guard growled. "They'll discover the tube. You fail if that happens."

Carstairs bit his lip. Another shot rattled the door.

They'd be on top of them in a moment.

"Save her!" Scrauts insisted and pushed him away.

Tephera reached out and touched the man's shoulder. "I shall never forget what you and your men did here today."

Carstairs took her hand, and they raced through the shadowy corridors toward the hidden cut-out where the turnwheel to the old tube lay in darkness. It took only moments for them to reach it, but already, heavy weapons fire pierced the air.

The captain handed his flux gun to the Chancellor. "Fire first. Ask questions later." He knelt on the floor in front of the wheel and heaved at it. But the heavy valve had not been used in years, and refused to budge.

More heavy fire. Closer this time.

They've breeched the doorway.

He thrust his body against the wheel, and it still resisted.

As a last resort, he threw himself on the concrete floor, leveraged his body against the wall, and kicked at the turnwheel with as much force as he could muster.

Bootsteps running.

"Carstairs," Tephera whispered. "They're coming."

He slammed his feet over and over again at the valve with increased desperation. *Something moved!* He kicked again and again. The wheel finally groaned and yielded. He continued turning it with his arms.

"Carstairs?"

The lid creaked open, and he grabbed the Chancellor, took her weapon, and pushed her down a series of metal rungs. Running boots approached, much louder now. He dropped into the tube and pulled the cap shut.

Then he waited.

Muffled sounds penetrated the covering. Carstairs held his breath. His heart hammered at his rib cage.

And then, the sounds faded until nothing but his heartbeat filled his ears. He exhaled and tightened the wheel closed.

"Chancellor?"

"Down here," she called, her voice resonating in the gloom.

Carstairs reached into his webbing and pulled out a torch that he wrapped around his head, and peered down.

Tephera stood in a few centimeters of water, gripping the metal hand rail with shaking hands.

He lowered himself, and at the bottom of the tube, she clasped onto him and held tight. Misplaced temptation filled his body, but when he brushed her straggly hair back and stroked her cheek, all he could think of was Piper.

"It's not over," he warned, and pulled away. He checked the tracker, determined which way led to freedom, and stepped through the narrow pipe, holding the Chancellor's hand.

THEY WANDERED IN SILENCE FOR WHAT SEEMED LIKE hours in the filth and pungent smell, but Carstairs knew from his timer that only twenty minutes had ticked away since they escaped the compound. And during this time, he questioned his decisions, past and pending, in deafening silence.

They eventually reached the end. Another set of rungs led to an overhead lid and turnwheel.

"If everything lines up, Tephera, we should be outside of the prison fence right now."

"What if they're waiting for us on the surface?"

He shrugged. "I don't like to play *what if*," he said. "If they are, they are. Wait here."

Carstairs scrambled up the rungs and fought with the turnwheel. This one released its hold after a few powerful tugs, and he eased it around. The cover refused to lift.

Carstairs killed the torch on his head. Rainwater seeped through a tiny crack at the lip.

"The lid's covered with grass and dirt." He worked at it until the grime loosened.

"Any sign of the guards?" Tephera asked.

"Hang on."

He curled around the turnwheel and pushed on it with his back. The lid relented, breaking the constraints of grass and shrubs. Carstairs raised the flux gun close to his cheek and poked his head out from the pipe.

To the north, floodlights and klaxons filled the surrounding air. From his vantage point, guards moved like busy insects throughout the compound, but none searched the grounds beyond the external fence.

That would change soon enough once they realized he'd made it out.

He squeezed onto the surface and the torrential rain showed no mercy on him. Then he reached down the tube, urging Tephera to join him. She climbed the rungs, took his hand, and he pulled her through.

Within moments, he found the runabout hidden in a hollow covered with shrubs and branches. They cleared the debris away and prepared to enter the craft.

Tephera stared at him over the roof of the shuttle. "We could have been something together," she said as the rain poured around them. "We still could, you know."

Carstairs, ignoring her, drew the weapon and set the power level to stun, aiming it at her scrawny chest. "Sorry to have to do this, Tephera. But you took my family from me a long time ago and cost me my career. I won't let you take the last shred of dignity I have remaining."

She glared at him. "How dare—"

The energy beam glistered in the thousands of raindrops falling around them. The Chancellor slumped on the soaked ground, staring vacantly into the black, turbid sky.

Carstairs dragged her behind some protective shrubs and said, "I can only do so much to help you. You're on your own now. I imagine the guards have picked up the heat signatures and are on their way to collect you." He propped her against a tree. Rainwater soaked through her thin prison clothing that now clinged to her bony body. "Oh, and you're the last person on this planet I would ever trust again. For anything."

He leapt into the shuttle and, rather than enter the coordinates for the drop off point, he flew the vessel on a route that would soon track to the Northern Airfield. Before easing into the stormy night, he sent an encoded message to Leda: *Asset available for pick up at the cache. Craft unavailable. Hurry.*

If Tephera's supporters arrived before the guards expanded their search, they'd be pissed at him. But if the soldiers found her first, who knows what might happen?

The command console's amber glow reflected in the windscreen as he meandered through the valley brush in full stealth mode. The cartel wouldn't be pleased, he realized, but perhaps he had already caused enough of a distraction to fulfill at least part of his contract, whether or not Tephera escaped. And he could always find a more conventional way to disrupt the order of things if needed.

I'll deal with that if it arises. In the meantime, the moment I'm on the Dauntless, *I'm going after Piper. No matter where she is.*

TWENTY-ONE

HEALERS IN THE MOANING BONES TUNNELS PLACED SALVE and a herb poultice on her lacerations, but her ruptured knee concerned them most. The surgical procedure she'd undertaken on Second Point may have sufficed at the time, but in the intervening clashes and troubles since, she aggravated it so much they could not repair it without considerable effort. In the short term, the herbs they administered were surprisingly effective in numbing the pain, and they insisted she rest for several days, if not weeks.

Piper wanted nothing to do with that.

They provided her with a tea-like liquid—a variation of the Bone Sip—to help ease the swelling, and she retired to a section of the tunnel where people slept. She lay down on an empty stone slab, and fell into a deep sleep.

She did not know how long she'd been out, but she awoke to a large, powerful hand pushing against her shoulder.

"Piper, we found her."

She propped herself up on her elbows under the pug-beaver skins to see Dolian looming over her. "Come. Get up. We leave for Edenfall shortly." He disappeared, and she threw on her jacket and grabbed her gear bag, slinging it over her back and stumbling through the array of beds and sleeping children.

She followed Dolian into a cave-like area in the tunnel. A large table sat in the middle of the room. Weapons lined the walls. Portable light stands dangled from above. Somehow, they'd jimmied a comms station into the corner.

Dolian stopped in front of a ragged fighter. "Piper, this is Janas. He brings news of Ariel's location."

The thin Hand greeted her and formed each word carefully as he spoke. "As I told Dolian, we spent much time tracking. The Heads are skilled at hiding, and they know how to avoid detection. But the resistance is strong. The network saw strange movements in and around the Lowertown quarter in Edenfall. Hands where there should be no Hands. Lots of traffic at this one house, mostly in the darkness. We investigated further and watched. After several days, we finally spotted her inside."

Janas turned to Dolian. "She did not appear to be harmed."

"That is a relief," the big Hand grumbled, clenching his fists. Then, to Piper, he said, "We have the coordinates of this building. Getting in and out without harming others will be difficult, but a full assault is the only way to free her."

Dolian's face oozed fear and concern. He did not want to harm Ariel, but only a surprise attack would allow them to enter the structure, neutralize the kidnappers, and bring her home. That made the entire operation fraught with risk.

Piper turned her attention to the map sitting on the table. "Is this the place?" she asked, pointing to a multi-storey building.

"Yes," the runner said, "in Lowertown. An open

square protects it from the rear. And they have sightlines across the streets in the front. They can see people approach from a great distance."

"Subterfuge won't work," she said.

Confusion spread over Dolian's face.

"Meaning," she continued, "we cannot sneak up on them. And they'll have spies along the streets and in the open square."

The men grunted.

An idea struck her and her eyes gleamed. "But what about from above?"

"From above?" Dolian asked. "Yes… of course! We approach from high up, crash into the roof creating a big mess. Big chaos. Then we rescue Ariel."

"Our true leader," Janas added.

"All right. This idea shows promise," Piper said, leaning over the map. "If your team can get us into Edenfall again without being seen, the element of surprise could work."

For the next hour, they drafted a more detailed plan and identified the largest operational risks. Dolian continued to show concern for his wife's welfare, but his determination trumped his fears.

Soon after, the shuttle launched its new mission, buffeted by the merciless wind, with Piper and the combat team wearing traditional Hand battle uniforms.

EDENFALL GLOWED LIKE A PATCHWORK QUILT IN THE dead of the Robosian night. Several quarters had been without power for days. Not so the Governor's mansion on the outskirts of the city where Larrin—backed by the Protorans—continued to assume government functions.

The shuttle pilot, flying stealth with transponder diffusers, pulled the craft into a steep vertical ascent. One of Dolian's men shouted back from the cockpit. "Target identified and locked-in!"

Dolian leaned forward in his flight seat, cradling his assault weapon. Piper sat across the aisle from him, clutching a thermal flux gun. Several scissor-bombs dangled from her battle belt.

When the shuttle reached its apex and descended toward the kidnappers' building, a strange thought passed through Piper's mind: *I bet Carstairs would love to be in on this*. She took comfort from the memory of his courage under pressure, and focused on the mission.

"Front shields on maximum," the pilot reported. "Get ready. Impact in three... two..."

Piper braced for the jolt of smashing into the roof. Even so, her body flew forward, held in place only by the many restraints.

Before she regained her senses, the fighters threw themselves from the shuttle. Weapons fire erupted amid shouts and wild warrior screams. Piper unfastened her straps and joined them, diving through the portal and smashing onto the crumpled roof, tumbling through several other broken floors before resting at the main salon on street level.

Dolian grabbed her by the back of the collar and threw her behind him as laser blasts screamed overhead.

"Many Heads descended to the subfloor," he said, sweat pouring from his forehead. "Ariel must be there. You and I will find her while my fighters secure this level."

She followed him, weapon humming, through a kitchen area to a door with a staircase leading down to the dark.

"We go quietly," he whispered.

Piper held him back and shook her head. "We behave like them. After me." She pushed past the fighter and raced down the stairs. A moment later, Dolian joined her.

The silent room sat in complete darkness. They crouched low, aiming weapons at the top entrance.

"Medgers, is that you?"

A hushed voice in the gloom.

Piper grunted.

"Medgers?"

Dolian whispered in a rough, disguised voice, "Is the Graves girl secure?"

A second passed and Piper worried he may have given them away. But the response from the darkness said, "Yes, she's here."

The weapons fire on the upper levels petered out. Someone shouted, "It's safe to come up. The threat is gone."

Piper exhaled and lowered her weapon, maintaining the ruse for the abductors' benefit. Men stirred behind her as they rose and plodded toward the staircase. Her knee screamed, so she limped to the side, allowing them to pass.

That's when she saw her.

"Ariel!"

The figure stopped, along with a pair of kidnappers. One man said, "Hey, what's going on here? Who are you?"

Before he knew it, Dolian picked him up and slammed his body onto the floor. Piper discharged her flux gun across the hostage takers' path. These men were not fighters, she understood. They slumped, dropping their weapons. She gathered them up while Ariel and Dolian embraced quickly, then they all raced up the stairs.

His team tied up the captors—the ones still alive—and helped Piper with her load of firearms. Outside the main window, several armed vehicles amassed up the street. She assumed they were government security forces.

They were not.

"Come on, Piper," Ariel shouted. "Those carriers are controlled by a dominant local gang."

She hesitated. "You go fire up the shuttle. I'll keep these creeps occupied, then I'll follow."

The moment she spoke, the first carrier landed on its skids outside the building. Several armed myrmidons tumbled out and took up aggressive positions. The leader approached with caution in a display of either bravery or idiocy. Piper wasn't sure which.

Dolian's team clambered through the debris toward the shuttle.

The myrmidon shouted, "You are surrounded! Do not attempt to leave the premises. Drop your weapons and come out with your hands up."

She needed a diversion to help the others escape, even if it sacrificing her freedom.

Piper grabbed a scissor-bomb from her waist and yelled, "Okay… I'm coming out. Hold your fire."

She crawled toward the entrance and knelt beside the door. She reached up to turn the handle, and the second the gate swung open, a volley of weapons fire blasted into the room. Piper lay prostrate on the floor, searching for anything that might protect her. There was nothing except an overturned table. She held the bomb at her side and pulled the pin.

When the attack died down, she took that opportunity to roll the activated explosive through the destroyed entrance. It clanked and bounced along the pavement before stopping. Then she scrambled toward the dangling staircase leading to the ship.

The scissor-bomb detonated, ripping the front half of the building structure away, exposing her to the dangerous street. Her eardrums rang, but she pressed upward with more urgency, leaping across an open hole in the flooring, and hauling herself up to the next level.

The shuttle's nacelles whined above her. The pilot had righted the craft and held it hovering just above the crash site. Piper pulled herself up, but her knee buckled, and she fell down hard. Myrmidons shouted below her. She waved at the shuttle to go, but the vessel remained in place.

Piper tried again to stand, but her leg refused to work. The muted sound of boots and weapons fire shattered the rhythm of the powering engines. She pressed her body against the floor, unable to move, resigned to her fate.

Two large hands grabbed her and tossed her over a man's shoulder like a sack of wheat. When the initial shock left her, she realized Dolian carried her back to the ship as weapons discharged all around. He handed her to another fighter, and after she settled against the bulkhead, the shuttle rose and screamed away.

The pain in her knee flooded her, such that she could fight unconsciousness no longer. The world around her faded to black.

THE INCOMING TRANSMISSION FROM DR. SHEILOR chimed on the bridge of the *Volantis*. Scyther mulled over the production numbers she'd sent him, and when his comms lieutenant announced her message, he muttered, "I'll take it in my private quarters."

Once there, he opened the channel to the Operations Centre at the Governor's mansion in Edenfall. "Doctor, are you well?"

"Yes, my Lord. Governor Larrin's team has seized control of most of the city, and continues to provide us with unfettered access to the holding pens. We're loading up a second transport ship to carry hundreds more back to Protor for immediate harvesting and reclamation.

Scyther leaned forward at the comms desk. "So the weasel is proving capable, and consistent. This is good." He noticed a flicker in Sheilor's ocular implants. "Something else concerns you, Doctor. What is it?"

She cocked her head and said, *"You may not have heard, my Lord, but it appears Piper Madison has taken up with a rogue fighting unit from the lands. Several Heads witnessed her rescue Ariel Graves from her rebel captors."*

"Yes, we received the same report. That woman is a constant irritant, but poses no real threat to our soldiers. And, Sheil, now that we have access to these animals, our focus must remain on helping our people survive. Madison can wait."

The doctor flustered. *"Liege, I understand. But if anyone could disrupt our operations here, it's the girl. Perhaps we should dedicate some resources to search for her and Ariel Graves?"*

Scyther heard that several of the Heads and a healthy number of Hand gangs considered the Graves girl to be the proper leader of Robos 7, and he wondered what she might be capable of undertaking while in exile. Given the lack of strength in the Robosian military, not much, so he dismissed that possible impact.

But Piper Madison could be trouble.

"Doctor, I'm expecting communications from Ambassador Welkin soon, and there may be another solution to deal with the Madison girl in the works. In the interim, I'll dispatch a small team to scan the lands for those two. The rogue fighters favor the old mine sites, so we can begin there."

"Thank you, my Lord. Do you still wish to delay your facial surgery?"

He lowered his voice. "I do."

"Understood. I'll report back later with more numbers from the regeneration rooms on Protor."

After he ended the transmission with Sheilor, his bridge comms officer hailed him. *"Lord Scyther, Ambassador Welkin is calling on a secure channel. For your viewing only. I shall patch her through."*

This was the moment he'd been waiting for. Floating in orbit around Robos 7, so close to the Asterian Battle Fleet, rattled him. Although the fleet refused to involve themselves in Robosian internal affairs, he realized that could change at a moment's notice. But if Welkin had secured agreement on his proposal from the Council, he would no longer have to concern himself with the Asterian warships or anyone else.

He rose from the station and assumed a commanding position in front of the comms monitor. "Ambassador Welkin, I have been awaiting your call with great interest. How are you?"

The Ambassador's reptilian face appeared alone on his screen, but he recognized her entourage of advisors and underlings surely hovered beyond the camera's vision.

"I am well, Lord Scyther, and I—noot—appreciate your asking." She gathered her thoughts and proceeded. *"Let us get down to business. As you are aware, I presented your proposal to stabilize Robos 7 and the Fairfield Industrial Sector to the Council."*

Scyther crossed his arms and raised his head.

"I believe your own representative has briefed you on the fulsome discussion that ensued."

Indeed, his Protoran Councillor had kept him apprised of the thrust and parry of vociferous deliberation within the Great Hall. Many presented both concerns and support in a full display of paranoia and logic. Her final report offered no prediction regarding the proposal's acceptance, merely stating a "very close" outcome.

"I understand, Ambassador, that the debate carried on for a couple of days before any vote was taken," Scyther said, leaning on his professional speech protocols.

Welkin concurred. *"But in the end, the members voted, and I would like to share the result with you before anyone else."*

"By all means," the Protoran leader said.

The Ambassador glanced aside, and continued. *"The Torfinn Galaxy Governing Council has approved your proposition to stabilize the Sector."*

"Thank you, Madam. I shall immediately—"

She interrupted him. *"It's not that simple, Lord Scyther. The approval comes with an appending document comprising several conditions."*

He approached the comms screen. "Conditions, Ambassador? This is... unexpected."

"I will send them to you post-haste, Scyther, but in the interim, a key requirement is your assurance that no harm shall befall any Robosian citizens. Yes, we understand there are several factions of fighters acting independently, and these groups must be stopped. But in terms of the others, both Heads and Hands alike, the Council demands assurances that their safety won't be jeopardized. That includes the obvious harvesting of individuals."

Scyther could not believe her words. So the useless Governing Council expected him to assist Governor Larrin and receive nothing in return? Madness. But he would not be denied.

"Madam Ambassador, I shall, of course, need to study the entire list of conditions to ensure they meet with our satisfaction. You recognize that my people rely on organics for our very survival. Do I understand the Council does not approve of our use of the reproduction farms, despite the Protocol our two planets agreed to?"

She exhaled and said, *"I'm afraid that is what the members wish, Lord Scyther."*

He paced around his quarters like a caged animal. *This cannot be happening.* He quelled his rising rage and said, "We shall study the conditions, Ambassador Welkin. Now, did you discuss that other matter involving Tephera Madison?"

The lizard queen's face tightened. *"Indeed, we did, Lord Scyther. Despite some sympathy for the former Chancellor, she will have no involvement in any Council affairs."*

He studied the subtle movements in her facial expression. *She's only sharing part of the story*, he thought. *Something's going on with the elder Madison, and this reptile wants to keep it hushed up.* "Very well, Ambassador. We shall talk again soon. *Volantis* out."

He stormed from his quarters, marching on his tingling leg toward the bridge. By the time he arrived, he had calmed down and allowed his logic and rational circuits to await the Council's conditions.

Until then, he would continue with the ongoing harvest.

Scyther entered the command bridge. The officers scurried about, huddling around the main viewer.

"What the devil is going on?" he growled.

"Liege," Commander Wesling said, "we have detected a single ship on course for Robos 7. Scrambling its transponder. She attempts to run stealth, but is no match for our tech."

"Obviously. Someone from the Battle Fleet?"

"Negative. But its origin is uncertain."

Scyther's frustration mounted. First, the Council disappointed him. Bunch of useless politicians. Then that secretive, weak reptile Welkin. Another ineffective do-gooder. The old Chancellor would never have allowed this madness to permeate every level of Torfinn life. And now, even more distractions. He needed to take his frustrations out on something…

"Orders, Liege?"

He turned to Commander Wesling. "Prepare three vipers for battle. I shall pilot one of them myself. We will blast that unsuspecting ship, whoever it is, into dust."

PIPER FIRST BECAME AWARE OF HER SURROUNDINGS when children giggled and darted about nearby. The throbbing hammered at her head, and her knee burned like someone had driven hot nails into it. She groaned and eased her eyelids open.

Dirty, smiling faces greeted her, then disappeared. Piper tossed the pug-beaver pelt away and stretched into a sitting position. She recognized the familiar caves and tunnels of the Moaning Bones.

The Healer she met earlier arrived with a tray of various medications. He placed them on the stone table beside her and said, "Drink the tea, Ms. Madison. The medicine will ease your pain."

She did as instructed and the effect was almost immediate. Along with the soothing concoction and ubiquitous Bone Sip, tiny bowls of food dotted the plate. She ate and soon felt strong enough to find Ariel and Dolian.

The pair appeared together at a secondary tunnel entrance by the far end of the cavernous space and marched hand in hand toward the planning cave. Ariel spotted Piper and ran to greet her.

"Thank you for coming to help us," she said, wrapping her arms around her.

Piper flinched as her aching body rebelled. "Did the kidnappers hurt you?"

"No," she said, "but like I told Dolian, I overheard them talking about the Protorans and their big plans for our planet. Come, join us in the planning room."

They headed toward the shallow cave. Despite being held against her will and all that had befallen Robos 7 since the death of their father, Ariel's confidence and maturity had blossomed, along with her leadership abilities. Until recently, she understood little about her own world, and even less about the other planets in the Torfinn Galaxy. Today, Piper thought, she displayed all the authority of an emerging, powerful leader.

From a reluctant bride to dreams of being a teacher, and now the *de facto* Governor-in-exile of Robos 7. Piper's pride in her half-sister had no bounds. Clearly, the last several months working beside Feryn and other ministers in the interim government helped her grow into this position.

Pride, she thought. *Mother never said she was proud of me.*

Once inside the cramped cave, Dolian and his advisors greeted them and they sat around the map table in the center of the room.

The big Hand cleared his throat. "These Protorans may be a worse scourge on our planet than the evil Heads." He glanced at Ariel and continued. "First, they support Larrin and his faction. Then, they use the captured Hands for their own organic needs." He bit his lip. "Their next step? Seizing those wicked breeder farms to create an army of flesh machines."

Piper studied Ariel observing the discussion. Her face remained expressionless.

"We have no choice," he continued, "but to destroy those facilities and make sure Scyther never rebuilds them."

Several fighters grunted their approval.

"Then it is decided," he said. "Let us prepare to move whoever remains there out and turn those farms into rubble."

Ariel leaned on the table. "It's not quite that simple." She faced Dolian. "My love, your resolve and passion to protect our people and planet are admirable. You and the fighters have shown nothing but courage throughout these troubles, and now, during this Protoran occupation. But," she added, "every report I read before the kidnapping suggests the Hands don't want to leave the farms. Do you know why?"

The room became as quiet as death.

"Because they are so used to living lives of servitude

that they fear everything else. Even if we convince them to go and eliminate the farms, we can't stop Scyther from building new ones."

"Then we shall destroy them, too!" Dolian shouted.

"Perhaps. But he will also continue harvesting our people—Hands and Heads—for his own needs." She searched his eyes. "Don't you see? He's doing that already. How many hundreds are being shipped right now to their regeneration facilities on Protor? Unless the Governing Council intervenes—which they won't—I believe we need to consider alternatives."

Dolian shrugged. "Ariel, there are no other options. We must fight these intruders."

"Yes, we have to stand our ground, but we must also regain control and governance of our planet. To build our new society together, Heads and Hands. And to do it so we can protect ourselves and not allow anyone who wants our resources to overrun us." She held Dolian by the arms. "Change comes slowly. We all need time to adjust without hurting each other. Our strength grows from working together, and right now, we're not."

The man pulled away, fuming.

Ariel spoke with a firm, controlled voice. "We cannot win a prolonged war against the Protorans. Every time we destroy those ugly farms, they will build new ones. If we continue that way, we'll lose and forever be enslaved."

Dolian softened and faced the others. The concern on their faces was palpable. "I have learned much about warfare in these past few months," he said. "What you say, Ariel, has merit." A veil of sadness and frustration fell upon him.

Piper took advantage of the pause. "What alternatives do you propose, Ariel?"

She collected her thoughts, then stated, "This will not be a popular choice, but I suggest we turn the farms over to Scyther, exactly the way he wants them, in exchange for peace."

The cave room erupted. Even the subdued, elder advisors sputtered. When the cacophony subsided, Piper said in a calm voice, "We can't do that. A government's primary responsibility is to protect its citizens. Leaving the reproduction facilities and the Hands to the Protorans guarantees they'll always live as breeders."

A look of resignation spread across Ariel's face. "It's what the people want, Piper. We cannot force them to abandon the lives they want, even if we find their choice difficult to accept, otherwise we're no better than Scyther." She turned to the others. "Let us resolve to make peace with the intruders. Look, it sickens me, too, but the sacrifice may only be short term. While the fighting ends, we'll work hard to convince the Torfinn Governing Council to order the Fleet to restore a proper government here and to support the Protorans with their need for organics. We must all obtain some benefit, or none of us will quit."

Dolian growled. "You said yourself, Ariel, the Council will never get involved in our local affairs. What makes you believe they might help now?"

"Because I have faith they may also desire peace over conflict. And I'm confidant Piper can convince them of our urgent need to stop the fighting."

"And if they refuse?"

She rubbed his shoulder. "We'll cross that bridge when we get there."

In all the flurry of activity and planning, Piper ignored the whisper stone vibrating in her pocket. She thrust her hand down and wrapped it in her fingers. Ariel's beliefs rang loud and true in her thoughts.

But something else fluttered in the mental mix.

Another set of jumbled, ghostly images.

Familiar expressions.

Only someone she knew intimately could produce

such words, such thoughts.

As the room continued debating the merits of Ariel's approach to the Protorans, Piper's heart skipped a beat.

TWENTY-TWO

"SO THESE ARE PROTORAN SHIPS, EH, QUIRP?"

Carstairs studied the various icons on the main viewer. Not only were several dozen of these alien vessels hovering in orbit, but the Asterian Battle Fleet lurked in the area as well, doing what they did best in these circumstances: nothing.

"Affirmative, Captain," the computer sing-songed. "Three viper-class attack ships have veered away from the armada."

Carstairs stood, hands on hips. Glowing icons stuttered across the viewer toward their position. "How did they detect us, Quirp? We're still sending out false transponder beacons, aren't we?"

"Affirmative, and unknown. Regardless, as you can see, they are heading our way."

"Open a channel to the armada, Quirp."

"As you wish."

Carstairs positioned himself in front of the comms

panel on the bridge. Once the ship mind made the link, he said, "Greetings, Protoran vessels. This is Captain Jay Carstairs of the *Dauntless*. We mean you no harm, and we have no interest in your business on Robos 7."

The viewer flickered and an odd, machine-like creature appeared. His face was a mix of flesh and some sort of rubberized compound. Both his eye sockets sparkled with an unnatural glow.

And this is a Protoran, he thought.

"Captain Carstairs," the alien in the viper said, *"I am Lord Scyther, leader of Protor and peacekeeper for the Robosians under the authority of the Torfinn Governing Council. What brings you here, and why are you flying in stealth mode?"*

Quirp's analysis of the vessels scrolled across the overhead screen. Carstairs glanced at the data, noting the heavy armaments and ridiculous upper velocity limit on these vessels. Their presence alone would challenge his ability to drop in on Edenfall and search for Piper.

He offered his most charming smile, and said, "Lord Scyther, I apologize if my stealth mode caused you any discomfort. These are dangerous times, as you know, and many rogue vessels patrol this sector. Flying under the radar promotes a long and healthy life for me, but I assure you, I am no threat to you."

Scyther stared at him with those illuminated ocular orbs, unmoving.

"And to answer your other question, I'm searching for a missing colleague. I am concerned for their safety with all the different factions running around shooting at each other. Perhaps if you'd like to escort us to Edenfall, I'll follow you in."

He muted the transmission for a moment. "Quirp, can we blast through these vipers?"

"Negative, Captain," the computer replied. "They are

faster, more nimble, and heavily armed. Even if you neutralized these ships, several more remain in the Protoran armada."

Dammit...

He unmuted the comms.

"—I repeat, who is this colleague you are searching for? Perhaps we have run across him."

"He's a she, actually," Carstairs countered. "Her name is Piper Madison."

Scyther glowered at him. *"I know this girl. She has caused me nothing but trouble. You say she's a friend of yours?"*

Carstairs, attempting to keep the conversation light as the *Dauntless* roared toward Robos 7, replied, "Well, I'm afraid it's a bit complicated. You see, she and I... okay, I started out on a contract, and then went through the whole boy meets girl, boy loses girl thing, and—"

"Silence!" the Protoran shouted. *"Captain, I have only one thing to say to you."*

Carstairs gulped. "What's that?"

"Surrender your ship immediately, or die."

A green bolt of energy burst from the nose of Scyther's viper.

"Shields to max, Quirp! Evasive maneuvers."

The *Dauntless* careened to starboard on a chaotic course that tossed Carstairs across the bridge like a leaf in the wind. He pulled himself into the pilot's command chair and buckled in.

The powerful bolt narrowly missed them, sputtering away into the dark.

"Any other ships from the armada joining in, Quirp?"

"Negative. Only these three vipers."

"And the damn Asterian fleet?"

"No change, Captain."

Carstairs took over the flying controls. "Quirp, keep

the weapons warm. I don't want to pick a fight with these washing machines, but I'll defend us without hesitation."

"Acknowledged."

"I'm heading into the Robosian atmosphere as soon as possible. We stand a better chance of losing them in the hills than we do up here."

The *Dauntless* powered forward and screamed toward the planet, lurching back and forth in an attempt to shake the attackers.

Carstairs' efforts did not work.

The vipers continued their aggressive pursuit, randomly firing energy bursts in his general direction. One such volley narrowly missed, exploding on the port side and diminishing the ship's shields.

"Captain," the ship mind said, "the Protorans continue to gain on us and our shields cannot hold if we get too many more close calls."

"Understood, Quirp. Let's hope we arrive at the hills and valleys before they get us."

The *Dauntless* entered the polluted Robosian atmosphere on a tick-tack line toward Edenfall. Remembering the city's western hills from a past visit with Piper, Carstairs reasoned that the area's high winds might help him evade the lighter vipers.

Two of the attack ships screamed ahead of him without any warning whatsoever. Scyther's face appeared on the comms viewer. *"Surrender, Captain. Ease your ship to the planet's surface. You already know you are no match for the vipers. Make it easy on yourself."*

A bead of sweat poured down the captain's cheek. He'd spent far too long avoiding the truth of his predicament and his desires to quit again. Fishmonger. Cartel contractor. Useless dry drunk. Tephera Madison's pawn. Black market pilot. Piper's erstwhile lover. And now Scyther's amusement.

"Quirp, is the channel open?"

"Affirmative."

Carstairs gripped the joystick in his hand. The other hovered over his own weapons bank. "Scyther, give me your best shot. But know this: you'll only get one before all hell breaks loose."

The Protoran leader hissed and laughed in an odd, metallic way. *Very well. Prepare to die.*

The air surrounding him burst in a flash of light, blinding Carstairs and jarring his bones as if a rockslide had rolled over him.

It can't end like this, he thought, gripping the controls and fighting to hold the *Dauntless* steady. *It simply can't.*

PIPER SLUMPED AGAINST THE COLD, WET STONE WALL IN the cave. All around her, Dolian and his advisors argued about Ariel's desire to hand the reproduction farms over to Scyther in an effort to bring peace to the planet.

Their speech rose and fell with the jabs and slices of the back-and-forth debate. But she only listened to that faint voice emanating from the whisper stone.

Jay Carstairs' voice.

She had no doubt it belonged to him.

"Everything alright, Piper?" Ariel asked, reaching out to steady her.

She concentrated her thoughts and frowned. "Are you familiar with whisper stone lore?"

Ariel shook her head.

"These gems were a myth, believed to transmit thoughts across space and time, allowing the holder to experience something like second sight... an uncanny ability to see and hear other people's thinking." Piper hesitated and shrugged sheepishly.

"Oh, no," Ariel shuddered, moving closer to her. "And you found one? Is that what's in your hand?"

Piper did not move.

"Are you hearing anything right now?"

"Yes."

Ariel's frustration with the planners surfaced. She said, "Listen. We will turn those farms over to the Protorans. I want you to work out the logistical details now."

The big Hand stopped arguing with the men and worked his jaw. "We will find a way that we can live with."

Then Ariel grabbed Piper by the arm and led her from the cave toward the back of the tunnel opening, where they could speak more freely.

They sat on granite blocks in the gloom. The effect of the healing tea dissipated, and Piper rubbed her knee, trying to bring some comfort to it.

"I understand little about war," Ariel began. "Not like Dolian and the fighters. But if this whisper stone is real and you sense the thoughts of others, it's an important weapon in our fight with the Protorans."

"Maybe, but so far, they remain silent. As machines, the Protorans don't think like us. They are impossible to know. Same with some of the Robosians. The rock has its limitations."

Ariel chewed her lip. "Can you read mine?"

Piper inhaled. "It's not that I want to. It simply happens, and I hear thoughts as if they were my own. When I found this gem on Hauntor, one of the first voices I picked out was yours. You shouted for help."

"Amazing..." She squeezed closer and whispered, "But you heard something else, didn't you? Just now."

"Yes. Carstairs."

"What... what did he say?"

Piper searched her mind for the words again, but they had vanished. "Nothing specific. Almost random thoughts having to do with the *Dauntless*." She concentrated more, and recalled another image. "And some other ships chased him... strange ones... wait.... I got it... Protoran attack vipers." She faced her half-sister, beaming. "He's coming here, Ariel!"

"We must contact him. I'll put an alert out through the network to scan for the *Dauntless*. And we have to send a message to Scyther about surrendering the farms, too."

"That's risky," Piper said. "Those are Dolian's people... the Hands, I mean."

"I know." A swath of shadows surrounded Ariel. "He's proud and caring, yet I see no alternative. This small mining group lacks the power to defy the Protorans without Council support. I'm still learning about galaxy politics, but I understand the constraints imposed by the Ethical Protocol." She slumped against Piper's shoulder. "Oh, Piper, what should I do? I fear he won't accept handing the reproduction facilities to the Protorans because of what it'll do to the Hands."

She brushed a strand of hair from Ariel's face.

"But they don't want to leave," she continued. "They believe their sole purpose is to breed workers to serve the Heads. Only now, it will be the machine men and, within a couple of decades, a never-ending source of organics for them. Meanwhile, they take whatever Hands they need, much like Father said."

"How do you mean?"

"The needs of the many outweigh the needs of the few."

Piper grabbed Ariel and helped her stand. To hear Ariel spout rubbish like their father did, spooked her. "We must destroy those farms." Ariel began protesting, but Piper hushed her. "Yes, even if Scyther builds more, I agree with Dolian. We have to fight back. This is a gross injustice here. We cannot allow it to continue, no matter the consequences."

Dolian approached from across the cavern. He scowled

and fidgeted with his weapons belt.

"What did you and the men decide?" Piper asked him.

He worked his mouth and stood tall. "We refuse to surrender anything to the Protorans. Instead, we will fight them, even if it costs us our lives. Even if no one else joins in."

Tears welled up in Ariel's eyes, but she would not let them flow. She stiffened her back and searched Dolian's rough, brooding face. "Very well, my love. I don't agree, but let's do everything we can to save the Hands at the farms. And then we will destroy them, so there's nothing left for the Protorans to use."

Tension in the air between the two thickened. Dolian placed a large hand on Piper's shoulder. "Will you fight with us, Piper Madison?"

"Yes," she said without hesitation. "It would be my honour."

SCYTHER'S INTERNAL MONITOR—THE VIEWSCREEN embedded in his mechanical brain and body—showed the *Dauntless* careening through the Robosian atmosphere on a trajectory heading into the blackened, dead hills outside Edenfall. The coordinated, massive energy blast that he and the two other vipers initialized had the desired effect on the useless Asterian vessel. From the telemetry data he received, the disrespectful captain could not maintain control and, within moments, would crash in the mountainous region.

"Zotal, follow the *Dauntless* and make sure she is destroyed," he transmitted internally.

"Acknowledged."

The viper closest to the surface fired its engine and tracked the *Dauntless*.

Scyther picked up a distress call from the vessel's ship mind. An old-fashioned mayday, a remnant from terran colonists in the Torfinn Galaxy, indicating urgent danger.

How quaint, he mused, *an archaic mind to manage the vessel's functions.*

Video appeared from Zotal's viper. The *Dauntless* had broken through the polluted Robosian atmosphere and hurtled toward the hills, seemingly with minimal helm control. Huge winds buffeted both ships, and the viper pilot struggled to maintain a direct trajectory.

Scyther, holding a position in the planet's exosphere, speculated about the captain's true motives for coming to Robos 7. He recognized that Carstairs, along with the Madison girl, caused great havoc among the mainstream Torfinn planets, so he reasoned the man's interest in Piper had more to do with some other hidden motive than simply caring for her well-being.

In that regard, keeping Carstairs alive for questioning would be prudent. But Scyther had grown tired of these meddlers. Larrin's slow thought process, and that of other Heads like him, provoked his contempt. No, ensuring the problematic captain died would benefit his people and, by extension, the entire galaxy. He might even win more favour with the Council.

"My Lord, the Dauntless *continues her rapid descent. They have lost most of the helm controls. Intel suggests weapons systems and shields are inoperative. Life support is minimal."*

"Good." He studied the video stream in his mind. "It appears they will impact in the valley. Follow them in."

"Yes, my Liege."

Smoke billowed from the plunging vessel. When the *Dauntless* hit the surface, it smacked the lowland hard on its belly. Sand and rock blasted from the front of the ship and she spun around, smashing into outcrops and fissures in the gorge.

The video stream shook as the pilot fought high winds and turbulence. But no humanoid could survive that tumble across the valley. Chunks of the *Dauntless* lay scattered throughout the land. Scyther discerned the separation of the main engines from the ship's body. Sections of the fuselage littered the place. A huge smoke plume mushroomed up from the crash site.

"Circle around and move in closer to the wreckage," the Protoran leader ordered.

"My Lord, I'll dive in close, but the winds are powerful, and I do not wish to put the viper in jeopardy."

"Understood."

The scout circled high into the dark sky, encountering more turbulence on the way. When it began its descent, it flew a few hundred meters above the valley floor but fought to hold a steady course.

However, Scyther had seen enough. Between the wreckage and apparent implosion, along with complete loss of communications telemetry, that damn captain would not survive.

"Leave the scum's body to rot," he said. "Return to the armada. We'll meet up there."

"Acknowledged, Liege."

Scyther maneuvered his viper with his mind and set a course for the *Volantis* and the armada in orbit around Robos 7. The coordinates of the other two ships flashed on his internal monitor as well. He continued checking various frequencies for any sign of life from the *Dauntless*, but all he detected was cosmic static.

Before the trio of vipers joined the others, the *Volantis* hailed him. Commander Wesling appeared on his screen.

"This must be important if you can't wait a few more minutes until I'm on the bridge, Commander."

"Believe me, my Lord. It is." The Protoran officer's eerie humanoid face—including his orbs—showed considerable strain.

"Well, spit it out, Commander."

"Sir, we picked up reliable intel concerning the breeder farms. We identified several Robosian scouts near those facilities. They are armed and appear to belong to a larger rogue faction from the lands. We're attempting to confirm that affiliation."

Scyther fumed. He felt the pressure in his organic heart build. "Commander, we must protect those breeders at all costs."

"Yes, my Lord. I put a squadron of vipers on stand by. We can order them to investigate as a show of strength to any of the factions."

"Good. Deploy those ships now. Assemble a troop carrier as well. If we're going to send a message, then let's make it a profitable one."

"Acknowledged, Liege."

Scyther prepared to cut the transmission as the armada appeared in visual range, but changed his mind. "Commander, has there been any word on the Madison girl's whereabouts? Or those of Ariel Graves?"

"Negative, my Lord. Several teams are involved in the search, but so far, they turned up nothing. The local Robosians are incommunicado."

"Very well. Keep at it. The minute Piper Madison appears on the grid, I want her taken alive."

"Acknowledged. Volantis out."

Scyther considered the possibility of a battle over the reproduction farms. Larrin assured him the rebel factions outside Edenfall would soon succumb to his strong-arm leadership. To date, that had not happened.

But what grasped him better than ever before was this: Piper Madison found resources his own people never could, and she accomplished goals his followers only dreamed of. He slowed his viper, causing it to hover above the planet.

One of the other ships contacted him. *"My Lord, is your vessel functional? You appear to have lost engines."*

"The ship is fine, Croon. But there's a change in plan. We will remain in low orbit above the *Dauntless* crash site."

"*Understood, my Lord, however, the chances of anyone surviving that impact are miniscule.*"

Scyther stroked his metal chin. "No doubt, but I have a hunch someone will come to investigate. Someone specific. Someone who has an active interest in the captain of that vessel."

And when Piper Madison shows up, he mused, *we will take her.*

TWENTY-THREE

DOLIAN ORGANIZED THE FIGHTER SQUAD INTO RANK AND file in the primary cavern. Nervous energy crackled through the air. Piper buckled her weapons belt and slung the filtering air mask around her neck. She joined the fighters and, to her great surprise, Ariel appeared wearing similar battle tackle.

The fighters froze.

"I'm joining you," she said with a serious tone.

Piper grimaced and bit her lip. "Your place is here, Ariel. You are the proper Governor, and this mission is far too dangerous to put your life at risk."

"Agreed," Dolian said, and motioned for the troops to follow him to the hidden shuttle hangar.

"These are my people, too!" Ariel struck a defiant pose. "I want to help, and before you say anything, I understand and accept the risks." She raised her chin and dared her husband to disagree.

He did not.

But Piper did. "Listen, Ariel, you are their leader. If something happens to you out there, who will save the planet? Who will oversee the reforms? Who will give the people hope for the future?"

Ariel's face slowly softened. "But I can't just sit around doing nothing. I'll go crazy."

Some children ran ahead of them, laughing and behaving like typical kids. Piper mused, "Perhaps a bunch of little ones could use some kindness and attention?" She thrust her chin toward the group.

Ariel brightened and said, "Alright, I can play with the youngsters." She winked at Dolian and blushed. "Should be good practice. Now go, and take care out there."

"Fighters, to the shuttle!"

They marched in pairs to an opening at the end of the cavern, but before they departed for the hidden hangar, a breathless messenger burst through the tunnel entrance. He spied the group and staggered toward them, waving his arm.

"Dolian," he gasped, gobbling his breath, "News... from the surface."

The line of fighters halted. An old, stooped Hand approached the runner with a skin of Bone Sip. He drank and spoke between breaths. "The Protorans... have shot down an alien ship over the Windy Peaks."

"Did you see it happen, Balzer?" Dolian asked.

The man wiped dirt from his sweat-stained face. "I have seen the wreckage. Only the protective cockpit capsule remains intact. The rest..." he shook his head and took another swallow of the liquid.

Piper glanced at Ariel. "A single seater?"

"No, Ms. Madison. A full light-cruiser."

Piper's heart sank. She buried the rising fear and regret. "Any sign of survivors?"

"None," Balzer said. "But I have the ship's name."

Ariel placed her hand on the man's forearm. "Tell us."

"We salvaged a piece of the fuselage that landed near the hidden lookout. We could only read part of it: *D-A-U-N-T—*"

"The *Dauntless*," Piper whispered.

"You know this ship?" the messenger asked.

"Yes." She glanced at the others. "We all do. She's Captain Carstairs' vessel."

Silence enveloped the group for a moment until the fighters behind them began shuffling their boots.

Dolian said, "We will grieve later. But time is short, and we must head to the farms."

"Wait," the man interrupted. "There's more. Intel intercepted Protoran transmissions. They detected our scouts at the reproduction facilities and dispatched a squadron of vipers and a ship full of troops."

"Dammit," Dolian scowled, "then let us hurry."

"It's too late," the runner cried, wiping his forehead. "Several attack ships touched down and set up defenses. More are coming."

Dolian faced his band of fighters. To a man, they showed no sign of quitting or retreat. "Men! Will you fight despite these invaders protecting the farms?"

As one, they shouted, "Yes!", and raised a cheer.

"Piper, you and I stay close together," he said, lowering his voice.

She checked on the nervous men, then the hopeful, trusting faces of the Hands left behind. Then she squeezed Dolian's shoulder. "I'm sorry, but I can't join you."

A look of astonishment crossed his face. "But you must, Piper. We need you."

She shook her head. "I have to see this wreckage for myself… to find out if…" Her lip quivered and she tensed. "Once I've confirmed… I'll meet you as soon as I can."

"I understand," the big Hand said. "Balzer, show Ms. Madison the ship. Keep her safe. Take others if you think it is necessary."

"Yes, Dolian."

She pulled away from the squad and watched them with a hint of sadness as they marched toward the tunnel exit. Within moments, the only sound in the cave was the fading *clomp-clomp* of heavy boots disappearing in the dark.

Piper turned to the runner. "Are you ready?"

BALZER EXPLAINED HE USED TO OPERATE THE RAIL CARS that brought ore up from the belly of the planet when the mine was operational, long before the breakdown of society.

They jogged together through a musty, dimly-lit tunnel until they arrived at the rail tracks. Since the death of Piper's father, the operation had ceased. Now, with Dolian's faction digging in, the entire site itself resembled an impenetrable fort.

They followed the line in a long spiral up to the surface. The acrid smell of pollution, along with the menacing winds, howled through the tunnel. Piper stopped to put on her headscarf and air filter, then they greeted a pair of sentries and slipped into the hazy daylight.

Balzer led the way over the mine compound toward an outbuilding. Piper followed a step behind as the whipping wind slashed across the dust and debris, challenging her vision. Inside the huge shed, a conventional ground vehicle awaited them. It resembled the clanky rover she used on Hauntor. Not as industrial, but with similar tires and treads. This unit appeared built for speed more than hauling.

"Quick," Balzer said, "before full darkness comes." He hopped onto the pilot seat, and she jumped into the side compartment. An automated massive door at the side of the building squealed open, and they disappeared into the wind.

The runner's vision in such a storm baffled Piper. Few

navigational guides showed on the vehicle itself—certainly nothing fancy like those on the Olavus   rover—and she concluded this Hand must know the terrain so well that he raced across it on instinct.

They rode for half an hour. She reached for her pocket again to touch the whisper stone nestled there, but received no more strange voices or images at all and wondered if the magnetic minerals in this region somehow suppressed its spatial properties.

Balzer pointed at a looming mass off to their right and steered the craft over more rock-strewn terrain toward it. Piper reasoned these must be the hills that followed the valley. They slowed to a crawl and a light—barely perceptible—flashed at them through the dust. Balzer moved closer and several figures wandered from the gloom to greet them.

Piper trailed them down a twisting path to an open cave where, once inside and out of the gusts, she removed her headscarf and filter. One of the men fired up a lantern and placed it on a flat slab containing half-eaten crusts of food and meat.

"Welcome, Ms. Madison," a tall man said. "I am Kendra." His features showed he was a Hand, but the other men resembled Heads, or possibly Hybrids.

Balzer said, "She would like to investigate the crash site. She may know the pilot."

The others grumbled, growing agitated.

"Has something happened?" Piper asked. "Please, if… if the captain is…"

"I doubt anyone survived," the man with the lantern muttered with a chill in his voice. "And there is danger here. Come and see." He waved to a monitor and comms station at the back of the cave.

"It looks like the planet," she said, studying the image. "Where are we?"

Kendra outlined a dark area on the land west of Edenfall. "The threat is above us, Ms. Madison." He zoomed in on the atmosphere. "The vipers that destroyed the ship remain, as if waiting in ambush for us to show ourselves."

Piper studied the local topography. The smear of wreckage strewn along the valley was inaccessible by shuttle or land vehicle. Hiking across the jagged outcrops also seemed impossible. That might explain why the Protoran ships hadn't seized the *Dauntless* wreckage. However, her instincts suggested they could have found a way to land, but they waited instead.

For her?

For Carstairs to emerge unscathed from the cockpit?

For the fighters to reveal their hidden locations?

She said, "But you have already seen the debris."

"Yes," Balzer answered. "Knowing the way makes it possible."

Piper again sensed the runner's uncanny awareness.

"But," he added, "I did not have time to investigate more. It is…" he chewed his lip, "messy down there, Ms. Madison. Conditions are extremely poor."

Warmth emanated from the stone in her pocket, and Piper reached in and withdrew it. The sensory gem glowed like a sapphire. Although no words or images came to her, she gripped the mineral and pictured him.

Carstairs, are you there?

The glow dissipated and disappeared. She clutched it and said, "Will you take me there, Balzer? I promise we won't stay long, but I have to know, despite the risks."

He glanced at Kendra and the others. Their grave faces showed nothing but deep concern and trepidation.

"Please," she implored.

Balzer grunted. "Okay, Ms. Madison, but we must leave now."

The group remained fixed in their positions, stoic and silent, like the surrounding rocks. Piper wrapped her covering over her head again and adjusted the filter on her face.

THE TREK THROUGH THE SCREAMING WINDS FOLLOWED A steep trail carved through the jagged breccia formations. Balzer tied a rope around their waists to avoid getting separated in the ferocious gale. Piper saw nothing more than a few meters in front of her, so she focused on Balzer's boots as they crept through the blackened hills. To the west, the sky began to darken.

They hiked out on the valley floor where the terrain flattened out, and marched toward the debris field. In the translucent, dying light, the wind shear relented and a large swath of land opened up. The trail of wreckage across the ground made her wretch. The *Dauntless* had become a second home to her, and now she lay shattered in ruins.

Balzer grabbed her arm and pointed to a rectangular object protruding from the soil.

The cockpit refuge chamber.

They raced toward it. As they approached the module, the magnitude of this section of the bridge shocked her. Far larger than she remembered, perhaps a newly modified safe zone for an entire crew. She surveyed the wreckage for life signs, but detected nothing.

Balzer found the manual override for the portal and, together, they heaved on it. The arm yielded, and the door cracked open. Piper yanked on it until the opening widened enough for them to enter.

The cockpit had no power. Not even an emergency light flickered. She tore the flashlight from her weapons belt and scanned the area. The main viewer had splintered in several places, and wires and conduits tumbled from the ceiling across the various consoles. The pilot's flight seat—

the one belonging to Carstairs—had been torn from its moorings.

But the man had gone.

"Perhaps they bailed out before the ship crashed," Balzer said.

Piper considered that, but didn't believe Jay would ever abandon his beloved *Dauntless*. "Let's move some of this crap. The captain may be buried underneath."

They pushed the fallen beams and consoles away, opening up the floor. Still no sign of the man.

Piper's hope of finding him evaporated.

"There's no one here," Balzer concluded. "And it grows dark. We must return to the cave before nightfall."

"Okay," she said. "I'll check one last time." She moved aft, picking her way over and around the clutter. The weapons console appeared intact, as did the supply cabinet.

She scanned the entire area again with her flashlight and staggered back toward the entrance when something grabbed her attention.

A boot?

Or was that her imagination?

She froze and stared at the heap of debris near the tactical post.

A gloved hand.

Oh crap! She thought. "Balzer, come here! I found him!"

The runner picked his way over the stack and joined her in removing various objects from the trapped body underneath. When they finished clearing the material away, Piper stood back in disbelief. Her throat seized and throbbed. Carstairs lay on the cockpit deck, facing the ceiling. His face was battered, bruised and swollen, and his one arm appeared crushed.

And this time, when the tears came, she allowed them to flow in a silent, endless stream.

Balzer reached out to her. "I'm sorry."

Piper fell to her knees by the captain's chest. She placed her palm against his lacerated cheek. He still felt warm to the touch. She closed her eyes and her body convulsed with the emotional release.

The nervous runner nudged her. "Please, we cannot stay."

She wiped her face with the scarf.

Perhaps her imagination or the emotion of the moment got to her as she finally understood how much she cared for the infuriating man, but she swore his chest rose ever so slightly. She watched it and leaned down toward his mouth.

The whisper stone vibrated against her leg.

"Balzer, did you bring any stimulant?"

"Yes, but—"

"Hand it over, now!"

She leaned across Carstairs' body and grabbed the hypo. Then, reaching for the man's neck, she plunged it through his mottled skin. Within moments, the captain of the *Dauntless* groaned and his eyelids fluttered open.

"Piper," he croaked, "is… is that really you?"

In that torrent of emotion, the hurt and despair, the hope and futility, she wanted nothing more than to hit the bastard and pound his chest. Her mind told her to strike him hard, to injure him as much as he had damaged her. But her heart would have none of it.

She clenched her fists and slammed them into a broken conduit beside her. She then bent down and gently kissed him on the mouth, tasting his blood and salt, and pouring out all the loss, pain, and passion she had long buried.

TWENTY-FOUR

"HELP ME MOVE HIM, BALZER." PIPER TUCKED HER ARM under the captain. They leaned him up against a smashed bulkhead. Not the most comfortable place, but it would have to do until they arranged transport. She couldn't look at his mangled limb without choking.

"Piper," the runner said, "we have no comms here in the valley. I will return to the cave for help." Balzer furrowed his brow. "If we are being tracked by those Protoran ships above us, they might attempt a landing on the surface."

"The winds won't protect us?" she asked, dabbing at Carstairs' face with a cloth.

"You have seen their vipers. If they break through the shear, they will reach this pocket of stable air."

Piper bit her lip. The pool of conflicting emotions swirling inside her chest muddled her thinking. Moving the captain now would prove fatal. By the look of his crushed arm, he may lose that altogether. And Balzer was right about the Protorans. If the machine men detected their presence here through the magnetic fields, they would surely hunt them down.

"You better go," she said, turning to the Hand, "before it gets any darker. I'll stay with the captain."

"Okay. I will return shortly if I can. He requires healing... and soon."

Piper agreed. "Go. If the machines show up, we'll deal with them."

Balzer picked his way through the debris and disappeared into the growing darkness.

"Looks like it's just you and me, Carstairs," she said.

The captain drifted in and out of consciousness. Piper scoured the smashed medical cabinet for anything that might be useful to ease his pain and came across a container of seriously potent narcotics. She pulled a spray tab out, loaded the hypo, and slammed it into the injured man's shoulder.

Moments later, he regained partial consciousness. The whisper stone in Piper's pocket vibrated, and she detected a faint voice in her mind. Only one. Only his. But it remained nothing but a jumble of mind soup.

"Where are we, Mads?" he asked, wincing as he turned his head.

"Inside the cockpit crash module," Piper replied. "We're at the bottom of some valley on Robos 7. The Protorans destroyed the rest of the ship."

He exhaled, and his breath wheezed. "Yes... I remember now."

His thoughts through the stone grew more coherent, and the dolorous voice she heard kept repeating: *I'm sorry... so sorry...*

"Quiet," she said, as guilt from reading his private feelings flooded through her.

"I've done a terrible thing, Mads." He struggled to find

the words, and the stone screamed in her brain. "Your mother…"

"Stop it," she begged. "I don't want to hear your explanation. You were only protecting your family. I get that now."

"No," he said, struggling to pull himself up, and failing.

The jumble of silent utterances somersaulted over themselves as they tossed around in her consciousness. The coherency of the ghostly voices fell into a state of chaos.

Prison… tunnels… Piper… Scyther… cartel…

They all meant nothing to her.

"I'm sorry I left you." He searched her eyes.

"Hush," she said. "Get some rest and focus on healing. We can talk later."

Carstairs shook his head. "I can't do that, Piper."

She pulled away, confused. The gem shared images now instead of words. The captain and her mother in each other's arms, standing in torrential rain. More recently than two decades ago. He protected her, like someone he—

Piper shuddered at the thought, trying to block the stone from transmitting his inner thoughts.

"Jay, don't…"

But Carstairs could no longer respond. He'd fallen unconscious again, slumping against the side wall, with his head flopping down on his chest. The stone stopped vibrating, and the images vanished.

THE RAGE OF DESPAIR AND HOPELESSNESS AND BETRAYAL coursed through her body. One moment, she wanted nothing more than to make him hurt. The next, she ached to be pressed beside him like on the *Dauntless*. Or when he rescued her from the insane Bortan leader. She held onto him at great length.

Did she interpret the spectral noises correctly? Was he still interested in her mother? Did he betray her again? Did

Tephera blackmail him into doing more evil?

After an hour passed, Piper left the resting captain and headed toward the broken pilot seat, searching for some mindless task to perform. The cracked main viewer needed replacing. Perhaps she might rig up a power source.

He left you, Piper, she reminded herself. *Abandoned you without even saying goodbye.*

She shook her head and tore open an access panel at the battered comms console.

And then he never bothered to ask how you were doing. Or offer to help.

The jumble of wires and fried circuits was irreparable, but a small power bus remained in decent condition. She pried it free from its holder and studied it under her flashlight. Perhaps it won't restore the ship's computer, but it might provide some lighting.

You sent him how many messages. Asked about his whereabouts how many times. Opened your heart to him. Wondered if he was even alive. And all he did was ignore you.

A power panel under the navigation console appeared intact. Piper slammed the power bus into it and searched for a secondary lighting source. She found an auxiliary circuit on the main board and activated it.

Low, ambient light blinked on, enough to allow her to kill the flashlight and get a better overall view of the wreckage.

You abandoned me, Jay, she thought. *How could you?*

Piper hopped onto the comms controls and lowered her head.

How could you?

The whisper stone hummed to life

Because I...

Rattling and clacking noises emanated from the portal.

"Finally," she said aloud, jumping down and helping

to swing the door open.

But when the first man entered, Piper froze.

This was not Balzer.

Not at all.

TWENTY-FIVE

"GREETINGS, MS. MADISON," SCYTHER SNEERED IN HIS metallic voice. "We meet again. And this time, you will not escape."

Scyther's enormous frame filled the portal entrance. Several armed Protorans lurked behind him and Piper figured there had to be many more waiting in the dark.

She kicked Scyther in the chest, causing him to stumble, and leapt across the wreckage toward the rear of the cockpit module. Carstairs remained propped up against the bulkhead, oblivious to the panic surrounding him. She unholstered her thermal flux gun and fired indiscriminately in the direction of the helm.

The broken captain stirred. He gawked around in a state of half-consciousness.

"Stay quiet, Jay," Piper ordered.

His crushed arm would not move, and he grimaced with pain as he shifted positions.

The voice from the front said, "You cannot damage us,

Madison. Don't you realize there is nowhere you can go to escape? Three of my vipers are on the ground, and the creature who brought you here has already been detained. Surrender now while you are able."

"Give me... a weapon," Carstairs groaned.

Piper knelt beside him and touched his face. The futility of the situation crushed her. Although confident that Scyther needed her alive and unharmed, she could not say the same for Carstairs. They shot down his ship and left him to die. Regardless, the Protoran leader was right: escape from the cockpit module was impossible with the Protorans guarding the only way in and out.

She had to decide on a course of action quickly.

"Scyther, listen to me," she shouted. "The captain requires medical attention. Can you give me your word that Dr. Sheilor will treat him?"

His response was swift and brutal. "I will not negotiate."

The sound of wreckage being cleared and clomping boots filled the stale air. *The bastards are coming,* she thought.

"Dammit, Scyther, you need both of us. Captain Carstairs holds as much sway as I do with the Governing Council. Check your records and you'll see. He offers you great value, but not if he's a corpse."

Scyther did not respond, but the clamour of his approaching men grew louder. Piper raised her weapon and fired into the ceiling, causing more conduit and part of a shield panel to collapse.

"Mads," Carstairs moaned, "I need a weapon."

She marvelled at the shattered man, wishing to remove his pain, and shook her head.

"Please?"

Before she answered, Scyther's voice bellowed through the cockpit. "Madison, I have reconsidered. I will spare the captain's life. We'll take both of you back to the *Volantis*. Dr. Sheilor can tend to his wounds."

Piper wiped a bead of cold sweat from her forehead and listened for any sign of movement. None came. "Do I have your word, Scyther?"

"You have my word. Now drop your weapon and show us your hands."

Carstairs stared at her. His pupils had dilated, and his blotchy skin turned ghostly white. Piper squeezed his hand and whispered, "It's alright. We live to fight another day."

THEY MARCHED SINGLE FILE TOWARD A VIPER NESTLED IN the soil on the valley floor. Two of the other Protorans retrieved a maglev gurney, loaded Carstairs onto it, and maneuvered it along in the rear. Piper's wrists were cuffed, and her legs had been shackled. They stripped her weapons belt and removed her jacket, and they also emptied her pockets and confiscated the whisper stone. She pretended it didn't bother her. Above her head, the winds moaned, stirring up dust and debris and turning the sky black.

"In here," Scyther said, entering his viper. A Protoran guard held her biceps in a powerful grip and forced her onboard. Scyther dumped her into a folding secondary chair and strapped her down before taking the seat in front of her.

"Where's the captain?" she demanded.

"He's on one of the other ships," Scyther responded, filling the pilot flight seat. "I gave you my word we shall repair him." He glanced over his shoulder. "I keep my promises."

Within moments, the ship lifted off, wrestling with the wind shear as they ascended between the hills. The straps around Piper's body prevented her from slamming into the bulkhead and ceiling, but the forces on her arms and chest almost crushed her.

After a hair-raising adventure through the gales, they

emerged from the Robosian winds and screamed across the atmosphere. Once in low orbit, when the ship's motion stabilized, Scyther contacted his flagship.

"Wesling, get me Dr. Sheilor."

Piper could not see the cockpit, and only caught a partial glimpse of the main viewer showing the viper's approach to the armada.

"Lord Scyther," the doctor said, *"You appear well."*

"I have retrieved the Madison girl and her friend the captain of the *Dauntless*. He requires extensive repairs. Please prepare a surgical team to address his wounds."

Sheilor's voice sounded much softer than Scyther's. More human. She said, *"Consider it done, my Liege. May I also remind you that you are overdue for your own maintenance?"*

"Understood. I will make myself available once I'm back on the *Volantis.*"

"Excellent. And I'll prepare the candidate for you. There is—"

Scyther interrupted her. "Stand by, Doctor. I wish to discuss that matter with you when we have a chance. In the meantime, this captain must be repaired."

"Acknowledged, my Lord. Sheilor out."

The viper continued on its course toward the *Volantis* in silence. Piper wondered if the stone might interact with the Protoran guard escorting her, but he showed no external sign of it. She wondered if the degree of machination in the Protorans influenced the stone's ability to read their thoughts.

At least Carstairs will be looked after, she thought.

An odd sensation roiled up from her gut and plagued her. "Lord Scyther," she said, "thank you. For helping the captain."

The machine man decelerated as the viper approached the docking bay on the flagship. "I believe the appropriate response is... you are welcome. Understand, Piper Madison, we are not insensitive brutes. We are simply trying to survive."

They eased into the belly of the ship, and Piper's mind burned on two actions: making sure Carstairs got healthy... and taking this fight for justice to the heart of the Protorans.

THE AIR QUALITY ONBOARD THE VOLANTIS WAS THE first thing Piper noticed when the equipment bay and passenger portal on Scyther's viper opened. A sweetness permeated the recycled oxygen, or perhaps what she sensed was the contrast between it and the foul pollution on Robos 7. Didn't matter. She inhaled a full breath and, in an instant, felt better.

A squad of Protoran soldiers and security officers awaited her removal, and they kept her wrists and legs shackled. She walked in short, choppy steps, shunted between shoves from behind and tugs from the front. The men escorted her through the docking bay and then along a wide, dimly lit corridor. She noted the markings on the bulkheads and doors as they marched, but could discern nothing from them.

Except for one.

A door containing the Torfinn symbol for communications.

For whatever reason—perhaps it was the designated intergalactic comms hub—they displayed it on this portal. All the others remained non-descript.

The soldiers halted outside a room with two oversized doors that hissed open on their approach. Dr. Sheilor stood inside, wearing a dark surgical coat. The men pushed Piper through and left her standing in front of the doctor.

"Welcome, Ms. Madison. Please don't mind these fighters. They are only doing their jobs." She shrugged, and something about her face caused Piper to question the doctor's commitment to the organic harvest and Scyther's desire to control Robos 7.

"This is a medical clinic?" she asked, glancing around the room.

"Yes, we carry a fully equipped hospital here on the *Volantis*. There is no surgery on Protor that we can't also do here."

Piper clenched her jaw. "Where's Captain Carstairs?"

"The captain, yes," Sheilor said, moving toward a biobed and checking the various monitors and other equipment. "The man is close to death, Ms. Madison. It's amazing anyone could survive that crash."

Piper's thoughts swirled, wondering where they'd taken him. Or if he even remained alive.

Sheilor continued, "Notwithstanding that, Captain Carstairs is in critical condition. His one arm was crushed, and he suffered internal bleeding. He's in surgery right now."

"What?" Panic rose in Piper's voice. "Why aren't you doing the operation?"

The doctor activated more biobed equipment and said, "Several top surgeons are aboard, and we each have our specialties. I am not needed at the moment. They must first address his internal injuries and then repair the damaged arm. And we'll look at everything else while we're at it, to make sure we haven't missed other breaks or tears."

The doctor returned to Piper and stood facing her. "It is in our best interest to keep the captain alive and healthy."

"So you can harvest his limbs, too?" she spat.

"If we must, yes. But I think with the addition of the Robosian Hands to our stock—along with the Torfinn politics that both you and he stir up—it would be prudent to repair him and allow him to function intact."

Piper swallowed. "You have such an odd way of speaking, Dr. Sheilor. As if he's some kind of machine."

She cocked her head. "But he is. Organic creatures are machines in their own right. They have operating parameters that must be respected, and they have fail dates. Organics originate via natural reproduction. That's the key distinction. Mechanical machines are constructed in factories." She studied Piper's face. "But make no mistake: we are all machines."

Sheilor nodded at the soldiers and two of them sprang into action. One removed Piper's cuffs, and the other unclasped her shackles.

She rubbed her wrists and stretched. "Thank you."

"Please," the doctor said, "you need repairs as well. We have detected a serious condition with your knee, along with several deep lacerations on your back and legs. I shall repair them."

Piper hesitated, and her face must have betrayed her, for Sheilor immediately added, "I'm a doctor first, and my only concern is to make you—and anyone else—well. Although I am Protoran, my first responsibility is to the health of the crew and our guests. Please, let's get you on the bed and take care of these breakdowns."

Two of the soldiers took her arms and helped her on the biobed. The doctor eased her down on her back and attached several scanning sensors to her fingers and above her heart. The equipment around the bed hummed and glowed with various biometric readouts.

"Officer, you and your men may leave now."

"Negative, Doctor," the man replied in a gruff voice. "Two of my guards shall remain inside this medical bay at the door. The rest will be outside."

"That isn't necessary," Sheilor said, "but do what you must." She turned her attention back to Piper. "I'm going to give you a spray of our own painkiller, Ms. Madison. You've had something similar before. You'll find this medication more pleasant than the barbaric concoctions available on Asteria."

Piper protested, but Sheilor moved quickly and administered the drug. Within moments, Piper's shoulders relaxed and the pain that flooded her body vanished. At the same time, she remained lucid, feeling no ill effects from the drug.

"This…" she said, staring at the lights on the ceiling and following the drug's effect as it coursed through her limbs, "… is amazing, Doctor. You're right. I wish we had this on Asteria."

Sheilor cut away Piper's pant leg and bandages around the knee and grimaced. She then removed much of the clothing around her torso and scanned the lacerations and contusions. Finally, the doctor leaned over Piper's face and, with the tip of her organic fingers, pinched the skin along her forehead and cheeks, scanning with her ocular orb.

Admittedly, the attention shown to her face unnerved Piper, but she had no reason to doubt the doctor's practices, and in fact, appreciated the thoroughness of the examination.

"We'll begin with the patella, Ms. Madison. It is of deepest concern to me. I won't know if I can restore it properly until I expose the joint and have a better look.

"Will you put me out for that?"

Sheilor chuckled, "Oh, no. You'll be wide awake. But you won't feel a thing with the local anesthetic on it."

The doors to the medical bay hissed open and heavy bootsteps filled the room. "Well, well, well!" the unmistakable, unnatural voice of Scyther bellowed. "Doctor, how is our young patient?"

The Protoran leader approached the side of the biobed. Piper turned her head the other way.

"I'm preparing to repair her knee right away, my Lord. We'll address the lacerations and bruising too, but I don't foresee any lasting complications, as long as there aren't any surprises in that joint." Sheilor pointed to the damaged leg.

"Splendid," Scyther growled. "And I understand the captain is in surgery as well?"

Sheilor did not respond. Instead, she continued with her examination and ran several other sensors over Piper's body.

Scyther continued. "Funny thing about that captain friend of yours, Piper Madison. Do you know what he was up to before coming to Robos 7?"

She knew enough about game theory to leave the Protoran to his own imagination, so rather than engage in conversation, she turned to face him and scowled.

"I'll save you the suspense." The man's hard lips quivered. "Your friend has been a busy man. Why, he undertook to rescue someone from prison on Asteria. Can you imagine that? And not just anyone, Piper."

She couldn't stop her curiosity, but fear consumed her. Scyther refused to speak, choosing to hover with that half-snarl of his.

"Who did he rescue?" she asked. And a familiar dread flashed through her heart. *It couldn't be...* She tried moving, but the painkiller prevented her from doing any more than shifting on the biobed.

"Ah yes! Sheilor," he said, addressing the doctor, "I believe our guest has figured it out."

"Don't say it, Scyther," Piper pleaded.

"Eventually, everyone in the Torfinn Galaxy will know, so I may as well tell you now. Not only did Carstairs break her out from the maximum security prison..."

"No... please..."

"... but your mother, Tephera Madison, has just been reinstated as Chancellor of the Governing Council. And you have your precious captain to thank for that."

TWENTY-SIX

"LIAR!" PIPER SPAT, STRUGGLING TO RAISE HERSELF FROM the biobed. "Carstairs would never get involved in any of that. And my mother's treachery with the Bortan Administrator ensures the Council would never let her return to power." She was confident about the second point. Not so much about the first.

Scyther folded his arms across his chest. "Well, you're mistaken, Piper Madison, on both counts. Your friend the captain did, indeed, rescue your mother from that hellhole of a prison. Evidently, she had many supporters organizing her escape for some time. It took a man of Carstairs' bravado—or stupidity—to pull it off."

"Lord Scyther," Sheilor interrupted, "my patient is not in a position to be disturbed. Can you not wait until we've repaired her damages?

The Protoran leader sneered. "Perhaps you are right, Doctor," he conceded. "We'll discuss the Chancellor's reinstatement later."

Piper's voice softened. "You lie," she whispered, the new truth dawning on her. "Let me speak with Ambassador Welkin."

Scyther grabbed an overhead monitor and swung it over the biobed. He ordered Sheilor to raise the bed so Piper could see the viewer. "You wish to confirm all this with the lizard queen, do you? How about this… I'll do you one better. Let's get your mother on the comms, shall we? Would speaking directly with her convince you?"

Piper's mouth opened, but the words refused to come. Scyther summoned a nearby underling and, working from a communications station in the medical bay, he established contact with the Torfinn Galaxy Governing Council.

Her heart sank as the stark realization of the truth smacked her. *How the hell did Carstairs' get mixed up in this?* Her thoughts returned to the cockpit refuge chamber, and the captain, who was unable to speak coherently. He kept muttering about her mother. She initially dismissed it as gibberish, but now questioned that assessment.

"My Lord, we have established communications with the Chancellor's office."

"Wonderful," Scyther said. "Open the comms and let's see who's there, shall we?"

The image on the screen flickered. Piper stared at it, hoping against all hope that Scyther was wrong and simply messing with her mind. But when the video stabilized, a nauseous wave inundated her. The person appearing on the monitor was not one of the Ambassador's aides; rather, it was Eebek, the Delaran, her mother's loyal former assistant.

Then, Tephera Madison stepped into view, dressed in her ceremonial Chancellor's outfit, standing erect in front of her familiar office, with a smug countenance reeking of self-satisfaction.

"Hello, Piper," she said in a thin voice. *"Despite our many differences, I am honestly happy to see you again.*

You bring me such joy."

Piper swallowed hard. The last time she met her mother in that prison cell, the woman had been humiliated and mistreated... a feral version of her erstwhile self. She seemed better now, albeit not healthy. She'd lost a lot of weight, and her hair ran askew, despite obvious efforts to make her up.

But her mother's eyes struck her the most. Clear and forever evaluating her surroundings. Full of confidence, and something else Piper could only describe as a cold desire for vengeance.

"You look well, Mother. But... what is going on? Where's Ambassador Welkin?"

Tephera smirked. *"The Erusian reptile remains here on the Council, but she has relinquished her post as interim Chancellor. Seems she wasn't quite up to the task and as a result, all hell broke loose in the cluster of planets, including the mess you left on Robos 7."* She scowled, waiting for a response. Piper refused to give her the pleasure of that moment.

"As you can see, the vast majority of Council members finally came to their senses, granting me a full pardon and reinstating me."

"I don't believe that," Piper said, biting her lip.

"My mandate is clear," the Chancellor added, ignoring her. *"I've been asked to re-establish order and peace to the Torfinn Galaxy, and return life to the way it was before you and your friend Carstairs poked your noses into other people's affairs."*

The combination of painkillers and the shock of seeing her mother ruling again caused her to slump on the bed and turn away from the monitor. But Tephera wouldn't surrender this moment easily.

"I understand, Piper, that the Protorans have offered to stabilize Robos 7. Not a small task given the chaos there,

but the Council approved Lord Scyther's proposed Breeder Protocol to maintain order in exchange for the reproduction farms and access to Hand organics. This will allow their people to thrive and survive. Win-win."

Piper glanced at the Protoran leader gloating beside her.

"Now, listen carefully to me, love."

She turned back to the monitor. Her mother had moved closer to the camera.

"What is it?"

"You remember I suggested you join me once... before the troubles with the Bortans?"

Piper stiffened.

"That offer still stands. And before you dismiss it outright, hear what I have to say. You come from an amazing set of parents. Your father ran Robos 7 for decades and, with much success, transformed the planet from a backwater to a prized industrial jewel in the galaxy. And you already know what I've accomplished as Chancellor of the Council over the years."

"What are you getting at?" Piper groaned.

"I'm trying to say that you possess natural skills and abilities. You have demonstrated those ever since you graduated from the ATI. Undoubtedly, Lord Scyther also recognizes your natural leadership, too."

"Indeed," the Protoran said, "your seed, Chancellor, has proved her worth as a formidable foe."

Tephera's voice changed, becoming more acute and directed. "Piper, I want you by my side to bring structure and stability to the entire Torfinn Galaxy. With your skills and my experience, we can accomplish great things together. In fact, I believe you recognize this to be your true destiny. You were born to lead, love. And I don't mean some ridiculous science team. I'm talking about the future of the Galaxy. To maintain the Madison rule here. To *continue bringing peace and prosperity to all the planets."* She attempted a warm smile without success. *"Would you at least consider it? It would make me so proud."*

Piper lay back down. Seeing her mother standing in her ante-chamber again proved challenging enough after the encounter with Zadicus Verman. But now, suggesting that she *belonged* in this powerful position, maintaining the status quo? How could she possibly accept the predestination to follow in her mother's footsteps? Yet, for some reason unknown to her, the need of her cruel mother's love set her on fire.

Dr. Sheilor broke the silence. "Lord Scyther... Chancellor... I must insist that you continue this conversation later. My patient requires surgery and rest."

Tephera glared at the doctor. *"Fine. Contact my office when she's feeling better. In the meantime, I'll prepare the ground work for Piper's integration with the Council."*

The screen flicked off. Piper stared at the overhead lights, numbed by the conversation. As long as her mother ruled the Council, the rest of the planets would remain under her authority. And for a moment, Piper yielded to the thought of joining her mother, and envisioned herself working beside her, restoring the Galaxy to its previous glory. More significantly, influencing the future direction of the cluster. Instead of despising the prospect, she eerily saw herself enjoying the lure of power. And of her mother's pride.

SCYTHER ANNOUNCED HE HAD MATTERS TO ATTEND TO on the bridge, and rushed from the medical bay. The room grew quiet, except for the hum and pings of the churning machines surrounding Piper's biobed.

She peeked toward the entrance at the two guards on duty. The Protoran painkiller affected her body with numbing, strange sensations, leaving her fully awake yet in a dream-like state. The pain—especially in her knee—had disappeared, but the side-effect was paralyzing. She wouldn't be able to stand even if her life depended on it. So taking on those sentries was out of the question.

"How are you feeling, Ms. Madison?"

Dr. Sheilor brushed up beside her and sat on a stool. She glanced at the monitoring devices and graphics surrounding the bed.

"I can't move, Doctor, but there is no pain." She bit her lip. "Except for... you know."

Sheilor's organic mouth and chin frowned. "I cannot understand what this sequence of events with the Chancellor has done to your emotional health, Ms. Madison. Since we cannot reproduce, our relationships are not like yours. We cannot grasp the concept of parental anxiety, for example."

Piper exhaled. "Has it always been that way?"

"You mean, could Protorans reproduce at some point in the past?" She thought a moment as if searching for information. "Nothing in my data banks suggests we could ever reproduce in the conventional way. Instead, we only remember being part machine and part organic. Effective functioning necessitates their interdependence. Perhaps we're all artifacts of whoever first created us."

"One day, you may change that," Piper said. Then, switching the subject, she added, "Have you heard anything about the captain's surgery?"

Sheilor's oculars flicked. "His internal functions have been repaired, and his arm is close to full restoration. Carstairs will need to rest for a short time to recover, but then he'll be as good as new. Better, in fact."

"That's a relief," Piper said. "Promise me you won't use his limbs for regeneration?"

The doctor demurred. "I cannot do that. Those decisions are not mine to make. My role is to perform the surgeries."

Something in the way Sheilor's voice sounded confused Piper, almost as if she regretted her duty.

"Doctor, have you truly exhausted all alternatives to harvesting organics? I mean, the ATI on Asteria, and many other institutions, make scientific advancements all the time. Have they looked into your needs?"

Sheilor stood and adjusted the sensor on Piper's abdomen. "Scyther says we have. He has received no cooperation from the other planets. Even when your mother ran the Council before her imprisonment, the members refused to help us despite her support." She stroked Piper's tummy with her organic fingers, pressing lightly here and there.

Sheilor leaned in close. "We're not all as single-minded as Scyther. We require a constant supply of organics, yet some find the idea of ceasing to exist intriguing, not frightening."

"Are you talking about yourself?" Piper asked.

"Sometimes, yes, Ms. Madison."

"Call me, Piper."

The doctor wavered a moment, then said, "Thank you. I am Sheilor. I do not worry about the end, whatever that means, because my brain is mechanical. Many of my parts are organic. I might be bothered more if I had offspring, like Asterians do. But I will simply stop functioning one day when the flesh runs out. My memories and experiences will remain on a memory chip and become part of our archives." She shrugged. "And that will be that."

Piper considered the Protoran predicament. She convinced herself that a solution must exist somewhere in the realm of synthetics, or perhaps in developing even more sophisticated mechanics that could offer the Protorans a life as full androids. Either way, they could find an alternative path to what it means to live. And if she joined her mother, then…

"Scyther cares deeply for all Protorans. Their well-being is what drives him, Piper. But when you're as imperiled as we are, fighting for everything we cherish, you can only think about cutting your way out. By force. I'm confident that if a realistic alternative existed, he'd abandon these farms and the Hands. But once his mind's made up, and he sees no alternative…" The doctor grimaced and moved toward a nearby lab counter.

"Sounds a lot like Jay Carstairs," Piper mused. "Perhaps we share more similarities than we realize."

Sheilor returned, clutching something in her hand. "As soon as the surgeon finishes repairing the captain, he will come here to fix your knee and other ailments. It won't take much longer. Meantime," Sheilor held out her palm, "can you tell me what this is?"

The faint blue whisper stone in her fingers glowed.

Piper gulped. The stone picked up something, causing it to glimmer that way, but she felt nothing… heard nothing. Perhaps the painkiller blocked reception, or the strength of whatever message hummed through the gem was too weak. Regardless, she didn't want it falling into Protoran hands. They may not have a use for the stone given their reliance on mechanics, but they could auction it off on the black market for untold riches.

"It's a good luck charm, Sheilor," she said. "I found it in one of my travels and I like the iridescence of it, so I kept it in my pocket for luck."

The doctor raised an organic eyebrow. "I can tell from your bio-signs that you are not telling the truth."

Piper blushed and tried a different tack. "I don't know what it is. But again, I find the colour soothing. That's all."

Sheilor turned the specimen around in her fingers, then brought it close to her ocular implant. "Interesting composition," she murmured. "Incomprehensible to me, but I think this stone has value to you, given your deception."

The two doors hissed open and a short Protoran entered, also wearing a dark surgical coat. His face contained no organics, and his ocular eye sockets glowed a deep orange. He ignored all formalities. "Is the patient prepared?"

"Yes," Sheilor said. "I'm sending you the data on her left patella." She blinked, then turned to Piper. "We shall address this magic stone later." She returned it to a tray on the lab counter.

And in that physical distance between the biobed and the worktable, no more than five meters, she began hearing the words, the sounds, the hum of the stone. She picked up readings, faint ones, but from whom? Carstairs? She concentrated harder, pushing the effect of the painkiller from her mind. No, these utterances were unlike any other and came from someone else.

Sheilor!

And they caused Piper to shiver with fear.

TWENTY-SEVEN

SCYTHER MARCHED INTO HIS COMMUNICATIONS ROOM
and sat at the head of a small table. Two of his bridge officers
joined him—Commander Wesling, and his Comms
Officer—for this three way meeting with Chancellor
Madison and the Captain of the Asterian Battle Fleet
flagship, *Nightingale*.

Several minutes passed while they established the
necessary links. The *Nightingale*'s commander, a one-
armed fellow named Phact, stood before his command chair
on the ship's bridge, reading a handheld device. To Scyther,
the man appeared agitated, shifting his weight, nervously
gazing around. Not how he expected a fleet captain to
behave.

"We should offer to replace that man's missing arm,"
the Protoran leader announced to his officers. "As an act of
goodwill."

The two men grunted.

When the Chancellor's link opened, she appeared in

her ante-chamber alone, and said, *"Gentlemen, I assume you know each other by name if not by face. Let's get down to business. Lord Scyther, what's the current status of the uprising on Robos 7?"*

"Chancellor," Scyther spoke, standing. "This planet continues to experience some upheaval, but I'm pleased to report that most of the rogue factions within Edenfall have either pledged themselves to Governor Larrin and joined him, or else they have been captured and tagged for the harvest."

Tephera Madison worked her jaw, demonstrating no emotion whatsoever. *"You have already begun transporting Hands to Protor to satisfy your most urgent requirements?"*

"That is correct, Chancellor. The creatures are particularly useful in addressing our needs. They are comfortable with lives of servitude, so their docility is a welcome relief from some uppity Heads—and others— we've had to deal with."

"What about the reproduction farms?" she asked.

Scyther accessed the latest reports from the land and replied, "Unfortunately, the facilities remain under rebel control. We have also detected pockets of guerrilla activity in the area, but this won't last much longer. I have sent a squadron of vipers and a transport ship with soldiers into the region. As soon as we're ready, we will secure those operations."

"Well done," the Chancellor pronounced. *"Tell me… have you located Ariel Graves yet? My reports suggest many on Robos 7 regard her as the true Governor. Not this Larrin worm."*

"She remains in hiding."

"I see. Word to the wise, Scyther… find her quickly, and make sure she never sees the Governor's mansion again. Do you understand me?"

"Completely."

"Excellent." She raised a data slate and studied it for a few seconds, then turned her attention to Captain Phact. *"Good to see you again, Captain."*

"Thank you, Chancellor. You seem well."

She smirked. *"You are too kind, but let's dispense with the greetings. ABF surveillance of the situation continues, and I understand you still uphold the Ethical Protocol. Tell me, from your perspective, how secure is the Fairfield Sector?"*

The commander grimaced. Scyther detected more on the man's face than he revealed.

"Chancellor, we feel the region is protected now that the Protoran armada controls Robosian space, and operations on the planet's surface are stabilizing. However," he added while pacing toward the screen, *"the situation here remains volatile. I don't share Scyther's confidence about quelling the rebel factions. And we have detected increased activity on Borta, suggesting they may be preparing for an intervention of their own."*

The relentless fussing is the problem with this one-armed Asterian, Scyther thought. *And now he vies for influence with our only hope for survival.*

"Captain Phact, we share an extensive personal history together. I know you wouldn't state your concerns to me if you had not addressed them with due consideration. I appreciate that."

The commander bowed.

"That said," Tephera continued, *"these times are fluid. My primary task is to restore order to the galaxy, and I count on your backing."*

"Of course, Chancellor."

"Good. Then this is how we shall proceed." She glanced at her slate again and turned to face the Protoran leader. *"Lord Scyther, the Council has clarified its approval of your proposal and reiterates its desire to have you support*

Governor Larrin as he restores order on Robos 7. You understand the only measure of success is to quash the factions, repair the air scrubbers in and around Edenfall, and to ensure the farms continue to run efficiently."

"Yes, Chancellor," Scyther answered, satisfied that she and the Council would allow him to protect his people.

"And Captain Phact, despite my deep respect for you, I don't share your concerns about the Sector. In fact," she said, referencing the slate, "I'm ordering you and the fleet to return to Asteria immediately. The Protorans now manage regional security, so you're no longer needed."

"Chancellor," the commander protested, "I must strongly advise against this action. Allow me to make my case for remaining here."

"That won't be necessary, Captain. Trust me, I'm aware of the strategic importance of the sector. However, we are concerned that the core planets, including Asteria, could be vulnerable to attack as long as the ABF remains in Robosian space."

The captain chewed his lip, but kept his protestations to himself.

"And Mr. Phact, I'm also ordering all the patrol ships under your command to retreat to Asteria as well. The sooner our cluster returns to normal, the better our lives will be." She scrutinized the commander. "May I rely on your support, Captain?"

The officer grunted and said, "Yes, Chancellor. My loyalties are with you and the Torfinn Council."

"Very good. Gentlemen, let's get back to work."

Phact broke his link first. Before Scyther punched his, the Chancellor added, "Lord Scyther, a word please. In private."

He dismissed his officers and stood in front of the comms screen. "Yes, Chancellor?"

"I'm not much to look at after the abuse I suffered in

that prison, so I may be out of line..." She hardened her lips and continued. *"What has happened to your facial skin?"*

"Ah, that," the Protoran chuckled in his metallic way. "I am scheduled to have it replaced any moment now. Our organics don't last forever, Chancellor, and require constant upgrades. But I assure you, when you see me again, this mess will be gone."

"Glad to hear, Lord Scyther." She ended the transmission, leaving the man alone in the room, contemplating his next steps.

He'd worked his entire life to make the lives of his people better, and more than ever, his attempts were failing. Perhaps there were other solutions he could pursue if he received the Council's full support. But Protorans had lived this way for centuries and built a successful society on Protor. To Scyther, it seemed blasphemous to reject all that now, despite the recent difficulties in securing the much-coveted organics.

But that will all change.

His internal comms pinged. "Yes, Sheilor?"

"Ms. Madison's knee has been repaired. We are ready for your facial enhancement operation, Liege."

"Good," he said, tugging the peeling skin from his face. "But before anything else, I need to look into the siege at the reproduction facilities. I'll come as soon as I am able."

PIPER REMAINED PROPPED UP FOR THE DURATION OF THE operation on her knee. The other surgeon cleaned out the mess from the Second Point outpost, and in practically no time, even repaired the extensive muscle and ligament damage throughout the joint. The only words he muttered during the operation were, "No need for any, Sheilor."

Dr. Sheilor assisted in the operation and, once she melded Piper's skin incisions, she asked, "Can you bend it?"

She struggled to control her knee, reeling under the painkiller's effects. Despite several attempts, Piper could not manipulate the joint.

"That's normal for humanoid creatures," Sheilor said. I will reduce the medicine's effect.

Piper's face flushed at the prospect of feeling the searing wound again, especially post-surgery.

Sheilor said, "Worry not. Most of the pain should be gone now that we've repaired the knee. We'll tackle the lacerations on your body next."

The short surgeon disappeared from the medical bay, leaving Piper and Sheilor alone with the two guards. The doctor administered a second hypo into her arm, and the suppressing drug took effect instantly, allowing her more freedom of movement. Although Piper felt a bit of aching, the pain was nothing like she'd experienced prior to the operation.

"Try moving it again," the doctor said, standing back.

This time, when Piper attempted to flex the joint, she found it moved with no discomfort whatsoever. "How… how can you perform surgery like this and not leave the patient in bed for a week to recover?"

Sheilor beamed. "We have developed and perfected many technological innovations over the years. Perhaps one day we'll share them with your doctors."

Piper continued flexing her knee and found that, with the decreased amount of painkiller in her system, she could move her body far more easily. Sheilor stood at the lab counter, tidying up some equipment. Piper inhaled and stated, "Help me convince Scyther to let me return home."

"Pardon?"

"Hear me out. I'm convinced that if the proper attention and resources focused on your regeneration problem, we could solve it without harvesting innocent Hands. I can talk to my mother about it. And I know many medical researchers at the ATI. Listen, they're already working on synthetic skins. If Scyther releases me, I promise to help you."

Sheilor finished up at the work counter and approached her. "But we already have a solution, Piper. The Hands. They are creatures of servitude. Beasts of burden who know no differently. Bred to serve others. We are only giving their lives meaning."

Piper propped herself up on the bed. "That's not true. If you saw them like I do, you wouldn't be saying that. For example, one of my father's servants, Koba, had dreams of being a pilot. He ended up saving our lives. And Dolian, Ariel Graves' husband, is a Hand. He's a master mechanic and a forceful leader of his people. And he likes to draw. Then there are those who mend ships and city infrastructure. Are they really servants? For many decades, they survived under the boot heel of the Heads until their emasculation."

Sheilor stared at her, speechless.

"They aren't animals, Doctor. These are sentient humanoids with dreams and desires of their own."

"Our indigenous creatures were nothing like that," Sheilor countered. "They lacked language, social groups, intelligence. But what you describe is..." Silence filled the room, and she shook her head. "I wondered why those brutes—I mean, those Hands—we used for immediate regeneration were so vocal and emotional."

Piper swung her legs over the side of the biobed. "Help me return to Asteria, Sheilor. I promise you we can find an alternative to harvesting these innocent people."

"It's not that simple," she said. There's more going on here than you realize.

The shocked look on Piper's face must have embarrassed the doctor. She sputtered over an apology. "Sorry, it's my lack of understanding your language, Piper.

Please, I only mean that the politics in play now are unpredictable."

Without warning, spectral words and images drifted through her mind, faint as the echoes of morning dreams. She glanced at the counter where Sheilor left the whisper stone, but saw nothing emanating from its box.

Visions of mechanical servos and electrical circuits flooded Piper's brain, followed by ancient, dusty memories of a little girl playing in rain puddles. *Could these somehow be Sheilor's thoughts? And were the images of the child remnants of various organics she'd used over the decades?*

"Sheilor," she asked, "do Protorans dream?"

The doctor approached the biobed and said, "I don't understand what that means. Sure, I understand the word's *meaning*, but I lack firsthand experience. None of us dreams." She cocked her head. "Why do you ask?"

"Just wondering. I thought you might want to leave this life behind and help me find a different solution to Protor's crisis."

Sheilor exhaled and said, "That's something only you fully organic creatures do. When Protorans sleep, we regenerate. It's a kind of full body cleanse, securing new power for the mechanics, rest for the organics. The way you think of dreaming is not what I can imagine."

"What I call a dream, you refer to as a goal. Let me go," she said. "Come with me. Let's work on the goal together."

Sheilor's eye flashed. "You make it sound tempting. I have always enjoyed the research aspect of medicine. But as long as Scyther leads our people and needs me, I could never abandon him. And as long as I need you, I cannot let you go."

The doors hissed open, and both Sheilor and Piper turned. A pair of guards entered the surgery, followed by Captain Carstairs, walking with a slight limp but otherwise healthy. Another two soldiers brought up the rear. The lead guard approached the doctor and said, "He insisted on seeing the young woman here. Wouldn't stop prattling on about her. I trust his presence is okay with you?"

"Of course, but keep your men nearby. We cannot afford to lose this fellow."

Carstairs stepped toward the biobed wearing a sheepish grin. His pale skin appeared clammy. "Hey, Mads," he said. "Can we talk?"

TWENTY-EIGHT

PIPER'S HEAD WHIRLED IN A CONFUSED TANGLE OF emotions. Carstairs almost looked like his old self, except for the awkward gait and sallow face. Compared to the broken man she found in the *Dauntless* wreckage, the one standing before her proved miracles existed.

Yet, at the same time, this madness about helping her mother escape the maximum security prison outside Capital City... was he truly involved in that? In her mind, no reason in the galaxy could justify that action.

Carstairs remained a couple paces away from the biobed. Everything had changed between them, Piper realized, and it seemed he understood that, too. His inner thoughts began flooding her mind, and she ignored them as much as possible.

"The first thing I owe you is an apology," he said in a low voice. "I have no excuses for my behaviour." He collected his thoughts and continued. "And I won't insult you by trying to justify what I did. Leaving you at the hospital like that… completely unacceptable." He snorted. "You should've heard old Quirp give me the gears about that."

Piper remained stoic, scrutinizing the man's face. She saw the pain behind his eyes, the shame and guilt oozing from his pores. And she knew the words tumbling over each other in his mind. Regardless, some things cannot be undone with a simple apology, no matter how heart-felt.

"Anyway," he continued, "the least I can offer instead of a poor excuse is an explanation."

His innermost thoughts fought through her consciousness and, to assuage her embarrassment, she increased her effort to block them out. But the whisper stone on the counter had other ideas, just like it did on Hauntor when it urged her to contact Ariel. The words Carstairs spoke floundered in comparison to the cruel honesty and passion she read in his mind, and in that moment, she knew his own trauma prevented him from coming clean… from becoming completely honest with her.

Could he ever say the words? Did he have the emotional maturity to even *understand* the words wrestling each other in his head?

Probably not.

Perhaps he was only capable of being exactly who he was, warts and all, and nothing more.

Piper clenched her jaw. Despite his flaws and weaknesses—and there were many—she ached to be by his side while he dealt with his own demons.

But regardless of the current circumstances, his inability to come clean was no foundation for a stable, long-term relationship. She could love this man without being with him, without enabling his questionable behaviour, without having to accept his unpredictability.

"I'm sorry," she said. "I missed much of that."

Carstairs stepped forward. "Piper, I had to leave, and I

refused to respond to your messages because I didn't know how to react. I hoped to, maybe…"

"Hoped to *what*, Jay?" she asked, searching his face.

He offered her nothing more than an apologetic gawk and shrugged.

The whisper stone left nothing to her imagination. She read his thoughts—all of them—the hurtful and the tender ones, the raw and the civil. The confused and the clear. The truth caused her to blush and her heart pounded. "Say the words, Carstairs. No more guessing games. Say the damn words."

He exhaled, as if debating within his mind, before locking eyes with her. "I can't. I don't know how."

She regarded him with a face of stone. She knew the words he wrestled with, sensed the internal struggle underway in his gut. But she wouldn't bail him out of this. He needed to be honest with her, and with himself.

He had to say them all.

He opened his mouth to speak. "I suppose you heard about your mother taking over the Council again."

"I have."

"And how I helped with that."

"I do now." She quelled the rising disappointment in her chest as he abandoned his emotions.

"My decision to accept a contract with the Black Bond cartel to open up the trade routes wasn't the best one I've made. And I had no idea it would lead to her grabbing power from Welkin. But yes, I rescued her. In my mind, I believed the Torfinn Galaxy needed stability and a firm hand to guide it. And if the Council put safeguards in place to keep her under control, perhaps it would allow Robos 7 to achieve peace."

"I see."

"What you may not know, Piper, is that I couldn't finish the job."

That's the confusing part in his mind.

"What are you talking about?" The spectral stone suddenly grew silent. She glanced over at the lab counter and saw Sheilor handling it, staring at the gem.

"After freeing her from prison, I left her in the rain. I contacted her supporters and told them where she was, but I couldn't complete the mission. Looking back, I see how much of a coward I was."

He took another step forward until he stood above her.

"But it crystallized something for me, Mads."

"What's that?" she asked, gazing up, urging her body to relax, now struggling to hear his inner thoughts when moments earlier, she wanted to block them.

"I don't know the right words. I'm not a poet. But I think I know what you're feeling."

Piper reached out and took his hand. It was cold and clammy. "Tell me, Jay," she managed to say.

He cleared his throat. "You see, I went through the same thing with my old man."

"What are you talking about?"

"Listen, I knew an older lady once who was taken off-planet and abandoned as a small child at some remote outpost. When I knew her, she was constantly looking for her mother. She finally find her on Coomus... used to fly out to her house every week, a long flight in her old beat up shuttle. She had hardly any credits to her name, yet she cleaned her mother's entire house for her, over and over again, to get just one thing."

Piper searched his eyes, wondering where he was going with this distraction. "What was that?"

He shrugged. "Her approval. The mother never once gave her an ounce of affection, not a thank you or a hug. Never once told her how proud she was of her. Still she went on cleaning. Tragic in a way, but children need their parents so much, even if they hurt them. Even if they're evil."

How was it possible to hate and love a man at the same time? He couldn't say the words she wanted to hear; instead, he stabbed her with a truth dagger to the heart.

Bastard...

Piper pulled him closer, kissed his cheek, and whispered in his ear. "We'll talk more later, but first, we have to send these Protorans packing."

Carstairs narrowed his gaze. "So, what are we waiting for?"

TWENTY-NINE

SOMETHING WASN'T QUITE RIGHT.

Carstairs stood in the medical bay, flexing his fingers and working his repaired elbow joint, while Dr. Sheilor scanned Piper's torso for what seemed like the tenth time.

But this repair job…

In his hazy recollection of being transported from the planet's surface to the *Volantis*, he dreamed that his right arm had been crushed when the *Dauntless* slammed into Robos 7. A mass of blood and splintered bone, with nothing recognizable except for broken fingers poking out from his jacket like mangled hickory twigs.

He told himself he was dreaming.

Perhaps he wasn't.

How did the surgeon repair this mess so quickly and effectively? How could he…

A sickening thought blossomed in his head. He steadied himself against an unoccupied biobed.

"Are you alright, Captain Carstairs?" Dr. Sheilor left

Piper's side and eased him to a sitting position on the bed. "Sometimes," she said, "post-operative complications are delayed. I'll scan you for any such abnormalities."

"That's not it, Doctor," he replied, biting his lip. "Tell me... whose arm did this belong to? Was it a Hand prisoner?"

"No, Captain. We didn't use any of those organics. They are too valuable to waste on..." She frowned.

He inspected his forearm and the fingers in particular. The digits were perfect in both size and shape. He glanced at Sheilor. Rage boiled in his chest. "No, not organic. This is a... a *mechanical* arm."

Two of the guards slipped in front of the doctor and steadied their weapons.

Sheilor scowled at them before saying, "Captain, I urge you to remain calm. We don't want these fighters complicating matters."

He agreed and settled on the biobed. But the armed men remained close by.

"Listen to me," she continued. "When they brought you in, you were barely alive. The combination of internal damage and extensive bleeding from your arm caused your heart to weaken. The surgeon repaired your internal organs and stabilized your breathing, but what remained of your limb was irreparable. Captain, there was nothing left to work with."

Carstairs flexed his wrist and elbow. "So I wasn't dreaming about the accident."

"We had no option but to attach an artificial limb... one that fits you and allows you to carry on with a normal life."

"It feels completely real," he said, pinching the synthetic skin. "Like, I don't even know it's fake."

Sheilor scanned the appendage. "Protorans have been doing this for a long time. We have a lot of knowledge to offer the other planets."

"And it feels much stronger."

"Up to twenty times more powerful than your human arm. Perhaps that might be beneficial in your travels."

Carstairs glanced at Piper. She now stood beside her bed, staring at the overhead monitors and holding her torso. "Everything okay over there, Mads?"

She faced the doctor. Horror covered her face. "Sheilor, why have you been..." she pointed to the monitor. "Why are you scanning my uterus?"

Before the doctor could answer, Carstairs clenched his jaw and tested out the strength of his new arm by launching a mechanical fist at the guards who escorted him to the surgery.

They didn't see a thing coming. And because he caught them gawking at Piper, the blow sent the pair sprawling across the floor. One dropped his weapon and Carstairs scooped it up, attacking the remaining soldiers stationed in the bay with wild, powerful swings of the gun's butt end. Another man prepared to fire at him when Sheilor intervened.

"No!" she shouted. "He must remain undamaged!"

This gave Carstairs time to raise his weapon, confronting the soldier. "You can't kill me, Gearhead," he said, "but that rule doesn't apply to me." He aimed at the man's legs and fired, slicing him down, and sending him buckling to the floor. Then he grabbed the soldier's gun and tossed it to Piper.

The doctor pleaded with her. "Piper... you don't understand. I need you here."

Her face turned ugly with rage and she pointed the gun at Sheilor. "You were examining my reproductive organs. Why?"

"Please, I must study them. Surely, you understand," the doctor begged.

"Well, I don't." Piper adjusted the intensity strip. She grit her teeth and muttered, "I hope this doesn't kill you."

The energy beam knocked the Protoran flying against the bulkhead, where she crumpled, spilling the contents of the lab counter.

"Come on," Carstairs urged. "We'll have company soon enough. Let's go!"

"Just a minute," she said, sorting through the scattered mess beside the work table.

"Piper, we gotta go..."

She cursed under her breath, kicked at the clutter and joined him.

They approached the entrance, sprang open the double doors—surprising a pair of confused guards stationed there—and sent them away in an energy-induced, stunned sleep. Carstairs glanced up and down the corridor. No other troops yet, but he knew their luck wouldn't last much longer.

"Quick," he said, "to the hangar." He began moving along the deck.

Piper remained in place. "No, Jay."

He stopped and turned.

"Listen, I'm more useful here on the ship. I'll feed a virus into the networks and computer systems. Cause some havoc here while you take care of matters on the planet. The machine men are occupying the reproduction farms. They have to be stopped. Find Dolian and help him."

"Forget it. We need to stick together. I didn't come all the way out here just to abandon you again."

She shook her head. "My staying here is best for disabling the *Volantis*. Go steal a viper and support the fighters."

Running boots echoed in the corridor, growing louder.

"Go!" she said, ducking back inside the clinic.

Carstairs bolted once the med bay doors hissed closed. He raced toward the hangar, taking out a shocked lone guard along the way. When he entered the launch deck, Protorans crawled throughout the area. Some performed maintenance on a trio of vipers. Others loaded a cargo scow. He glanced around and found what he needed... a viper standing by near the loading dock.

The Protoran mechanics stopped and watched him with curiosity, unsure of how to react. His appearance came as an enormous surprise, and they didn't immediately recognize something must have gone horribly wrong in the med bay. Before they figured it out, Carstairs blanketed the area with a wide swath of low-intensity energy beams, stunning them all. Several workers slid off the vessels and landed in a heap on the metal grating. Others slumped over or collapsed onto the bulkheads.

Carstairs sprinted across the bay and leapt into the warming viper. He studied the cockpit and recognized the various common elements that all Torfinn ships possessed. Once he isolated the main thruster ignition, his operational intuition of the ship's functions kicked in. He raised the vessel off the deck, positioned it in front of the massive launch doors, and fired an energy burst at them until they cracked open, sucking everything into space that hadn't been tied down.

Including the unlucky, stunned Protorans.

The viper slipped from the hangar into the black. He floated along with the other ships, bodies and debris until he cleared the launch. With the flick of a helm switch, Carstairs engaged the main power drive, and the combat craft screamed away from the *Volantis*.

The big ship soon opened fire on him, but he evaded their volleys through random course micro-corrections. He avoided the nearby armada in orbit by diving straight toward the planet and easing his angle of descent just before entering the Robosian atmosphere.

His first stop, if he didn't get blasted out of the sky by the gearheads, was the Moaning Bones mine site. He sat back in the flight seat and admired his new mechanical arm.

"Maybe this is okay after all."

PIPER STEPPED OVER THE BODIES OF SEVERAL STUNNED Protoran guards. Dr. Sheilor remained unconscious, slumped by the wall near the biobeds. A row of closets and cabinets stood tall against the far bulkhead, and she unlatched one, holding her weapon close, and ducked inside just as the doors to the medical bay whisked open.

The muffled sound of footsteps running throughout the clinic reached her, along with incoherent muttering. Sweat poured down her cheeks in the dark, stifling closet. A soldier began searching through the storage compartments, slamming the doors open and closed. Piper gripped the stock of her weapon and held her breath as he came closer. But an amplified, artificial voice shouted, "Leave this! Follow me."

More movement. Heavy boots stomping away. The sounds dissipated into the corridor, and the facility grew silent again, save for the familiar chimes and tones of the medical equipment.

Piper cracked the door and crept out. The soldiers had all left. Only the unconscious guards that Carstairs fought remained. And Dr. Sheilor.

She glanced at the bodies on the floor and realized the best way to hide was to disappear in plain sight by becoming a soldier herself.

Piper rifled through the open closets, searching for spare Protoran uniforms and coverings. But all she found was surgical clothing, stacks of various circuits in boxes, and some extra medical equipment. Nothing that could remake her into one of *them*.

Cold sweat collected on her forehead. She'd have no other choice than to strip parts from a soldier. The man crumpled on the floor near Carstairs' biobed wore a full face protective mask. Piper approached him and, before she dismantled the head covering, she spied a doorway leading off the main bay.

Curiosity got the better of her, and she abandoned the soldier and headed for the door. It opened into a walk-in storage room stuffed with mechanical body parts. Arms and legs of various sizes hung from metal bars like sides of meat. Picking through them caused Piper's stomach to twist. They weighed a lot more than she imagined. As she pushed through the macabre selections, looking for disguises, the limbs swayed behind her as if suddenly alive.

At the back of the supply area, shelves lined the wall. She ripped through them and discovered boots, leggings, and full sets of uniforms, including protective masks. She quickly stripped, found an outfit in her size, and turned into a Protoran. Next, she buried her own clothing underneath a pile of jackets and slipped out of the room.

A fallen soldier began stirring and sat up. *Here's the test,* she thought. She gripped her flux gun and marched right by him out the double doors, then waited. The man never flinched, and did not follow.

She learned as a youngster to avoid consequences from the most outlandish activities by performing them in the open. Stealing furniture from the Council chambers, for example. Or taking a ship without permission when she attended a seminar on Coomus. This was no different.

Piper marched down the corridor until she came to the portal marked with the Torfinn communications symbol. After glancing both ways, she stepped inside.

Dim lighting bathed the Hub. The main console sat against the opposite wall, and a smooth table occupied the center space. She located a control panel near the door and activated the full lights. The mask she wore had little in the way of ventilation, so she pulled that back off her face.

Communications systems were usually well-protected given the type of information that often flowed through them. Nothing like weapons or life support, but secure nonetheless. She accessed the network and identified the input to the underlying electronic codes and protocols soon enough, but accessing them proved much more difficult. Her training in deep space comms helped her navigate through the outer firewalls, and then she found exactly what she needed: a low-level power access port.

After tracing the circuit path on the monitor, she keyed in an over-riding code to introduce a virus into the ship's networks—one that would lay dormant until the bridge pressed the *Volantis* into action. Then, all primary operations would cease. Shortly thereafter, life support for the Protoran organics would fail, and the heavy cruiser's loss of power would send it tumbling toward Robos 7.

The sound of boots running through the corridor startled her. Piper grabbed her firearm and faced the door, but the troops didn't stop.

A few minutes later, she'd created the viral code and prepared to launch it into the network. But before she pushed it through, a series of feeds at the top of the monitor caught her attention. Each had a label: Corridor. Bridge. Weapons Bay. Hangar. Torfinn Council.

That last one gave her pause.

She clicked on the feed and the blue and white cluster symbol appeared, along with a record of previous connections. The most recent link was marked "Chancellor's Office". Piper licked her lips. The temptation to open the connection to her mother's workplace teased her. But if she established contact, what would she say? What *could* she say? Carstairs little story floated through her mind.

More shouts and a flurry of movement in the corridor filled the room, but she ignored it all, focusing instead on contacting her mother, and imploring her to end this madness on Robos 7 by revoking Protoran access to the Hands and the reproduction farms. She needed an alternative solution, one that wouldn't jeopardize her mother's standing. The thin assurance Piper could offer the Chancellor—namely, joining her—held a bag full of possibilities, but no guarantees.

Still, she could speak with her in private before unleashing the virus and shutting everything down.

A round symbol on the screen opened the link. Piper swallowed hard, reached out, and hit the button.

THIRTY

SCYTHER SCOWLED THE ONLY WAY HE KNEW HOW: BY stretching his organic lips back across the mottled skin around his mouth and baring his metallic teeth. He rode the elevator from the bridge to the main deck, marched down the corridor, pushing Protoran guards aside, and barged into the medical bay.

The sight enraged him. He adjusted the fluid levels coursing through his circuits and circulatory system to control his anger. Half a dozen soldiers occupied the biobeds and benches. One lay on his back receiving treatment from Sheilor who, to his mind, could barely remain upright herself.

"Status of these men, Doctor?"

Sheilor responded without shifting her attention from the injured patient. "Mostly stun injuries. The lot by the door will be fine shortly. Those two on the bench have additional wounds to their organic arms, courtesy of Captain Carstairs. And this unit," she said, pointing a microprobe at the man's chest, "may not survive. He has severe damage to his internal circuitry and eighty-three percent of his organics no longer function. I turned off his mechanical systems to repair his limbs, my Liege."

Her clinical approach soothed Scyther's frustration. He hated his inability to process and control these organic emotions he'd picked up somewhere through the generations. But after focusing on the cold, hard equations, he regained his rational demeanour.

"Thank you, Doctor. I am… sorry for having snapped."

Her warm eyes told him everything he needed to know.

Scyther faced the recovering guards and said in a low voice, "Men, return to your squads immediately. We'll discuss how those two escaped—again—in due course."

The Protorans gathered into a single line and staggered out the doorway, leaving only him, Sheilor, and the unresponsive patient in the clinic.

"I'll wait until your work is finished, Sheil," he said, keeping his distance.

Several minutes passed before the doctor set her instruments down and backed away from the biobed. "I've done all I can for now, my Lord, but this soldier may not continue to exist. The internal damage was extensive even before his fight with the captain."

"Thank you." He took her by the arms. "That Carstairs is a tricky organic, but did you hear?"

Confusion spread across her face.

"Well, after leaving this mess, he found a way to the hangar deck, stole a viper, killed a bunch of mechanics by vacuating them into space, and disappeared on Robos 7."

"A remarkable specimen," she said in a monotone voice. "No wonder Piper is attracted to him."

"Indeed. But here's the interesting thing, love."

Scyther paced around the surgery, fingering different pieces of equipment as he walked. "When he left the *Volantis*, he was by himself."

"That means…"

"Yes, Sheilor. Piper Madison remains on board. I've issued a ship-wide search, and when we find her, I shall enjoy peeling away her skin and giving it a new home."

The doctor grabbed a scanning device and applied it to her own organics, focusing on her recently acquired legs. "My Lord, I would like to ask an honest question, and I trust you will be open to it, knowing that my only interest in this conflict is the preservation of our people."

Scyther halted and turned to face her. "Of course. What is it, Sheil?"

She chose her words carefully and said, "Ever since we got mixed up with the Robosians and their internal affairs, nothing but evil has befallen us. Our soldiers are in harm's way. We have made enemies of many rational Heads on the planet. And for what? A handful of organic prisoners? A series of reproduction farms that won't realistically be useful to us for years? And now that Tephera Madison is Chancellor again, well, I feel we've lost whatever sympathy we garnered with the Council under Ambassador Welkin."

Scyther folded his arms across his chest. The only reason the doctor remained unpunished after such clear insubordination was because he respected her opinion above all others. But though he appreciated it, he was not prepared to accept it.

"Doctor, you've been at my side when I begged the Council for help. You remember their reaction. Even with Chancellor Madison's leadership, the members refused to hear us, preferring that we disappear because, one might imagine, we are… *different*." He moved closer to her. "But no more, love. No more. We will control those farms and dominate those infantile Hand prisoners. And in this way, our future shall be secured."

Sheilor placed the scanner back in its holder and lowered her head. "I understand, my Lord. I feel... heard."

He took her in his arms and said, "It won't be forever. Once the planetary government stabilizes and we have what we need, peace will return to Robos 7 and to Protor. This particular moment in history is fluid, unfortunately. And unpredictable." He kissed her lips and whispered, "And once we find Piper Madison, you'll have her limbs to use for regeneration, and I'll have her skin."

The doctor placed her organic hand on his chest. "Scyther," she cooed, "would you mind if I used some of her... other parts, too? For experimentation?"

"My love, you may do whatever you want with the remaining bits after we've harvested what we need."

"Thank you, Liege," she said, stepping away. "Now, I must attend to my patient."

"And I need to find Piper Madison."

In the muted light of the Communications room, Piper waited for the link to be established with her mother's office at the Torfinn Council Chambers on Asteria. Contacting her was a long shot, but she had to try. Finding another solution to aid the Protorans and stabilize the galaxy was crucial.

Besides, she also wanted to explore a potential role at her side, in case it might offer her an opportunity to right some of the many wrongs she'd encountered. Or, if she was truly honest with herself, a way to gain her mother's love.

Several minutes passed without a response. Piper worried that she may run out of time before being discovered. She reached for the kill button on the monitor, but before she pressed it, the screen flashed and the Torfinn insignia appeared. When it flared again, her mother emerged, standing before a large painting of Asteria's two moons. Piper recognized the art from the many times she visited her at work. She always liked that piece.

"What a surprise," the Chancellor said, smiling broadly. *"How are things going on the* Volantis? *"*

Piper leaned toward the monitor. "Mother, I'm sorry. I'm short on time, so I'll be brief.

Tephera's warmth disappeared. *"What have you been up to?"*

"Nothing, but please listen. The Protorans need help finding an alternative to using the Hands as source material for their organics. What they're doing on Robos 7... it's criminal. I want you to reconsider giving Scyther the green light to exploit these people. I'm asking you to make them stop right now, and to find another solution."

The Chancellor tightened her lips in silence.

"I'll help, of course. I know plenty of research scientists at the ATI and throughout the galaxy. If you truly want me to work beside you, this is exactly the kind of thing I'm good at." She stared at the screen, then added, "What do you think?"

Her mother did not answer immediately. Rather, she spent several moments considering the request before responding. *"I appreciate your concern for the people of Robos 7... in particular, your half-sister. But look at what you're asking. That planet is an industrial dung heap. It always has been. The Hands are imbeciles, and the Heads aren't much better."*

"You're wrong," Piper interjected, feeling the heat rise in her chest.

"Let me finish. You see, with few exceptions, the people are redundant. Yet, they take it upon themselves to behave like children who suddenly find themselves alone in a candy store. So off they go, getting uppity, wrecking everything your father built." She sipped from a glass of water and licked her lips before continuing. *"I believe we*

are fortunate the Protorans availed themselves to restore order. And all they ask in return is the organics they require to survive. So answering your question, Piper, no. We will not reconsider allowing them to run that garbage dump."

Piper slumped back, running through various arguments in her head to counter her mother's stubbornness, and realizing that fighting her with logic would prove useless. She'd already decided, and the more Piper belaboured the point, the more her mother became entrenched and recalcitrant.

"Is there anything else?" Tephera asked sharply.

"No," Piper said, "I suppose there isn't."

Suddenly, the Chancellor mused, "Curious about what Carstairs did to me at the prison?"

She sensed a trap, some kind of mind game her mother enjoyed playing. Use an innocent question as bait; then, strike decisively to score a big psychological win.

But she couldn't help herself. She already knew the captain's tale. Perhaps now she'd get a different perspective.

"Tell me," she murmured.

The Chancellor snorted. "The asshole went through all this effort to rescue me from that hell hole. Basically dragged me through tubes and filthy old corridors before escaping on the other side of the walls and fences." She cocked her head. "Do you know what he did next?"

"Took you to a hiding place, I imagine," Piper said, feigning boredom.

"Not quite." Tephera's cheeks reddened as she continued with her story. "He stunned me with one of those thermal flux guns. Me." She tapped her chest, shaking her head. "Then the bastard left me in the woods under a torrential downpour to suffer. And he took off in the shuttle, leaving me wondering if I'd survive. Fortunately, my supporters found me before those useless prison guards did, and they got me the hell out of there."

Filling in the details caused Piper to wonder about a hundred different things, but she had to end the transmission before the Protorans discovered her. "Are you saying Carstairs helped you escape and then abandoned you?"

"That's exactly what he did. Never could finish a job properly, that man. Listen. Come join me in the Council office. There's so much I can teach you, and your skills are needed here. You'll serve the members and the planets far better from Capital City instead of gallivanting around the universe, getting all self-righteous about presumed injustices. I'll contact Scyther and tell him to send you home. How about it?"

Before Piper could answer, the door to the comms hub burst open and half a dozen soldiers poured in, weapons raised. She killed the link moments before they grabbed her, but had no time to release the virus. The one task she needed to perform sat inert and useless in the ship's network.

A heavy set soldier growled, "Piper Madison, you have gone too far this time."

THIRTY-ONE

CARSTAIRS PILOTED THE STOLEN VIPER AROUND THE FAR hemisphere of Robos 7, opposite Edenfall and the Protoran ships patrolling that airspace. As far as he could tell, no vessels from the *Volantis* followed him through the atmosphere, but he knew they'd come looking soon enough. He had to reach Dolian and help dismantle the siege of the farms before his luck ran out.

He flew only a few meters above the planet's surface, maintaining a route that snaked along polluted rivers and mountain ranges until he approached the Moaning Bones mine site. Long before the hills came into visual range, defensive weapons throughout the land opened fire on him. Carstairs studied the cockpit in front of him but had no idea where the ship's shield activations were located.

One of the rebel torpedoes slammed into the viper's tail end, sending it spinning like a top, and slamming in the surface dust on its belly.

When the ship skidded to a halt, he muttered, "I seem

to make a habit of getting shot down on this forsaken planet." The attack craft listed near the mine. He began hitting random switches and buttons on the forward console, hoping to communicate somehow with the rebels, but these ships operated primarily through transceivers built-in to the Protorans' mechanical bodies.

Fighters soon appeared around him, and hammered on the ship's portal. Carstairs opened the door and raised his hands above his head. A gang of armed men peered nervously into the viper.

The captain announced, "It's me, Jay Carstairs of the *Dauntless*."

At the mention of his name, the rebels froze. One leaned in and studied his face. "I am the Hand Durklin. It *is* you!" the rebel said. "How did you...?"

"Long story. The Protorans repaired me on the *Volantis* and then I escaped in this viper. Where's Dolian?"

The man's brow furrowed. "He and a small group of men are at the reproduction farms. The plan is to... dismantle them before the machine men occupy the facilities for good."

"Take me to him. The gearheads must be stopped!"

They stepped out of the damaged viper into a swirling maelstrom. Carstairs followed the Hands to a modest carrier vessel, and they flew to a location near the facilities where they hid the runabout among the scorched hills. Durklin handed the captain protective clothing and weapons before the squad headed out into the winds.

When Dolian recognized Carstairs, they embraced, then settled into the hidden observation post the Hands had built into the rocks. The surrounding outcrops and hollows protected the shelter from the elements, and the captain instantly understood the grim nature of their mission.

Protorans guarded the perimeter of the buildings. As a show of strength, the invaders positioned several vipers around the farms. The rebels knelt together and surveyed the area.

"The machines are already inside," Dolian said. "And they are many."

"This is suicide if we try to overthrow them now," Carstairs thought out loud, assessing their numbers. "What about the Hands?"

Dolian shrugged and rubbed his chin. "They refused to leave. This life is all they've ever known. But since the machines entered the facilities, we have heard nothing from our people." He faced the captain with grim determination. "They may already be dead, Jay."

"Possibly, but the Protorans are not murderers. Sure, they take whatever organics they want, but they don't kill indiscriminately."

"True or not doesn't matter," Dolian grunted, pacing. "The soldiers are the outsiders. They threaten our existence. We have no choice now but to eliminate the facilities. If we remove what they desire, perhaps they will go somewhere else."

Carstairs surveyed the wind-swept rocks. The Heads who used to run the planet relied on these breeders to maintain a population of labourers and servants. Destroying the farms now would jeopardize anyone in there… Hands, machine men… everyone and everything.

"If you turn this place into rubble, Dolian," Carstairs said, "you'll condemn those still inside to their death."

"Yes."

"And you're comfortable with that?"

"Captain," the Hand leader muttered as if by rote, "the needs of Robos 7 are more important than the lives of a few Hands. It pains me to say it, but that is the truth. We must all make sacrifices in time of war."

Carstairs felt like Dolian hammered him with a metal pipe. "But don't you see? The Heads controlled and manipulated you the same way. They chose who to sacrifice. They claimed the needs of the many always outweigh the needs of the few. It suited them because they were the ones deciding your fate." His shoulders slumped. "And now you're arguing the same thing."

"Do not fight me on this, Captain. We all agree to wipe out the farms, whether the people inside survive or die."

The fighters shouted their agreement as one. Perhaps they were so conditioned to accept their subservient fate, they could not allow another group to run their lives again. Even if it meant dying so that others may live.

"I do not expect you to understand. But please... do not get in our way."

He scrutinized Dolian's face and saw the man's determination and resolve. "Okay, I am with you, my friend. How can I help?"

"Go with these men and prepare to fire the Heavy Pulse Device."

Carstairs hesitated a moment. He understood the damage this weapon would cause, and how it could easily wipe out the entire farming footprint, and then some. The Hands retrieved this massive cannon from Governor Graves' myrmidons when they threatened to destroy the Moaning Bones. If Dolian deployed this firepower, nothing would survive. But destroying the facilities could also stop Scyther's aggression on Robos 7, at least temporarily.

"Very well," Carstairs said, and followed half a dozen fighters out of the observation post where they uncovered the HPD and wheeled it into position.

The extreme and relentless howl challenged them. The captain, recognizing his new, artificial arm was far more powerful than his old one, performed much of the lifting and moving of the enormous weapon.

A ragged-looking fighter checked a scanner showing

the topography of the area. He confirmed the Device's location and moved away, then he yelled above the furious wind, "The reproduction facilities are on target!"

The fighters, including Carstairs, lowered their heads in silence for those innocent people who were about to die.

A moment later, the Robosian fighter gave the order to fire, and the world burned as bright as the sun.

THIRTY-TWO

"MY, BUT YOU'RE A SLIPPERY GIRL," SCYTHER MUSED when the soldiers hauled Piper into the medical bay. The Protorans dumped her prostate on an empty biobed. Her hands were cuffed behind her back and heavy shackles encompassed her ankles.

"Mind the face," the Protoran leader said to the guards. Turning to her, he asked, "Did you have a pleasant chat with your mother?"

Piper's outrage roiled. She wanted nothing more than to wipe that smug gearhead's smirk on the grated floor. Instead, she calmed herself with a few deep breaths and answered. "Scyther, we can still figure something out. From what I've seen and learned, your people are not warriors. We can help find a solution. You don't have to torment another planet. Existence is not a zero sum game."

He marched to the biobed and lifted her head by the chin. "The Governing Council had plenty of opportunities to do right by us. And they refused. All you can offer, Ms.

Madison, is more talk. More humiliation."

Dr. Sheilor approached them, clutching a data slate. "The regeneration room is standing by, Liege. Shall we begin?"

Scyther brushed his organic fingers across the peeling skin on his cheek. "Yes. It is past the time. Men, take the girl to the chamber."

"Wait a second," she shouted, "you're not taking anything that belongs to me!"

"See, that's where you're mistaken, Ms. Madison. I require new flesh, and yours is healthy and fresh. You have it. I need it. So I shall take it. Then, logically, we wouldn't want your limbs to go to waste, so we'll remove those, too." He motioned for the men to come.

Half a dozen soldiers lifted her off the bed and dragged her into the corridor. She struggled against their grip, more out of instinct than anything else.

"Be careful with her." Sheilor chastized the brutes as they manhandled her through the ship.

Piper's patience wore thin. "Does my mother know what you're planning to do?"

"Naturally," Scyther sneered. "In fact, she told me earlier that she never really had any intention of bringing you onboard as a protégé. She was simply... what's the term? Oh yes, *toying* with you."

"Liar!" she spat, struggling against her bounds.

"The exact words went something like, 'Do with her as you please'. I think she may be seeking revenge for the trouble you caused her with the Bortan Administrator. Remember that?"

"I don't believe you, Scyther," she growled.

The big Protoran shrugged in that awkward, sly way of his. "In the end, whether you believe me or not is moot."

They entered the ship's regeneration room. The lighting remained dim, except for the machines and pieces of equipment that hummed and glowed. The soldiers removed her cuffs and shackles, then tossed her on a hard, metal examination table and pinned her on her back.

Sheilor tied down her arms and legs with thick leather straps, then leaned over her. "In a few minutes, you won't feel a thing." She prepared a hypo, stroked Piper's cheek and said, "Turn your head, will you?"

She refused to cooperate, thrashing back and forth until Sheilor asked one of the soldiers to hold her head steady. The man's grip on her temples was so forceful, Piper feared her head might explode.

The doctor stared into her eyes, holding the hypo above her like the sword of Damocles. "This truly won't hurt at all," she said. The injector dangled close to her neck, and Sheilor concealed it in her fingers. Next, she sprayed the anesthetic into her clothing—not her skin.

"I don't—"

"Quiet, Ms. Madison," Sheilor whispered. "In a few minutes, you'll be in dreamland and that will be that. Know that your limbs and flesh help our people survive." She patted her patient on the forehead, then moved away to prepare Scyther for the transplant. Two other Protorans occupied biobeds in the regeneration room, appearing to be in stasis, apparently awaiting her arms and legs.

The Protoran leader hopped on a biobed and allowed himself to be secured. Sheilor placed a bright lamp over his face and injected another hypo solution into a piece of flesh that hung behind his metallic jaw.

"I'll be with you in a moment, my Lord," the doctor said. He grunted and remained still. Sheilor returned to Piper. The soldier who held her head stayed there, getting in the doctor's way. "If you don't mind, I need more room to perform the extraction. Go stand by the door... or in a closet, will you?"

The guard grunted and backed away to join the others

at the entrance.

"Are you beginning to feel light-headed, Ms. Madison?" she asked in a loud voice.

Piper, unsure of how to react, sensed the doctor kept her conscious for a reason, so she played along to determine Sheilor's goal.

"Feeling... drowsy," she replied in a slow voice.

"Good. This is normal. The solution won't take much longer now until you're under. Then we'll begin the operation." She glanced at the men and leaned in closer. "I want to ask you a few things in private before I fulfill my duty," she whispered.

Piper ignored her. "Just let me go so I can help you."

The doctor frowned. "Even if I were inclined to, I could not free you. I am Protoran. Scyther is my leader and my best friend. He can be frustrating at times, and stubborn, but his commitment to our people is beyond reproach."

"You love him?" Piper found the whole notion of affection between machines ridiculous.

"Yes. I have for a long, long time."

An odd thought crept into Piper's mind. A question. *What is this feeling? What does it mean to a machine? To a human?* She had no answer.

"So, what would you like to know?"

Scyther grunted again and hissed in his sleep. "He's under now," Sheilor said, then quickly added, "Piper, why do you and your mother fight?"

She considered the matter, buying time to figure a way out of this mess. "Well, it's not unusual for mothers and daughters to see the world differently. Mine is skilled in her political work, but I always wanted my own life. Make my own decisions."

She loves you.

The words appeared in her mind as if she spoke them aloud. Could the missing whisper stone have opened up a dormant mental pathway?

"But she loves you," Sheilor said, "and you must love her, too."

"I suppose," Piper agreed, "but love and respect are very different things. And just because we're family doesn't mean I *like* her. In fact," she added, "I'd do anything to put her back in that prison where she belongs."

I want to be a mother... to hold a child I create.

Piper wondered where this thought came from. It was too coherent to be from Sheilor. Perhaps all the excitement and madness she'd been through with Tephera had taken its toll, and some desire for motherhood somehow surfaced.

Sheilor reached out to stroke Piper's abdomen. "Are you a mother?"

"Hell, no," she snickered, "I'm not there yet. Maybe some day."

"So your internal parts... the ones used for reproduction... they are functional?"

Confusion spread across Piper's face. "Of course. And when the..." Her voice trailed off as the full realization of Sheilor's intentions dawned on her. She pulled against her restraints in a futile attempt to escape.

I can't do it on my own.

The soldiers beside the bulkhead stirred and regarded Sheilor, but she seemed to have no fear. "It's a normal reaction for humanoids," she said to them. "It will pass."

Piper fumed. "That's why you studied my ovaries... why you're keeping me alive. You want..." She struggled anew against the straps. They refused to yield.

"Yes," she whispered, placing her hand on Piper's shoulder. "I deeply desire a child of my own. And assimilating your parts into my body allows me to have one. These others... these Hands and Heads are unsatisfactory. I will have your genetics."

"You have the whisper stone!"

Sheilor reached to her side and extracted the gem. It glowed in a brilliant blue. How it came to read Sheilor's thoughts so clearly was a mystery to Piper since she'd only heard bits and pieces from the doctor earlier. The only conclusion she drew was that the stone *had* somehow found a pathway between the machine's inner consciousness and her own.

Piper slumped back on the bed, her thoughts swirling, defeat beginning to settle in. She would turn 25 in a couple of months, and thought little about starting a family… didn't even have a reliable partner. The closest she'd come to that was Neris, and he set her free to become a farmer in the valley. Nothing reliable about that. And Carstairs? A potential mate despite being twenty years older and an emotional child. What kind of father would he be?

Regardless, now that Sheilor coveted her reproductive organs, some deep instinctual desire filled her. She refused to give any of herself to these beings, no matter how desperate they were or what she had to do to fight back.

But escape was impossible. Carstairs was, presumably, down on the planet. Protoran soldiers, like the doctor, dedicated themselves to Scyther's cause. The straps binding her to this bed would not yield at all. And her mother had apparently abandoned her, too.

And that damnable Carstairs.

Unable to verbalize his deepest fears and desires.

Turning to *doing* things instead of *thinking* about things as a way to cope in this world.

And the realization struck her like a frigid winter wind: maybe Carstairs had it right.

Maybe actions were far more important than words. Remove the ability to act, and you may as well become wallpaper.

A great sense of peace fell upon her. She would die at the hands of these Protorans. She preferred collaborating with them to ensure their survival, but that wouldn't happen now. All she could do, she had already done, and nothing remained but to accept her fate with grace and courage, knowing she had given the fight all she had.

No regrets.

Piper turned to Sheilor and said, "Help yourself to any parts you need, doctor. I'm done."

THIRTY-THREE

WHEN CARSTAIRS REGAINED CONSCIOUSNESS AFTER THE Heavy Pulse Device unleashed its fury on the reproduction farms, dirt and debris covered much of his body like a thick blanket. He pulled himself up, wiped his eyes, and fought to get his bearings.

The brilliance of the HPD's payload dissipated, and the normal, muted light and winds returned. A fighter grabbed his arm and led him to join the others. He recognized Dolian among them. A small troop carrier sat nearby.

"Come! Let us search the area from above." Dolian's words fluttered in the wind.

Carstairs followed the rebels and boarded the craft. It immediately lifted off and flew toward the coordinates of the farms.

But there were no facilities remaining.

He fixated on the night-vision monitor showing the massive crater on the planet's surface. Bits and pieces of Protoran vipers lay scattered like kindling for kilometers across the scorched ground. They recorded no life forms at all.

"I hope this was worth it," he muttered, loud enough for the others to hear.

"It is regrettable," Dolian muttered, "but necessary."

They flew over and around the crater, scanning for any survivors. The smouldering hole reminded Carstairs of the cratered moons of Nusomia, black and dying.

"There is another place to look," Dolian said with a strange, knowing grin on his face.

The vessel veered to starboard and headed toward a range of distant hills. Carstairs figured they must be searching for Protorans hiding in the rocks, but as they approached the base of the mountains, the monitor began pinging wildly.

"The hell is going on?" The captain fumbled for his flux gun and prepared for a new battle. The fighters' hearty laughter filled the cabin.

"Jay," Dolian said, "These are the survivors. The *Hand* survivors."

Carstairs scratched his head. "What? How?"

"The Hands built an underground tunnel network from the lower levels of the farm buildings to this place," he explained. "We found out about them only after they contacted us."

The ship circled the landing area. Carstairs squinted at the ground, but the wind and dust made seeing anything impossible.

"I don't get it, Dolian. If the people could have escaped earlier, why didn't they?"

"Most refused. They do not know any other life, and the farms were their homes. When you're born into servitude, it is difficult to change. And fear of the unknown is a powerful emotion." He grew silent a moment before adding, "I am fortunate. I came to meet Ariel, then you and

Piper. My world is much larger now."

When the vessel landed, fighters tumbled out to greet the Hands. They said many perished in the blast, refusing to leave. And some who escaped appeared lost now that their purpose had been obliterated.

Dolian reassured them that life would be better. He organized additional ships to shuttle the survivors to the safety of the Moaning Bones. While that operation unfolded, Carstairs found a moment to speak with him in private.

"I must return to the *Volantis*. Piper is still on board, and I want to help her disable that ship."

The rebel leader frowned. "We have no vessels capable of space flight, Captain."

Carstairs gazed through the dust at the smudged outline of rocky hills. He imagined Piper on the *Volantis*, putting her life at risk again for what she felt was right and important. He wanted to join her more than anything else, and resolved to do precisely that.

"Then I'll just have to find one."

PIPER STARED AT THE CEILING, AWAITING HER FATE. THE regeneration room hummed with machinery and Protorans. This time, unlike previous incidents when she stirred up crap, she suffered it without Jay Carstairs' involvement.

A commotion in the corridor grabbed her attention. The doors to the operating theatre hissed open and the Protoran bridge officer, Commander Wesling, raced in, assessed the environment, and announced, "My apologies, Doctor, but I must speak with Lord Scyther on an urgent matter."

Sheilor approached the man. "I'm afraid that's out of the question, Commander. As you can clearly see, our leader awaits regenerative surgery. No one is to disturb him."

The officer glanced at the big Protoran lying on the biobed across from Piper. "That is unacceptable, Doctor. You must bring him back online."

Piper craned her neck for a better view. "What's the emergency, Commander?"

When he scanned her with his ocular implant, his face suggested he understood her fate, and saw no risk in answering. "The Robosian rebels have destroyed the reproduction farms. There's nothing left. It seems the Hands inside abandoned the facilities before fighters obliterated the place. Our evaluation of the area reveals a network of deep tunnels where the buildings once stood. Doctor, all of *our* people were vaporized in the attack."

"Impossible," said Sheilor, returning her attention to the medical equipment. "Those uppity types are feisty, but they don't have the firepower to level an entire facility that size." She froze and glanced at Piper. "Do they?"

Piper remembered the caliber of weapons deployed at the Moaning Bones when the Governor's myrmidons captured her during the initial uprisings. Although the heavy devices were restricted and controlled by the governing Heads, she knew Dolian and the fighters would protect themselves with any weapon they could find. And they clearly had.

"I don't doubt Commander Wesling's report at all," she said. "In fact, I bet he's got video evidence to prove it."

The man agreed. "Would you like to see it, Doctor?"

Sheilor leaned against Scyther's biobed. Her shoulders slumped. "That isn't necessary. Despite the risks, I shall awaken him. It should only take a minute." She grabbed a hypo from the supply table, adjusted it, and shot the solution into Scyther's flesh. Turning to Piper, she cocked her head. "Did you know about this attack?"

Piper sensed another opportunity to bring the conflict to a peaceful resolution. "Not exactly," she said, remembering Sheilor's ability to detect lying. "I didn't have the specifics, but Dolian and his fighters were committed to thwarting your reliance on the farms, returning the planet to Robosian control, and installing Ariel Graves as the proper Governor. This is only the beginning."

Scyther stirred on the biobed. Sheilor loosened the straps holding him steady. "Is... is it complete?" He touched his face, then looked with confusion at the doctor. "What happened?" he asked, gaining strength.

"Trouble on Robos 7, Liege," she said, inviting Commander Wesling bedside.

The groggy Protoran leader swung his legs over the bed. "Status report?"

The officer recounted how the rebels deployed a massive weapon that destroyed the reproduction farms, leaving nothing but a monstrous crater where the facilities used to be. The explosion also wiped out several vipers, and hundreds of soldiers stationed around the perimeter.

Scyther's face burned like a fire blown by the wind. He sat on the edge of the biobed in disbelief.

"But there's more, my Liege."

"What else could there possibly be?"

Wesling cleared his throat and said, "We received word from Asteria that Chancellor Madison—" He flashed a stone-faced look at Piper. "Tephera Madison has been relieved of her command again."

The news hit Scyther like a punch to the gut. "That can't be," he said. "How...?"

"The Asterian Battle Fleet, Liege. Ambassador Welkin announced that the fleet commander on the *Nightingale* could no longer support the Chancellor. Neither could the captains of his ships. Some remain here, to escort us back to Protor peacefully. The remaining cruisers, including the *Nightingale*, returned to Asteria and forced the Chancellor out."

Piper felt a measure of relief that someone with authority finally stepped up and refused to honour that ridiculous Ethical Protocol. She wouldn't have imagined Phact would be the one to do it, given his history with her mother. Perhaps she underestimated him. A mistake she would never repeat.

"Scyther, I say again, you can change this. I know in the past the Council hasn't been receptive or respectful, but you've made your predicament clear now. They get it. Let me help you find a solution that doesn't involve harvesting Robosian prisoners or relying on reproduction farms."

The big Protoran grimaced and straightened his back. "But we still have the detainees. They will allow our most needy patients to survive. And we can always build more breeder facilities."

"Don't you get it, Scyther?" Piper pushed against the restraining straps. "It's over now. Sure, you might replace those farms, but the rebels will just turn around and destroy them, too. There's only one way out of this mess. Release me and I can help you find another option."

The Protoran remained silent and stoic, mulling the situation over. The doctor reached out to him and stroked his face, peeling off more of his skin. "My love," she said, full of resignation, "young Madison speaks reason. We cannot sustain our presence here. If the Fleet now protects Welkin, it won't be long before the Council installs a proper government on this planet."

The big man turned and scanned her.

"We must find an alternative," Sheilor said, "like Piper offers. We have accomplished much in raising our plight with the Council. It's time to stop the loss of life in this battle."

No one foresaw his rage.

In a sudden move, Scyther leapt from the biobed and struck the doctor with such force that her body cracked and flew backward, slamming into the bulkhead.

The impact broke her spine and limbs.

Her half-organic, half-machine frame twitched and sputtered. What served as blood for her humanoid parts oozed onto the floor beneath her.

Scyther slumped against the bed, despair filling his face. "No…" he whispered. Then, with his body trembling, he screamed and raced to his lover's side. He lifted her limp arms and dropped them right away.

Piper turned to the stunned commander and said, "Wesling, cut me loose from these restraints."

The man hesitated, then slashed the straps from her body. She approached the grieving Protoran leader and, not knowing what to do, touched his metal shoulder. "I'll talk to Ambassador Welkin immediately about your needs."

His body convulsed with emotion under her palm. "No," he repeated.

He stood and faced her. His peeling face grew more grotesque by the second, and his hands clenched.

"You brought the chaos here, Madison," he growled in a measured voice. "If you hadn't interfered, my people would have hope for their continued survival. Now what? We're beholden to the whims of the ridiculous Council for help?" Scyther shook his head. "Not a chance. And you're to blame."

"My Lord," Commander Wesling said, "I'll have the other surgeon attend to Dr. Sheilor."

"No," he replied. "Salvage her memory chip. Let her rest in peace, then return to the bridge."

"Yes, Liege." the officer plucked the device from Sheilor's chest, turned and exited the room.

The big man's rage bubbled again. "My people and I will die soon, Madison. But I, for one, am eager to take you with me." The man crouched, preparing to spring. She eased away, angling for the main doors. But the furious

Protoran pounced, lashing out at her with his powerful arms.

Piper anticipated the blows, unlike Sheilor, and she rolled with the impact, diving across the floor and hopping up, striking a defensive pose. "Don't do this, Scyther. The fight's over."

"It will never be over!" he croaked. "As long as I function, I fight." He marched toward her, reached out, and grabbed her in a vise-like bear hug, squeezing her breath away.

Piper fought against the man, but she was no match for his brute strength. He squeezed harder and harder until stars floated across her vision.

"Time for you to die, Madison, as slowly as possible," he grunted in her ear.

The black world of unconsciousness encroached, and she battled to stay alert and break free.

But it was no use.

Her ribs cracked, shooting fresh flames of pain through her chest.

"What the—?" A commotion by the theatre's entrance caused Scyther to release her. Piper fell to the floor, gasping for air. The hum and sparkle of a discharging thermal flux gun filled the surgery. She looked up in time to see Scyther with a shocked, broken look on his face before he teetered and collapsed.

A soldier helped her to her feet. When she turned, Commander Wesling stood at the entrance, holding a smouldering weapon. Behind him, several Protorans stood at attention.

"Wesling? I don't understand."

"This insanity is over, Ms. Madison. I have seized command of the *Volantis*, and wish to join you when you contact the Ambassador. Time is running out for our people, and serving Lord Scyther in this manner is not helpful." He marched to the big man's body, knelt down, and pulled something from it.

She clutched her chest, staring at Scyther's shattered corpse splayed on the floor. "Is he...?"

"Yes. Permanently offline." He held out his hand. In it was a memory chip the size of a pebble. "What's left of him is here, to be preserved along with Dr. Sheilor, for historical purposes so that when we are all gone, someone, perhaps, may learn about us."

"You're not finished yet," Piper grunted, clutching her ribs. "Help me find some painkiller, and we'll call the Council together."

Piper staggered over to Sheilor's fractured body. She touched the doctor's cheek. One of her hands was clenched in a fist, and poking out from between her fingers was the glowing whisper stone. She wrenched it away and stuffed it in her pocket.

THIRTY-FOUR

SEVERAL DAYS LATER, PIPER AND COMMANDER WESLING, along with a contingent of Protoran doctors, gathered outside the Torfinn Galaxy Governing Council chamber discussing the strategy to make synthetic organics a priority among all cluster planets.

Ambassador Welkin and her entourage exited the hall and approached the group. Piper suppressed a chuckle, seeing the Erusian's diminuitive stature standing beside the tall Protorans.

"Commander Wesling, it will not be... *noot...* easy moving forward to preserve your entire race."

The man lowered his head.

"But," she continued, "the Council has finally made your plight a priority, and with Ms. Madison's passionate support, the ATI and other scientific organizations throughout Torfinn have already begun working on solutions."

Wesling straightened. "We appreciate your advocacy,

Ambassador. Let us hope the page has turned on this unfortunate chapter in our collective history."

"Indeed… *noot*… if we dwell on the past, we are condemned to live in it. I look forward to working together." With that, she took her leave.

"Well, Wesling," Piper said, "I'll get back to work, too." She held her healing ribcage.

The Protoran officer thanked her. "And I shall return to the *Volantis*. The medical team will remain here on Asteria and assist your scientists with the organic research." He stepped toward the exit, hesitated, and added, "I am saddened by the loss of life before coming to this shared understanding."

"Me, too, Commander. But like the Ambassador said, we can't keep living in the past. Look forward… always forward."

They exited the Council building together. Wesling boarded a nearby shuttle for the flight back to his orbiting ship, and Piper hopped on a scooter and flew out to the Asterian Maximum Security Prison.

When she arrived at the check-in, everything about the institution had changed. Workers had erected new fencing and walls. They constructed additional watchtowers, and deployed advanced surveillance technology. Soldiers now replaced the guards.

Two of them escorted Piper through the imposing corridors to an area reserved for the most dangerous criminals. In the middle of the row sat Tephera Madison, behind bars, staring at the floor in silence.

"I wondered if you'd come," she croaked in a hollow voice, without lifting her head.

Piper's gut wrenched. Despite everything her mother had done, and all she'd said to her, the inexplicable bond toward Tephera remained strong. "I came to say goodbye and to wish you well."

The elder Madison peered up. A deep sadness covered her face. "Oh? Where are you off to now?"

"I haven't figured that out yet. Carstairs will arrive soon, and we'll find some place to explore together."

"You know, Piper," she murmured, "he and I—"

"Don't say it, Mother. There are no more mysteries between you two for me to solve." She tapped the whisper stone in her pocket.

Tephera stepped awkwardly toward her, leaned against the cage bars and stroked Piper's cheek. "Farewell, love."

Conflicting emotions threatened to rage through her chest. She quelled them by focusing on her mother's true, innermost thoughts propagating through the stone into her mind.

"Goodbye, Mum."

And for the first time since she was a child, peace filled her completely.

THAT AFTERNOON, PIPER LAY BACK ON THE GRASS relaxing in the warm Asterian sunshine outside the Pilot's Lounge at the Northern Airfield. She checked her comms device again to see if Carstairs had updated his ETA.

He had not.

It wouldn't be him to do so, anyway.

And the stone revealed nothing.

Earlier, she poked her head inside the bar and noticed how quiet the place had become. A few older pilots, likely retired, carried on a drunken conversation at the far wall, but there was no sign of Gazzer, his entourage, or any of the other younger pilots. Cullin the bartender greeted her with a shrug and a smile.

The return of the Asterian Battle Fleet to the planet had an impact on the trade routes again, along with the newfound stability of the Governing Council. Turned out her mother brought the people and the planets together after all, but not in the way her supporters intended. Her presence consolidated all the fence-sitters against her, and opened the door for much needed reforms.

Piper stuffed her hand in her pocket and fingered the dormant whisper stone, debating whether to keep or destroy it. The gem gave her the power to read other people's thoughts and to see their truth. But that posed a terrible ethical dilemma, especially if she didn't disclose her abilities. Still, the stone already proved helpful, even if she heard more than she wanted.

Perhaps it would be better to turn the thing over to the Council and remove the temptation?

What would Jay Carstairs think?

She pulled her fingers out, leaving the whisper stone hidden away, then folded her hands on her stomach and dozed, listening to the hypnotic lull of various spacecraft landing and departing.

Piper must have fallen asleep, for she awakened with a start when someone kicked the soles of her boots. She shielded her eyes from the brilliant sunshine.

Carstairs stood before her, bathed in light. "Mind if I join you?"

She turned on her side and patted the grass. The captain dropped to the ground, leaned over, and kissed her forehead.

"What's the update from Robos 7?" she asked.

"Good news, Madison. Ariel is the newly minted Interim Governor with the full support of various groups and several influential ministers. And, with a remnant of the Fleet remaining behind to keep the peace, it seems the Robosians have had enough of the chaos and are committed to resolving their differences."

"That's wonderful," Piper replied, admiring him. He appeared well-rested and surprisingly presentable in a clean, light blue flightsuit. "What about Dolian?"

Carstairs chuckled. "That big stiff managed to bring the groups of rebels together under his leadership. His ability to take on the Protorans, rescue his wife, and save us made him a hero. The planet needs someone like that to rally behind. Even the Heads are impressed."

Piper stroked the captain's arm. "I always thought he was smarter than others gave him credit for. He performed wonders with the *Dauntless*, remember?"

"Sure do," Carstairs said. "And speaking of that..."

She bolted up, wincing at the strain on her ribs, and surveyed the airfield for the old vessel. After its complete destruction on Robos 7, she wondered if the Hand mechanics could piece it back together.

"Relax, Mads. The ship we knew is gone. I salvaged as much as I could, but there was precious left. However..." He pointed to the far end of the field at a solitary light cruiser that looked as if some giant kid had dropped it there and sat on it. The vessel leaned to one side. Massive dark streaks scorched its fuselage. Piper swore the thing would never get off the ground.

"Seriously, Carstairs? *That's* your new ship?"

He grinned from ear to ear. "The old girl's a beauty, don't you think?"

They strolled together, holding hands, across the field toward the battered cruiser. Piper inspected the entire exterior. The dimensions were similar to the *Dauntless*, but this was definitely an older cruiser that had seen much better days. To her surprise, her confidence in the ship's ability to fly increased as she inspected it more closely.

"Let me show you the inside." The Captain pulled a manual lever tucked into the body and hauled out a folding ladder. He shrugged and quipped, "Not all the electronics are up to date yet."

The worn interior of the ship needed a good cleaning, but seemed functional. Carstairs showed her the locations of the key consoles, including navigation, comms, tactical, and helm. "And," he said, inviting her to sit as he flopped into the command chair, "I've got a little surprise for you."

Piper sat beside him. "I can only imagine," she replied with more than a hint of playful annoyance.

"That's your cue!" he shouted out in the cabin.

The control panel sprang to life. All lights flashed on and the suborbital engines rumbled.

"Greetings, Ms. Madison. I am pleased to see you again."

"Quirp? Is that really you?"

"Why, yes, Ms. Madison. Who else would it be?"

The two laughed.

"I pulled the xanthalite crystal from the cockpit refuge wreckage," Carstairs explained. "Quirp was mostly intact. The Hands fixed him up and adapted him to this bird."

"I am completely restored," the ship mind chirped.

"And where'd you get this boat?" Piper asked.

He ran his palm over the helm console in front of him. "Turns out the cartel didn't care at all how the trade network opened up, so they paid me for my services." He pulled a face. "Well, not entirely everything. I owed a lot of credits for various messes I'd made, so by the time I had my share, this old beauty was the only thing I could afford. I figured we could fix her up together. Come up with a new name."

"You did, hm?" Piper smiled seductively, leaving her seat and stroking his cheek. The whisper stone hummed merrily in her pocket, filling her head with his innermost desires, causing her to blush.

"If you don't mind, that is."

"I can't think of anything better, Captain." She kissed him on the lips. "Now, how about you show me what you've done with your quarters?"

"As you wish," Carstairs whispered, lifting her up in his arms, and carrying her away.

Acknowledgements

AS WE OFTEN SAY IN THE WRITING WORKSHOPS, WHILE each of us has to do the writing alone, it takes a community to create a novel. I would like to thank the many writers in the Ottawa Writing Workshops who shared their insights, thoughtful suggestions, and support throughout the writing of this novel.

About the Author

DAVID ALLAN HAMILTON IS A WRITER AND INSTRUCTOR living in Ottawa, Ontario. He has edited and published numerous collections of stories from participants of the Ottawa Writing Workshops since 2017, helping hundreds of writers and novelists feel that sense of achievement from accomplishing their dream.

David previously enjoyed a career with the Federal Public Service and has been a contract instructor at Carleton University. He holds a B.Sc. (Honours) degree in Applied Physics from Laurentian University and a M.Sc. in Geophysics from the University of Western Ontario and has undertaken graduate literary studies at the University of Sheffield. He is also a licenced ham radio operator. His own stories often combine his deep love of the natural world and the endless possibilities of science fiction.

You may contact David at the following:

David@davidallanhamilton.net
davidallanhamilton.net
Facebook.com/davidallanhamilton

Available From
David Allan Hamilton

Ross 128 Universe

Alien in the Grey
The Crying of Ross 128
Echoes in the Grey
Three Days of Darkness
The Lonely Scars

Piper Madison Series

The Hands of Robos 7
Requiem for the Graves
Breeder Protocol

Other

The Quantum Awakening

Don't Miss

The Crying of Ross 128

An alien distress call, nervous world leaders, and scientific betrayal

September, 2085. Listening for alien signals is a welcome respite for Jim Atteberry, an English professor at City College who's marking a pile of boring undergraduate essays.

But when he detects a subspace distress call from the Ross 128 system, Jim becomes a pawn in a global scientific conspiracy bent on stealing the alien technology for political domination. Jim and his colleague Kate team up with Dr. Esther Tyrone at the Terran Science Academy to confirm his findings and warn the aliens. But are the Rossians truly in distress, or setting a trap for an ambitious, naïve Earth?

The Crying of Ross 128 is the opening installment in the Ross 128 first contact trilogy. If you like science fiction with credible stories, compelling characters, and mysterious aliens that will keep you guessing, you'll love author David Allan Hamilton's page-turning trilogy of near future alien encounters.

www.ingramcontent.com/pod-product-compliance
Lightning Source LLC
Chambersburg PA
CBHW021457240626
47154CB00002B/404